D1492383

MOHAWK VALLEY

Ronald Welch

MOHAWK VALLEY

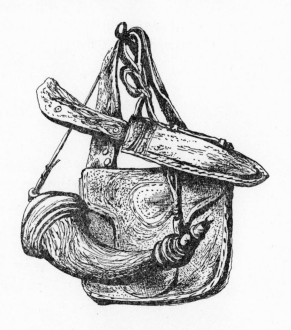

Illustrated by
WILLIAM STOBBS

London
OXFORD UNIVERSITY PRESS

Oxford University Press, Ely House, London W.1

GLASGOW NEW YORK TORONTO MELBOURNE WELLINGTON
CAPE TOWN SALISBURY IBADAN NAIROBI LUSAKA ADDIS ABABA
BOMBAY CALCUTTA MADRAS KARACHI LAHORE DACCA
KUALA LUMPUR HONG KONG TOKYO

First edition 1958
Reprinted 1962, 1967

PRINTED IN GREAT BRITAIN BY
MORRISON AND GIBB LIMITED, LONDON AND EDINBURGH

for my Canadian niece
MARILYN SYLVIA EVANS
of Montreal

AUTHOR'S NOTE

So far as I know there is no such place as Ashwater in the Mohawk Valley. Otherwise I have tried to keep to the main historical events of the period, including the details of the fighting at Ticonderoga and Quebec.

The story of Duncan Campbell of Inverawe can be found in the history books, but I have never come across any mention of how Wolfe discovered the existence of the path to the Heights of Abraham. The conversation with the French sentry did actually take place, but the speaker was a Highland officer in the leading boat.

The naval officer, Cook, was afterwards the famous explorer, Captain Cook. He made the first accurate soundings of the St Lawrence, and helped to pilot the fleet up the river to Quebec.

CONTENTS

Part One
ENGLAND

Part Two
AMERICA

Part Three
QUEBEC

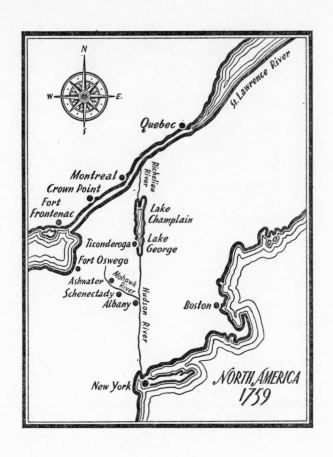

Part One

ENGLAND

Chapter One

CAMBRIDGE, 1755

ALAN CAREY pushed back his chair from the table so that he could stretch out his long legs. He did it cautiously, for his friends liked to remind him that he could seldom move without knocking over a piece of furniture. He glanced at the clock. Half-past one already. He would stop playing soon, and go to bed. The candles were low in their holders, and the air in the room was warm and stuffy.

Hugh Goring, their host for the evening, passed a new pack of cards to Harry Napier, who was the banker. Harry ripped off the paper wrapping, and the cards pattered softly on the table as he dealt the next hand. Alan gave one look at his cards and dropped them. Not even worth the smallest of bets. He was always unlucky at cards, he thought ; how much had he lost so far tonight ? About twenty guineas, he supposed. Well, he could pay without worrying, which was one consolation, for he had barely touched his month's allowance.

' Alan ? ' Harry asked.

Alan shook his head, and edged his chair back another few inches. He was not built for sitting at a card table for several hours ; six feet and more with shoulders and arms to match became a little cramped. His head was aching, too, but he emptied the glass that Hugh had just refilled, and watched the others as they played the hand. He knew them all well, for they had been at school together, and this was their second year at Cambridge.

The five wigged heads were bent over the cards. Alan wore no wig ; he detested the hot, tight feel of a wig on his head, and wore his own black hair, tied at the back to resemble a wig. The young faces were tired and strained in the yellow candlelight. What a way to spend a summer evening, Alan thought.

3

Hugh Goring, on his immediate right, was pushing forward a pile of white counters. His fingers were shaking, Alan noticed. Poor Hugh ; he had lost more than anyone, and he could least afford to lose. Fifty guineas would not harm the others, but they might well be disastrous for Hugh. He was a fool to play for such high stakes, but Hugh would never draw back or refuse to join in with whatever his friends were doing.

Harry Napier glanced round at the stakes against him. He showed little concern. But he was far and away the most level-headed gambler there. Alan had to admit that, though he disliked Harry. They irritated each other ; they had always done so, even at school. There was Harry, neat, brisk, and competent, a self-assured and decisive young man, and there was Alan, overgrown and vast, often clumsy and shy, the Mammoth, as he had been called at school, and by many at Cambridge, too, with little self-confidence, and cursed with a violent temper, though his friends did admit that he did not lose it so frequently now. No, he and Harry were the perfect pair to squabble, Alan decided ruefully.

Harry turned his cards face upwards on the table. From Hugh there came a swift hiss of indrawn breath.

' Luck's against you, Hugh,' Harry said as he raked in the counters from all round the table.

He dealt again, quickly and deftly. But no one could imagine Harry doing anything clumsily or inefficiently, Alan thought irritably as he picked up his cards and fanned them out between his big, powerful hands. There was a slight nick on the back of one card, he noticed idly ; new pack, too. Another bad hand, worth one counter perhaps.

Hugh was staring intently across the table, and Alan grinned. If Hugh hoped to learn anything of the value of Harry's hand by the expression on his face, then he would be disappointed. Harry was much too good a card player for that. But Hugh was always so earnest, a good-looking young man with charming manners, always ready to help, or to make himself pleasant.

' Double the stakes, Harry ? ' he asked.

Harry glanced at his own cards, and nodded indifferently.

Hugh pushed out another heap of counters, and his fingers were trembling as he did so. Then he laid down his cards, face upwards.

' Can you better that, Harry ? ' he said triumphantly.

' Not this time, Hugh.' Harry pushed across a large heap of counters, stacked the cards with a flick of his brisk, capable fingers, and dealt again.

Alan watched the cards as they slithered over the polished surface of the table. One good hand, and he would go to bed. He was a poor gambler ; he became much too excited, and if he did put down a large stake, it was often on the wrong hand. He would have gone half an hour ago but Hugh had opened a fresh bottle of wine, and Alan had stayed. That simple, casual decision was to change his life.

Another bad hand ; a poor pack, too, for there were nicks on the back of two more cards. He would not have noticed them unless he had got into the habit of holding his hand well down in his fingers, so that the cards almost disappeared in his great paws. The Ace of Spades and the King of Clubs. He stiffened. The Ace and a King ! With the little finger of his left hand he touched the cards again. The nicks were in the same place on each card, right at the top. What card was it in the last hand that had been nicked ? Yes, it had been a Queen.

Alan's heart began to thump, a sure sign that he was excited or alarmed. But there was no doubt in his mind. His boredom and sleepiness had vanished now, and his brain was working quickly, though his friends said he was as slow to think as an ox. The cards were marked. The whole pack must be marked, every court card there.

He kept his head down with an effort. This would be an unpleasant affair if anyone noticed. But would they notice ? Possibly not. It was only because he held his cards, like a gorilla, Harry had said once, that he had felt the slight nicks. It was a hundred to one that anyone round the table had ever handled marked cards before. Only by chance had Alan done so, during the last vacation, when he had been staying in London with his elder brother George, and he had been shown a marked pack in one of the clubs, kept there as a curiosity.

Bets were being made on the hand. Alan's eyes flickered from face to face, the familiar faces he had seen so frequently for the past seven or eight years. Who had marked the cards ?

Harry ? Possibly, for he had won heavily. No, it was impossible ; not Harry with his biting scorn for anything underhand or dishonest. James Dundas ? He was immensely wealthy ; why should he cheat for the sake of a handful of guineas ? He could have covered all the stakes on the table with the same casual gesture with which he tipped a servant.

Edward Rankin ? No, he was not so rich a man as James, but his allowance was a very large one, and he was too transparently honest to cheat, and far too indolent a young man to spend hours marking a pack of cards.

Stephen Rawle ? No, not Stephen ! Alan dismissed the idea with horror. Stephen was his closest friend, the man with whom he was always at ease. He had practically grown up with Stephen, for his father, General Rawle, was an old friend of the Earl of Aubigny, Alan's father, and they had served together under the Duke of Marlborough. No, Stephen would never cheat ; Alan would have staked his last guinea on that— not Stephen, solid, dependable, and as trustworthy as the Bank of England.

Hugh Goring ? Yes, of course, it must be Hugh ! It could not possibly be anyone else. This was a new pack, fresh from the wrappings. They were in Hugh's rooms, and these were Hugh's cards. Only he could have had the opportunity to mark them. And it was not at Harry's face he had been staring, but the tops of Harry's cards.

He was watching Harry now with the same strained look in his eyes. Nothing unusual in that, perhaps, and no one would remark about it. You might learn a great deal from a player's face.

' Double again, Harry ? ' Hugh asked. His voice was pitched higher than usual, Alan thought.

Alan threw in his hand. What should he do ? Shout and stop the game ? Expose Hugh ? He pulled a handkerchief from the deep pocket of his long-skirted coat, and wiped his forehead. But it was not the heat of the room that had brought out the prickles of perspiration.

Harry had noticed nothing. He was shaking out the lace ruffles at his wrists, very much at his ease as he watched the bets being made. From the box by his elbow he took a pinch of snuff with a delicate flick of his fingers. Oh, yes, Alan thought with a sudden burst of irritation, Harry was quite the young gentleman of fashion already. He would not have been out of place in a London club.

Alan shifted his long legs again. I must stop this, he thought, as the counters were pushed forward. But only Hugh knew how many court cards lay on the table. He was betting on a certainty, and betting heavily, too.

But exposure would ruin Hugh. Even if he did not have to go down from Cambridge, he could hardly face his friends again. And loss of friends to Hugh, the friends he had made at school and at Cambridge with his charming manner and his quick wit, would be complete disaster for him.

He had never made any secret of his ambitions. Politics, or perhaps the army, he had said so often. But for those careers he would need money and influence, and Hugh had neither. Disgraced, there would be no pocket borough waiting for him, no commission in a good regiment, nothing at all without the backing of the families represented around his table tonight. Even Mammoth Carey, with all his painful shyness and lack of social graces, could help him, perhaps more so than anyone there, for Lord Aubigny had six pocket boroughs at his disposal, and had been a soldier of distinction with powerful connexions at the Horse Guards.

Hugh had won again. He was laughing as he piled up the counters by his side, a tense, shrill laugh. But why should the others suspect that? They were all young enough, and anyone would be delighted at such a wonderful run of the cards.

Oh, I'll leave it, Alan decided wretchedly. If he had cried out, he could imagine the faces of his friends, and the explanations he would have to give. They would have hailed him with amused disbelief. What, the Mammoth an expert on marked cards ? Stick to your boxing and wrestling, Alan, they would have shouted. And Harry would have made one of his cutting, icy remarks about the social gaffe that Alan had made, accusing Hugh of cheating. Really, my dear Alan . . . No, keep quiet, Alan decided. And that was the second decision he made that night that was to affect his future so drastically.

Harry was picking up the discarded cards. Alan watched the deft fingers. They hesitated. Alan gulped. Harry was feeling the cards, the two cards that Alan had thrown down, the Ace and the King.

Harry looked up. His eyes met Alan's. Alan was bending forward, great shoulders hunched, his face white and anxious, for his face was always a true guide to his emotions. Harry slowly turned over the two cards and dropped them on the table, and stared at Alan again in accusing silence.

' Look here, Harry,' Stephen Rawle said quickly, ' you can't do that. You shouldn't see Alan's discarded hand, you know.'

Harry shrugged his shoulders. He did not bother to look at Stephen, and he was still watching Alan. Then he started to go through the whole pack, throwing out all the court cards, indifferent to the buzz of comment from the other players. But the remarks died away as he ran his fingers over the tops of each card. Alan heard again that swift hiss from Hugh.

' Marked ! ' Harry said, and tossed the cards across the table with a contemptuous flick of his hand.

' Marked ! ' The chorus went up all round the room. Hands reached for the cards, and under the neat bagged wigs, startled faces peered down as fingers felt for the marks.

' Your pack, isn't it, Alan ? ' Harry said quietly.

' Mine ! '

Harry picked up the torn wrappings. ' Your name is on the direction.'

Alan nodded. Yes, he remembered. They were his cards, and Hugh had asked him for the loan of two spare packs the morning before. He started to explain, not daring to look at Hugh, stammering, red-faced and embarrassed at what he had to say. He saw Stephen watching, startled and worried, but the other faces were cold and unfriendly, and Alan broke off abruptly.

' I am sure the others will excuse you, Alan, if you wish to leave us,' Harry said. ' Another hand, gentlemen, with a fresh pack ? '

Oh, yes, it was very neatly done, Alan thought. Trust Harry to handle an awkward situation with such polished smoothness. Alan stood up, a huge figure in the candlelight, his pleasant face with its big, square jaw jutting out dangerously, a furious, uncontrollable flood of anger welling up inside him.

' Are you accusing me of cheating ? ' he demanded furiously.

Harry turned his head and looked up at him with a studied indifference. ' They're your cards, Alan,' he said. ' I saw your face when I picked up your hand. I shouldn't make a scene of this, if I was you. You can rely upon our discretion.'

He turned back to the others, taking another pinch of snuff as he did so. Oh, he was enjoying this, Alan thought, clenching his fists. The wigged heads nodded ; all except Stephen's. His freckled face was creased with worry, his sandy brows wrinkled with utter disbelief at what he had heard.

' Of course, you will understand that you must not play cards again at Cambridge,' Harry added. ' If you give us your promise, then nothing will be said outside this room. Eh, gentlemen ? '

The heads nodded again in solemn shocked agreement. The stupid, pompous fools, Alan thought, sitting there like a bench of judges, agreeing with everything that Harry suggested, just because they had always listened to Harry, their natural leader since they had arrived together as timid new boys at school.

His fury boiled over. ' You damned liar ! ' he roared, and jerked his chair aside. ' You know perfectly well that I didn't mark those cards.'

He took a step forward, but Stephen caught at his arm.

M.V.—2

' Now, calm down, Alan,' he said soothingly.   ' I don't believe this nonsense, for one.'

But Alan pushed him away impatiently.   ' I'll call you out for this, Harry.   You——'

' Why should I fight a cheat ? ' Harry asked insolently.

The table toppled over with a thud, and Harry recoiled, too late, though, to prevent Alan's hands from fastening themselves around his throat.   But they were pulled apart, Alan growling like an infuriated bear, and Harry trying to repair the damage to his once neatly arranged stock.

' Afraid as well as being a liar ? ' Alan said.

' Oh. have it your own way,' Harry said.   ' Hugh, act for me, will you ? '

He turned his back on Alan, and three other backs turned, too.   The sight of those hostile backs was like a douche of icy water on Alan's smouldering temper, and he stumbled out of the room and down the stairs to the darkness of the court below.

There was a faint glimmer of light from the porter's lodge by the gates of the college, and Alan walked heavily towards it, turning there to reach his staircase in the corner.   He clattered up the bare, wooden stairs to his rooms, slamming the door behind him.   His servant had left one candle alight on the mantelpiece, and Alan lighted another from it.   He heard feet run up the stairs outside, and Stephen burst into the room.

' I've arranged it for you, Alan,' he said, and dropped into a chair.   ' Eight o'clock on the Backs.   In that field opposite Trinity gates.'

' Swords or pistols ? '

' Pistols.   I insisted that it was your choice of weapons, because Harry really started the whole business.   You're hopeless with small-swords, so I said pistols.'

Alan slumped into a chair that creaked under his weight. Stephen looked at him in concern.

' Who marked those cards, Alan ? ' he asked.   ' If they were marked at all.'

' Oh, they were marked,' Alan said.   ' It was Hugh Goring.'

' Hugh ! '

' Yes, I lent him those cards ; he was short of two packs. Who else could it have been ? It takes time to mark a whole pack. Besides, I noticed him staring at Harry's hand just before he won two big bets.' Alan sighed wearily. ' And like a fool I said nothing.'

' You should have stopped the game.'

' And ruin Hugh ? You know what it would have meant for him. Would you have done it ? '

' Yes, of——' Stephen broke off and shrugged his shoulders. ' Oh, I don't know, Alan. I should have done the same as you, I suppose. This is a beastly business. What do we do now ? Shall I speak to Hugh and Harry ? '

' You can't very well do that until after we've met in the morning,' Alan pointed out. ' I'll have a word with Hugh, then.' He clenched his fists and scowled at the candles.

' Well, we'd better go to bed and have some sleep,' Stephen said. ' I'll call for you at half-past seven. We're using my pistols, by the way. You've fired with them, haven't you ? '

Alan nodded, and showed Stephen out, before walking back slowly to the mantelpiece and staring down into the empty grate. He had never fought a duel before ; nor had Harry, for that matter. Alan smiled, despite his gloom. His father would want to hear about it all, for Lord Aubigny was a famous duellist with a European reputation as a swordsman.

Well, he was no hand with the small-sword, that was certain, though he was a fine shot. But standing fire was a very different affair from shooting on the range ; at least, that was the stock phrase of any duellist. He would find out for himself in the morning, Alan decided, and went into his bedroom, taking the candles with him.

He slept heavily, and awoke with a start to see the sun streaming in through his windows. He sat up and rubbed his eyes. His head was aching, and his mouth was dry ; too much wine the night before, Alan thought, as he reached for his watch. Five minutes to half-past seven !

He hurled the bedclothes to one side and rolled out of bed. He had forgotten to leave a message for his servant to call him early. Stephen would be here in a minute or so ; he was a punctual person. Alan began to dress with frantic haste.

Anyway, it was a lovely June morning. Below his windows the dew was sparkling on King's lawn, and he could see the sun glittering on the river as it ran slowly between King's and Clare bridges.

But there was no time to admire the view or the weather. What clothes should he wear ? Dark colours, his father had always said, especially for a duel with pistols. Hurriedly Alan ran his eyes over the contents of his wardrobe. That would do ! He took out a dark-grey coat with huge cuffs and tight waist. Waistcoat next, but all his waistcoats were brightly coloured. He would have to button the coat up well, and . . .

Stephen Rawle burst into the room. ' Not dressed, Alan ? ' he exclaimed. ' We'll be late ! Looks bad, you know.'

' All right, all right ! ' Alan said testily, for he was not feeling so calm as he had hoped. ' Give me a hand with these clothes.'

He snatched up a shirt, pulled it over his head, held out a hand for the breeches which Stephen was holding, and started to put one leg into them.

' Stockings first ! ' Stephen said. ' Here ! '

Alan grunted crossly. Fool that he was. Of course he must pull on the long white stockings first, for they came up over the knee, and it was quite impossible to roll them up under the breeches. He struggled with them, then the breeches, his fingers fumbling clumsily with the buckles at each knee. His fingers were shaking. Was it just excitement and haste ?

Stephen was handing him a white stock, and Alan fastened it round his neck with savage jerks. Then the waistcoat with its endless number of buttons, each one obstinate and in-furiating, especially when an impatient and nervous Stephen tried to help.

' Sit still, for heaven's sake ! ' Alan snapped. ' Who invented these infernal buttons ? Sit down, Stephen, and don't walk around like a hungry lion.'

'But we shall be late, Alan ! You can't be late for a duel.'

'I know that. Throw me that coat.' Alan thrust his arms into the grey coat, trying to shake out the lace ruffles at the sleeves of his shirt as he did so. But ruffles were not meant to be treated in that unceremonious way, and Alan pulled at them roughly.

'Don't bother about those,' Stephen pleaded.

'I'm not going to turn out like a tramp, even if we are late,' Alan said obstinately. 'It's your fault, you should have called me earlier. Tie my hair at the back, can you ? '

He tried to stand still and control his rising irritation and impatience while Stephen's fingers, as shaky now as his own, tried to tie the black bow at the back of Alan's neck.

With a growl of relief when he had finished, Alan rummaged for a hat and a stick.

'You don't want a stick, Alan,' Stephen protested.

'Yes, I do,' and Alan picked up a long Malacca cane, clapped the three-cornered hat on to his black hair, and clattered down the stairs with Stephen at his heels, long coat-tails flapping as they hurried across the court below.

They crossed the lovely bridge of Clare without sparing a glance for the carefully tended gardens, the peaceful river, or any of the stately buildings of the colleges on either side. They raced down the long avenue and emerged on to the road at the far end.

There was no one about at this hour, and Alan lengthened his stride, until Stephen, who was a head and shoulders shorter, was half running to keep up with his long legs. Under his left arm he was hugging the flat mahogany case containing the duelling pistols.

Harry Napier must be on the ground already, Alan thought, for there was no sign of anyone on the road ahead of them. Anyway, Harry was a Trinity man, so he would not have so far to walk. They passed the gates at the end of Trinity avenue, and crossed the road. Neither spoke, and they strode along in gloomy silence.

As fashionable young men they were familiar enough with

the etiquette of the duel ; they talked frequently about well-known meetings, and exchanged tales of famous duellists. But this was the first time that either had been brought face to face with the stark reality of an engagement. The shock had stripped away their air of fashionable sophistication, leaving two young undergraduates hurrying along a lonely road at eight in the morning, silent, depressed, and more than a little frightened of what lay ahead.

' That gate,' Alan said.

They went through the open gate, up the narrow track beyond with trees on either side, until they reached an open space with a level expanse of closely clipped turf. A small group of men stood near the hedge on the right.

They all turned as Alan and Stephen arrived. On one side, standing alone, was the short, active figure of Harry Napier, dressed in a dark-green coat, his three-cornered hat pulled down well over his forehead. Near him was his second, Hugh Goring, and Alan saw that Dundas and Rankin, who had both been present at the card party, were there, too.

Detached from this little group was a much older man, with a wooden case under his arm.

' Doctor,' Stephen muttered. ' James Dundas said he would find one.'

Alan nodded curtly. He did not like the look of the doctor, a portly and shabbily dressed fellow. He tried not to think of the contents of the man's case, the neat rows of shining instruments, the probes, the knives, and the forceps, all waiting to be used. He shivered suddenly, and began to feel sick. He should have had something hot to drink before he left his rooms.

He bowed to the others. They ignored him coldly, and his lips tightened. So that was the line they were going to take. He stood aloof, while Stephen and Hugh opened the case of pistols, and began to load the deadly weapons. Alan wanted to pace up and down, but that would be an obvious sign of his impatience and growing nervousness. But it was hard to stand still, and to control the faint trembling of his knees.

A warm breath of brandy was wafted across his face, and a hoarse voice greeted him. It was the doctor. Alan bowed stiffly. No respectable doctor would have turned out at such short notice, if indeed he would have come at all, for the University authorities were beginning to take a stern line over duels between undergraduates. At closer quarters this particular doctor looked even less prepossessing than at first sight. A stubble of dirty grey hair covered his mottled face, and he did not look as if he had shaved or washed for some days. His eyes were bleary with drink, and his fingers were shaking.

'Doctor Joseph Brown, at your service, sir,' he said, and bowed again. 'You need have no fear, my dear boy. I am well accustomed to these little affairs. A dig with my forceps, and the bullet will be out before you can say William Pitt.'

Alan bowed again, even more stiffly. The prospect of those grimy, shaking fingers probing into his side to find a bullet made the feeling of sickness well up like a flood in his stomach, and he gulped.

Would they never finish loading those pistols? Alan clenched his fists and then pushed them into the deep pockets of his coat. He would not have staked much on the steadiness of his hands now. His pistol would waver up and down as if he were suffering from a fever, and his heart was thumping now, pounding away under his shirt with the loud regularity of a hammer.

Stephen was pacing out the distance on the grass, and dug his heel in to mark the spot. Then he hurried over to Alan, while Hugh crossed to Harry.

'Twenty-five paces, Alan. Goring insisted on that. You fire when I drop my handkerchief.'

He held out a long-barrelled pistol, his fingers grasping it gingerly by the muzzle. 'Careful,' he muttered. 'It's cocked, and it's a hair trigger.'

But Alan knew all about duelling pistols, and their exceptionally light triggers, so that they would fire at the merest touch. His big fist closed over the heavy butt, and keeping the muzzle pointed to the ground, he walked over to

his mark. It was a relief to move, but his legs were shaking, and the feeling of sickness was overwhelming.

He gritted his teeth, and turned sideways to face Napier. Twenty-five paces had never seemed so short before, as he stared into Harry's face. Napier had half turned, too, his neat, dapper figure tense and still. He was avoiding Alan's glance, his eyes fixed on the trees by the hedge.

'Ready, gentlemen?' Stephen asked in a voice that quavered a little.

Alan gulped and nodded. What would it be like to be hit by a bullet? he was thinking. But his father had told him. A smashing blow, numbness, and then a red-hot, searing pain as if a skewer had been thrust into you.

Stephen's hand was rising slowly with the white handkerchief. Harry was up at the aim already, but all that Alan could see of his pistol was the round, black muzzle pointing straight at him. He could not take his eyes off that menacing, motionless threat. With a jerk he began to come up to the aim himself, but his arms were shaking now as violently as his knees, and he closed his lips tightly in a frantic effort to choke down the horrible sensation of nausea. His heart was racing, thump, thump, thump, so loudly that everyone there must hear it.

But all control had gone. The pistol dropped from his trembling fingers. It hit the soft turf, and exploded in a flash and a swift gush of white smoke. The terrific crack of the explosion made Alan start back with a cry of horror. The bullet whizzed into the hedge, and then there was silence.

Alan took a deep breath. Harry had come down from the aim, and was watching him. So, too, were the others, a circle of cold, contemptuous faces. Alan stared round ; he opened his mouth to speak, but a loud shout came from the direction of the road, and three running figures burst into view.

In front was a man in the gown and white tabs of a University don. Behind him were two burly figures in dark coats and breeches.

' Proctor and bulldogs,' a voice muttered, but there was no move to run, for the only way out of the field was blocked.

' Your names and colleges, please, gentlemen,' the Proctor said.

He stopped in front of Harry. ' Sir Harry Napier of Trinity,' Harry said. He made no attempt to conceal the pistol still hanging down by his side. It was far too large a weapon for that.

' And you, sir ? ' the Proctor asked, turning to Alan.

' The Honourable Alan Carey of Clare, sir.'

' Please hand your pistols over, gentlemen.' The bulldogs took possession of the pistols, handling them carefully, for Harry's was still cocked.

' You will return to your colleges immediately, gentlemen,' the Proctor said. He turned, and with his two officials behind, disappeared down the track to the road.

There was a pause. Then the group broke up without a word. They walked slowly away, while Alan watched them go. No one turned to speak to him, not even Stephen, Alan noticed, as the stiff backs marched away from him, until he was left there alone in the field ; a coward, now, as well as a cheat.

Chapter Two

THE EARL OF AUBIGNY

ALAN left the Bear Inn at Cowbridge soon after eight. He had spent the night there, the last stage of his journey, for he should reach his home at Llanstephan that after-noon if he rode steadily.

The morning was fresh and fine, with a promise of heat once the sun was fully up, for the sky was a deep blue already, and clear of clouds. It was as pleasant a day as anyone could wish for on a long ride, but neither the weather nor the prospect of reaching his home gave Alan any feeling of contentment.

He had been sent down from Cambridge. He was riding home to Wales in disgrace. But the reason for his punishment, the duel, was the least of his troubles. The accusation of

19

cheating he could explain, but his pitiful cowardice the next morning was something he could not bear to think about.

He was still bewildered by the events of the last few days. He felt like a man suddenly flung into a whirlpool, carried remorselessly from one rock to another, and without a single hand held out to help him. The card party, the marked cards, the duel, his loss of nerve, had all followed each other with a grim and relentless fatality.

But that had not been the end. He had been summoned to the Master's Lodge for a brief and formal interview. The Master, once so friendly, had spoken to him with a frigid politeness. Perhaps the story of his cheating and cowardice had already reached the Master's ears, Alan thought, as he was told that he would be sent down for the rest of the term.

He was becoming a little more accustomed now to this chilly politeness. But it still hurt savagely. He preferred the turned backs and the silence, even the silence of Stephen Rawle who had not spoken to him since the duel.

In a few hours he would have to face his father. What would be Lord Aubigny's attitude ? Anger, contempt, a bleak indifference, or pity ? Anger, Alan hoped. That would be far easier to meet than contempt or pity.

Just before noon he trotted down the long gradual hill into Carmarthen. By the bridge he pulled into the side of the road to allow the stage-coach to Swansea to pass, the coachman pushing his team of greys hard to make the most of the level before they would be forced down to a walk up the long incline. Alan rode past the tollhouse and stopped again.

To the left was the road to Llanstephan, an hour's ride away. But he was hungry, and his hired horse could not go much farther without a rest. Alan rubbed his cheek with his riding crop, and watched two men in coracles fishing in the river below. If he went to the Ivy Bush Inn, he would be recognized. Probably old David Thomas, the innkeeper, would question him curiously, for he would wonder why Alan was home before the end of the University term.

Alan shook his reins, and cantered over the bridge into the narrow streets of the town. He could not go on avoiding people as if he were a leper. As an ostler came out and took his horse, Alan smiled bitterly. To judge by the way his friends at Cambridge had treated him he must have caught some disease far worse than leprosy.

He ate by himself in a corner of the coffee-room, and listened to the quick, singsong Welsh voices around him, for he could understand a good deal of Welsh. It was pleasant to hear these farmers talk. At Cambridge the conversation had been about nothing but the possibility of war with France, and the manœuvres of politicians at Whitehall. But in Carmarthen the price of wheat and the prospect of a fine summer were far more important than the threats of the French in North America, or whether the Empress Maria Theresa had really made an alliance with King Louis of France.

David Thomas greeted Alan in the yard when he strolled out after his meal.

' There's one of his lordship's horses from Llanstephan here, Mr Carey,' he said. ' Will you take him? And I'll send that hired hack of yours back for you.'

' Thank you, Thomas. I hired him from the Castle Inn at Swansea.' Alan fidgeted while the ostler strapped on his saddlebags. His heavier baggage was following by carrier. All of it, for Alan knew now that he would never return to Cambridge. That was the one definite fact in his future that he could foresee. He wished he could be as certain of the rest.

To his relief old Thomas asked no questions nor made any comments on his journey home. Alan trotted back over the bridge again ; the men were still fishing, a little farther down the river now, as he paid his toll and took the road to Llanstephan.

He rode steadily, his gloom increasing as each milestone was passed, and as each familiar landmark came into sight. He had always loved riding down this road, particularly when he had been away from home for a long time, spurring on his horse, or urging the coachman to hurry. But today he could have wished the distance was twice as great.

The road followed the river, and then eventually the river widened into a broader estuary, and Alan could see the sun glistening on the sea, with the grey ruins of Llanstephan Castle rising up against the blue skyline. Alan set his teeth. Best get it over quickly, he decided. The lodge gates were open, thank goodness, so there would not have to be any explanations for Evans when he came out.

He cantered briskly along the curving drive through the park, with the old castle high above him on the crest of the hill. The Careys had long since built themselves a more comfortable home, and here it was at last, a stately Elizabethan house, yet friendly enough with its warm red bricks and the many windows glittering in the late afternoon sun.

A liveried footman appeared at the great doorway, and a groom came running from the stables as Alan's horse clip-clopped up the gravelled drive.

'Why, it's Master Alan!' exclaimed the footman, and, 'Why, it's Master Alan!' echoed the groom.

'Hullo, Will,' Alan said to the groom. He ran quickly up the steps to the doorway. 'Davies, take my saddlebags to my room, will you?' and he brushed past into the hall to avoid any more questions.

But once inside the house he hesitated, and looked round uneasily, bracing himself for the sight of a familiar face, or the sound of a surprised voice. He did not have long to wait. From the landing above there came a shrill, excited cry, and the rustle of silk down the stairs.

'Alan! Why, it's Alan!' His sister Anne hurried across the expanse of polished floor as rapidly as her hooped skirt would allow her. 'Alan, what are you doing here? You don't come down until the end of June.'

'Hullo, Anne.' Alan looked down from his great height into his sister's startled face, and smiled wryly. Here were the first awkward questions. Better Anne first, and then there was only his father, for his mother was dead, and his elder brother George was in London.

Davies, the footman, was crossing the hall just behind with the saddlebags. Alan jerked his head in warning. Anne's expression of surprise turned to one of alarm. If her brother's sudden arrival could not be explained within hearing of the servants, then the news must be bad. She turned, and led the way to a small ante-room on the other side of the hall.

'What is it, Alan?' she asked immediately the door was closed. 'It's trouble, isn't it?'

'Yes, Anne. Where's father?'

'In the library.'

'Anyone staying here?'

'Only Mr Pitt. He came two days ago.'

Alan frowned. He wanted no witnesses when he met his father, least of all Mr Pitt, the Paymaster to the Forces, and one of the most popular politicians in the country.

'Father's alone, Alan,' Anne said. 'Mr Pitt is working at his papers in the Long Gallery.'

Alan squared his broad shoulders and turned towards the door. But his sister caught him by the big cuff of his coat.

'Alan, what is the matter? Why have you come down in the middle of the term?'

'I'll tell you later.'

'No, now, Alan, now!'

Alan shrugged his shoulders. Anne could be obstinate when she wished, and it would be easier, in some ways, to tell her first.

'I've been sent down,' he said.

'Sent down!' echoed Anne. 'What have you done, Alan?'

'I fought a duel.'

Anne's worried face cleared, and she laughed. 'Is that all? Oh, Alan, you are stupid! Father won't be angry with you for that. He fought dozens of duels. You've heard General Rawle tell us about them.'

General Rawle. Alan winced; that was Stephen's father. He opened the door. 'It's worse than that,' he said harshly, and strode across the hall towards the double doors of the library. His sister's hand flew to her mouth as she watched him pause by the door, draw himself up like a man about to dive into cold water, and then open the door.

The tall windows of the library looked out across the park to the sea. Warm sunlight filled the room, brightening the colours of the carpets, falling richly on the sombre leather of the tiers of books that rose from the floor to the moulded ceiling. Two wing armchairs were standing on either side of the wide fire-place, though there was no fire burning there on this lovely June day. Clamped to the wall above was a faded and tattered French standard, captured by the Earl at the battle of Malplaquet.

In one of the chairs under that proud trophy was a tall, thin old gentleman in a blue coat and a gaily coloured silk waistcoat. His white-wigged head was resting against one wing of the chair, his long, white-stockinged legs stretched out comfortably on a stool. He was sound asleep, breathing quietly, his face relaxed and peaceful.

Alan walked quietly towards the fire-place, and stood for a moment looking down at his father with a mixture of affection and apprehension. The Earl must be nearly eighty now, he was thinking, for it was fifty years since Major the Earl of Aubigny of Cadogan's Regiment of Dragoons had ridden out with the staff of the Duke of Marlborough from a German village on that misty morning when the French batteries were rumbling across the wide plains of Blenheim.

The Earl stirred. His eyes opened and travelled slowly up from Alan's riding boots, his thick grey brows rising in surprise as he recognized his son.

' Why, Alan ! ' he said. ' You should be at Cambridge.'

Alan took a deep breath. ' I have been sent down, sir.'

' Oh, I see,' the Earl said slowly. ' You had better sit down and tell me all about it.'

Alan did as he was told. His knees were beginning to shake as they had done on that morning in the field on the Backs.

' Why did the Master send you down, Alan ? ' the level voice asked.

' I was fighting a duel, sir.'

' Indeed ! ' The Earl half smiled. ' Well, that's no great matter, Alan. I suppose I must have fought half a dozen duels by the time I had reached your age.' His mind seemed to drift back momentarily to the past, as old men's often do. Then, ' It was pistols, I hope. You're no swordsman, despite all my lessons. You're a fine shot, though, better than I was, I fancy, and I was considered a dead shot with duelling pistols.'

' It was pistols, sir.'

The Earl nodded his satisfaction, and reached for his snuff box. His eyes were somewhat faded now, but they were still shrewd and alert. He noticed the tired face of his son, the tightly clenched fists ; there was no slackening of the tension despite his mild comments. There was more to come, and two deep lines appeared on the Earl's forehead.

' You didn't kill your man, Alan ? ' he asked sharply. ' That's a vastly different matter. It wouldn't have mattered so much in my day, perhaps, but times have changed since then.'

' No, sir. No one was hit.' Alan had not raised his head. He was inspecting the intricate pattern of the carpet beneath his feet.

' Then there is something else you have to tell me ? '

' Yes, sir.'

' What is it, Alan ? '

Alan covered his face with his hands. ' I . . . I can't tell you, sir,' he said hoarsely.

The Earl contemplated his son in silence. But not for nothing had he earned the ungrudging respect and affection of a regiment of Dragoons.

' You can tell me anything, Alan,' he said firmly.

Alan looked up quickly. As he saw in his father's face the deep understanding and kindness there he realized that here, at last, was one hand stretched out to help him. The dreadful weight of depression and loneliness that had pressed down on him for the last week seemed to roll away.

' It's bad, sir,' he said.

' So I gather. Well, I've faced some unpleasant things in my life.'

' It started at a card party.'

M.V.—3

' Oh, money, is it ? ' the Earl said, almost with relief. ' We had one gambler in the family. But that's another story. You lost, of course ? '

' Yes, sir. But I can pay. That's not the trouble : I wish it was. Just before we finished playing I noticed that the cards were marked.'

' Did you know who had done it ? '

' I was pretty certain that it was our host, Hugh Goring.' Alan explained his reasons.

' You exposed him, Alan ? '

' No, sir, I didn't.'

' You should have done so immediately,' the Earl said decisively. No one could imagine his hesitating so fatally as Alan had done.

' I know that now, sir. But like a fool I kept quiet. I was sorry for Hugh. He's got no money, and no connexions. He wants to go in for politics or the army, and he'd made friends at Cambridge who could have helped him.'

The Earl grunted. ' Including you, I suppose. Well, what happened then ? '

' Harry Napier noticed the marks on the cards, too.'

' Napier ? Napier ? ' queried the Earl.

' Sir Harry Napier, sir. He has estates in Norfolk.'

' Ah, yes, I remember the family now. I knew his grand-father. Fine soldier ; Major in Webb's Regiment of Foot. Killed, poor fellow, in the attack on the village at Blenheim.'

Alan waited patiently. His father had a vast acquaintance and a remarkable memory for their names, though he was apt to judge their worth by their presence or otherwise in that glorious army that had swept so triumphantly over Europe under the great Duke. For there was only one Duke for the old Dragoon officer, the Duke of Marlborough.

' Harry accused me of marking the cards.'

' You ! Why you ? '

' They were my cards, sir. I'd lent some new packs to Hugh. And Harry saw me watching him when he was feeling for the nicks on the back of the court cards. I suppose I must have looked afraid, because I was still hoping to keep Hugh out of it.'

The Earl grunted again. ' Then you lost your temper, eh, and called Napier out ? '

' Yes, sir. Stephen Rawle acted for me.'

' Stephen ? Oh, yes, Donald Rawle's boy.' The Earl smiled, for General Rawle had served with him for many years in the same regiment.

' We met the next morning, and . . .' Alan dropped his head again, his face working pitifully.

His father was watching him intently, and nodded as if he now knew the answer to some question that had been puzzling him.

' You discovered that standing fire for the first time is a vastly different matter to shooting at a target,' he said.

Alan was startled. ' How did you know that, sir ? ' he exclaimed.

' Never mind that. What did happen ? '

' I . . . I couldn't even come up to the aim, sir. My hand was shaking so badly that I dropped the pistol, and it went off as it hit the ground.'

' Yes, it would, of course, with a hair trigger. And then ? '

' The Proctor arrived with two bulldogs. I suppose some-one must have warned him. He took our names.'

' And the others there ? '

' They walked off and left me there. I don't blame them,' Alan said bitterly. ' Even Stephen hasn't spoken to me since.'

The Earl took snuff reflectively. ' What do you intend to do next ? '

' I don't know, sir. I was sent down for the rest of the term only. But I can't go back. I can't possibly, sir. You won't make me do that, will you ? ' Alan asked pleadingly.

' No, no, you need not go back to Cambridge.'

' But what can I do ? A coward and a cheat ! That's what everyone will say. It will be all over the London clubs in a week. George will hear about it soon.'

' I have no doubt that George will know how to deal with anyone foolish enough to tell him,' the Earl said dryly. ' He may not be exactly up to my standard with the small-sword, but he is still a very fine fencer. It would be a brave man or an extremely stupid one who will tell George that his brother is a coward or a cheat.'

' But you will have to tell him, sir,' Alan burst out. ' What will he say ? What must you think ? I've disgraced the family, all of you ! '

' My dear Alan,' the Earl said soothingly. ' If you have visions of me cutting you off with a shilling, and showing you the door with a dramatic flourish from the Drury Lane Theatre, then you have sadly misjudged me. Do please credit me with some little intelligence. I have been about the world, you know, and this is not my first experience of such matters.'

' I'm sorry, sir.'

' Now, let's discuss this calmly,' the Earl said, helping himself to snuff once more. ' The first notion that you must get into your head is that you are not a coward at all.'

' What ! ' Alan gasped. ' But you didn't see . . .'

' No. But I can tell you exactly what happened. You found yourself standing opposite a man who was about to fire at you. You were frightened. If any man ever tells you that he was not afraid under such conditions, then he is a liar ! I've seen really brave men shake with uncontrollable fear when they heard a cannon ball scream over their head for the first time. I did myself, and not for the first time only.'

' But you saw hundreds of actions, sir. You fought dozens of duels. They say you had no nerves at all,' Alan protested.

The Earl snorted. ' Nonsense ! I was frightened many times and always in duels with pistols. Now, with small-swords, that was different, because I knew what I was capable of with a sword, and I knew quite well that there were few men in Europe who were my equal.'

Alan was still not convinced. ' But you didn't run away, or show you were afraid, sir.'

' I dare say not. I was lucky. I don't suppose you will run away the next time. You know what it feels like to be afraid now, and believe me, Alan, that is a lesson well worth learning. I remember when I drew up the regiment at

Malplaquet with the rest of our cavalry for the final charge against the French. The whole of the Maison du Roi, the finest French cavalry they had, were spread right across the heath facing us. Their batteries opened up on us as we advanced. I always used to have a fear that my horse would go down, and there I would be on the ground with the rest of the regiment galloping behind me.' The Earl shrugged his shoulders. 'But I'd had the same fear before, and I'd heard cannon balls before. That helped.' He glanced up at the French standard on the wall, and his nostrils flared as if he could still smell the acrid tang of gunpowder, and his whole face lit up, his eyes shining, as he saw once more the long lines of horsemen thundering over the wide heathland of Malplaquet.

Alan nodded, though not so gloomily as before. 'But I'm branded now,' he said hopelessly. 'I'm ashamed to look anyone in the face. How can I make a fresh start, sir?'

'Ah, I have an idea that might solve that problem,' the Earl said. The French clock on the mantelpiece chimed the hour, and he rose to his feet. 'Time to dress for dinner, Alan. I'll talk to you again this evening. By the way, Billy Pitt is here. Did Anne tell you?'

'Yes, sir.'

'I'll tell him something of this. He's a clever fellow, and he might have something useful to suggest. Now, off you go, Alan, and get out of those riding clothes.'

Chapter Three

MR PITT

A LAN paused outside the drawing-room to shake out the
lace ruffles at either wrist, and to ensure that his long
stockings were unwrinkled.

His best clothes were still on their way from Cambridge, so
that he had been forced to make the most of what little was
left of his wardrobe at Llanstephan. He hoped his appearance
would pass muster, for the Earl held decided views on clothes.
He would run a critical eye over his family and guests as if he
were still inspecting his regiment of Dragoons on the parade
ground.

The drawing-room was filled with the warmth and light of
the evening sun as Alan went in. The Earl and Anne were
sitting by the great Elizabethan bay window. Standing near
them was the tall, somewhat ungainly figure of Mr William
Pitt, Paymaster-General to His Majesty's Forces. He was
talking vigorously in his deep, resonant voice, but that was no
surprise to Alan. On the previous occasions when he had met
Mr Pitt, that politician was always talking, dominating the

conversation, though he never had much difficulty in doing that, for he was invariably well worth hearing.

He greeted Alan pleasantly, but soon returned to the subject of his conversation. Indeed, throughout dinner he never left it. There flowed from him a steady flood of virulent criticism of his colleagues in the Government. It was an astonishing performance. Every sentence, almost every phrase, was accompanied by some extravagant gesture of his hands; every shade of emotion in his trained voice was reflected in his dark, restless eyes. The most accomplished actor in London would have envied the relentless precision with which he drove home each point with all the deft skill of a craftsman hammering in a row of nails.

The long meal came to an end. As two footmen lighted candles and placed heavy decanters on the table, Anne rose, curtsied to her father, and left the men to their port. Mr Pitt stretched himself luxuriously, holding a brimming glass up to the light. The pleasantest hour of the day had arrived, when a gentleman could relax over his bottle of wine, and talk and drink, until the bottles were empty or one's head could stand no more.

' Now, what are we going to do with Alan ? ' he asked.

Alan cleared his throat nervously. His future was about to be settled, and he sensed that his father had not only discussed the question with Mr Pitt, but had probably reached a decision.

' You must make a completely fresh start,' the Earl said.

' But where, sir ? '

' In America ! ' and Mr Pitt waved a long arm out dramatically as if he were sweeping Alan across the Atlantic.

' America ! ' Alan gasped. He looked in bewilderment from one to the other.

The Earl refilled his glass and pushed the decanter towards his guest. ' Drink up, Billy,' he said. ' You haven't got to face the House in the morning.'

' But why America, sir ? ' Alan asked.

' What else, Alan ? The Army might be awkward ; you

would meet too many people you know. I had thought of India, but one of the family out there is enough, I suppose.'

Alan nodded. His other brother, Rupert, had been in the Carnatic for some years now with the East India Company.

'Besides, I have some estates in America,' his father went on. 'I expect you know that the Crown made big grants of land over there at various times, and my grandfather was one of those who benefited.'

'Whereabouts, sir?'

'In the state of New York, as they call it now. On the Mohawk River.'

The names meant little to Alan, as indeed they meant little to most people in England then. His face must have given him away, for Mr Pitt snorted.

'I can see, Alan,' he said, 'that you are as ignorant of the American colonies and what they mean to us as my imbecile colleagues in the Government.'

'Tell us, Billy,' the Earl said, his eyes twinkling with amusement.

Mr Pitt seemed to gather himself together, and he turned on to his audience of two the full force of his extraordinary personality. He might have been about to address a crowded House of Commons.

'On the other side of the Atlantic,' he said, 'there is a whole continent, an entire new world! So far we have merely scratched out a foothold on a little corner of it. The rest is . . . empty.' A flourish of his hands sketched out in Alan's imagination the impression of an immense void.

'The potential wealth of North America is incalculable.' Mr Pitt repeated the word, 'Incalculable,' his trained voice rolling out the long syllables with relish. 'And it is there waiting for us to take.'

He paused, as if expecting some suitable comment. The Earl obediently gave him his cue. 'And what are we doing?' he asked.

'Nothing!' Mr Pitt cried in tones of anguish, so heartfelt that Alan could feel his own growing distress, so completely was he identifying himself already with every word that was being said.

'What can you expect from Pelham and his brood?' and Pitt mentioned the leader of the Government with such biting contempt that Alan loathed the unfortunate politician from that moment.

'Pelham!' and Mr Pitt rolled his eyes upwards with a gesture that might well have made his hearers think he was referring to Judas Iscariot. 'All he and Newcastle can think about is the defence of Hanover. Fiddling little alliances and campaigns in Germany! What value are they to England?' he demanded.

'But if we go to war in France or Austria, or even Prussia, as we did last time,' the Earl said, 'then we must defend Hanover. We can't abandon all Europe, Billy.'

'Of course not, Charles,' Pitt said quickly. 'But Europe is a secondary consideration to us now. Our main interests are elsewhere today.'

'Where?'

'At sea. All over the world. We must have command of the sea, and then we can smash the French!'

'France again,' the Earl muttered.

'You should know that, Charles,' Mr Pitt said. 'Yes, France.' He was in full flood now, his glass of port forgotten. He was speaking with an intensity that was almost frightening; even the mildest phrase was delivered with an air and a tone of overwhelming importance.

'France is our greatest trade rival. Trade, world-wide trade, together with the command of the sea, will make us the greatest and richest power in the world.' He pushed away the decanter at his elbow, and leant forward. 'There are four great trade centres: North America, the West Indies, India, and Africa.' He pointed a commanding finger at Alan. 'Do you know what the American trade consists of, Alan?'

Alan tried to answer. But Mr Pitt had not expected a reply. He swept on without a pause. 'Fur, fish, and naval supplies.'

'Now, this is my plan.' He lifted the white napkin from

his lap. 'Here is the American coastline,' and he spread out
the napkin on the table in front of him. 'We hold that
coastline. Two thousand miles of it!' His busy fingers
picked up a handful of nuts from the silver dish near Alan.
'Here, here, and over there,' and the nuts were laid out in
a long curving line, 'the French. Inland along the St
Lawrence, through the Great Lakes, and then down the River
Ohio to the Mississippi. They control Canada, and reach
right round behind us, from north to south. What does that
mean?'

This time neither Alan nor his father attempted to produce
an answer. They waited obediently, partly mesmerized and
wholly fascinated.

'We are pinned to the coast,' and Mr Pitt's hand fell with
a thump on to the napkin. 'The French can block every
move we make. We're like a man clinging to the edge of
a cliff; the French are standing on the top above. Can we
climb up and walk inland?'

He paused dramatically, one large, white hand in the air.
'No!' he trumpeted, and the hand came down with a crash.
'They can stamp on our fingers and kick us into the sea!'

The napkin was hurled from the table. Lying on the gleaming surface was the crescent of nuts. Alan drew a deep breath.
The Earl was staring down gloomily at the nuts.

'Isn't an attack being made now on one of these French
forts?' he asked.

'On Fort Duquesne. Here!' and Pitt placed his finger
on a nut in the centre of the line. 'General Braddock has
some regular troops and a force of colonials with him.'

'Braddock,' the Earl said thoughtfully.

'What is your professional opinion of him, Charles?'

'Oh, he's a good soldier. But . . .' The Earl shrugged
his shoulders. 'I feel uneasy about this fighting in North
America, Billy. There are no roads as we know them; just
hundreds of miles of forest land. The tactics we used in the
Low Countries and Germany won't be much use on the other
side of the Atlantic.'

'Exactly!' Mr Pitt thumped the table in his agitation.

' I can guess what Braddock and his men are doing ! Blundering about in the forests with their red coats against French trappers and Red Indians who can make themselves invisible behind a leaf ! '

' What would you do, then ? '

' If I was given full powers,' Pitt said without any hesitation, ' I should build up our Navy and Army. Neither is in a fit state to fight a major war. You know that, Charles. You learnt your soldiering under Marlborough. Then I would concentrate on Quebec. Here ! ' and he picked up a nut near the edge of the table. ' That is the key to Canada. From there we can capture all the other French forts.' The crescent of nuts was swept up in one large, white hand. ' The whole of North America will be ours. Trade, wealth, world-wide power and riches ! '

The Earl rubbed his chin, his shrewd eyes on Pitt. Perhaps he knew that behind those bombastic phrases and the resounding, over-confident voice, was the flash of genius, the torrential energy and the far-reaching inspiration that might well change the history of the world.

' We must hold France in Europe, too,' he said a little doubtfully.

' Of course, Charles. We must have an ally. Prussia, if you like, and a small army to cover Hanover. It belongs to the King, so we must do that much. But the main effort, the decisive blow, must be at sea, then in Canada and India. Those are the places that matter, not a few hundred square miles in Europe.'

' Oh, you're quite right, Billy,' the Earl said. ' But will you ever be given full powers ? '

Pitt's expressive face relapsed into a mask of despair. ' Not until the Pelhams have made a muddle-headed mess of the whole business. Then the country will call for me.' He paused, and for the first time that evening he spoke quietly and naturally. ' I know that I can save the country. And that I alone can.'

He pushed back his chair. ' If you will excuse me, Charles,' he said briskly. ' But I still have many letters to write.'

There was silence in the candle-lit room when the door closed. It was broken by a loud clink of glass as the Earl reached for the decanter.

' " I know that I can save the country ", ' he muttered. ' Have you ever heard such fantastic arrogance in a man before, Alan ? '

Alan shook his head. ' No, sir. But . . .' He half smiled at the absurdity of the idea. ' But I think he's right.'

His father laughed. ' So you've fallen under the spell, too. You're not the only one, Alan. I did, some years ago. You can't stand against Pitt. It would be as useless as a single infantryman trying to push back a squadron of Dragoons.' He sighed. ' But he's quite mad, of course.'

' Mad, sir ? '

' Haven't you noticed ? No, I suppose you don't know him as well as I do. There are times when he is completely unbalanced.'

' But, surely, sir, he's brilliant. He's a . . .'

' A genius ? Oh, yes, he's that, I'm sure. I believe every word he says. That's why I shall back him when the right time comes. I control six seats in the Commons, including George, and he'll need no prompting. I can speak in the Lords, too.' The Earl sighed again. ' But I could wish that Pitt was more stable, calmer. The greatest man I ever knew, the Duke—' and there crept into the Earl's voice that note of reverence without which he never mentioned Marlborough. ' The worse the crisis, the greater the responsibility, then the calmer he became. I remember when our infantry were repulsed after their first attack on the village at Blenheim. We all turned to watch the Duke.' The Earl smiled grimly. ' There wasn't a flicker on his face. He might have been watching the Foot Guards on parade at St James's Palace.'

He emptied his glass and pushed the decanter towards Alan. ' No ? Well, let's move into the library. This room seems empty now that Pitt's left it. Besides, I want to talk to you about America.'

They crossed the hall, and Alan walked forward to open the door of the library. But the Earl had paused to take snuff, and he was looking up at a painting of the Duke of Marlborough that hung on the wall. Alan followed his glance. The calm, handsome face of the Duke stared back at them impassively, and the Earl sighed, inhaled the snuff, and sneezed loudly.

' Curse this stuff,' he said. ' I've never really liked snuff.'

' You do want me to go to America, sir ? ' Alan said as his father settled down in his wing chair.

' It's the answer to all your problems, Alan. Stay there for a few years, and then come home. This business will have blown over by that time.'

' If Mr Pitt is right, there's going to be some action in America soon,' Alan said.

' Oh, yes, you'll find it interesting enough. But that's not the only reason why I want you to go. It's these estates of mine. I'm not at all satisfied with the way they are being managed, and last week I had a disturbing report from my agents in Boston.'

He opened a drawer in the desk by his side, and brought out a pile of papers and maps. Alan moved the candle, and they both bent over the map which the Earl was spreading out.

' My lands are there,' the Earl said. ' At a place called Ashwater. About three thousand acres or more, I believe, but most of it is still forest land. It's real importance is that it is used as a fur depot. You heard what Pitt said about the fur trade. There's a great deal of money to be made, and the returns from Ashwater are remarkably small.' He pushed the map away. ' I'm not so worried about the money. If I lost the Ashwater estates tomorrow I should not be greatly inconvenienced. But I do dislike being cheated ! '

Alan could well believe that, and he grinned. ' Who manages the depot for you, sir ? '

' A man called Hepburn. Mr Elijah Hepburn. I've never met him. In fact I know hardly anything about him at all. But there's something wrong, and he may be the cause.'

' Yes, I see, sir. And you want me . . .'

' I want you to investigate this Mr Elijah Hepburn for me.'

Alan shook his head doubtfully. ' I'll go, of course, sir. But I know nothing about the fur trade.'

' That doesn't matter,' the Earl said decisively. ' You're not a fool, and you can soon learn enough to find out whether Hepburn is a rogue or an honest man. I'll give you full legal authority to act in my name.'

Alan bent over the map again. He pored over the thin lines of the roads, very few of them, too, he noticed, and the widely scattered names of villages and towns. The area was a vast one, he realized with a start when he referred to the rough scale in miles at one corner of the map.

' You can sail from Bristol and land at Boston,' his father said. ' Then by road to the Mohawk Valley. That should be interesting. I wish I was twenty years younger. I would come with you.'

' I wish you could, sir,' Alan said. He started to trace out with his finger a possible route to the Mohawk River from Boston. His lips framed the names on the map, curiously familiar, some of them, and yet so strange to find on this map of a continent completely unknown to him. ' Worcester, Northampton, Troy, Albany, Massachusetts, Schenectady,' stumbling a little over the last two.

' What's that long lake to the north, sir ? ' he asked.

' Ah, that's Lake Champlain.' The Earl bent eagerly over the map. ' There is no definite frontier in that area between us and the French. That's the cause of most of these disputes. Now, look here, Alan. I've been studying these maps lately. Billy Pitt talked about an advance on Quebec and the line of French forts through the Great Lakes as they call them. I know what I would do if I was given orders to attack Quebec.' His eyes were gleaming now that his old professional interests were aroused. ' You see this river ? '

' The Hudson, sir.'

' No roads, you see, or precious few of 'em. So you must use the rivers. Now, the Hudson runs right up to within reach of Lake Champlain. Through the lake, and you reach the Richelieu River. See where that brings you out.'

' On the St Lawrence just above Quebec,' Alan said.

' Exactly. Of course, the French have built forts on Lake Champlain to cover that route. Here they are. Ticonderoga Crown Point.'

Alan stared curiously at the names. Ticonderoga. It was the first time he had heard of it. He little knew then how familiar it would become to him.

The Earl leant back in his chair. ' Give me the army we had in the Low Countries in 1705, and I would be at Quebec before the French could say Lake Champlain,' he said.

Alan grinned. ' What about those forts, sir ? I expect they're pretty strong.'

' No doubt. The French know something about soldiering. But they can't be as strong as some French fortresses we stormed, or as hard a nut to crack as the Schellenberg on the Rhine. But the Duke put us inside that before the Bavarians had time to think. Speed, terrific force at the right point, Alan.'

' You've got to find the right point, sir.'

' That's where a great general comes in,' the Earl said. ' We haven't got many at the moment. Billy will have to search around for someone if he wants Quebec in his pocket.'

He went off to bed soon after that, leaving Alan with the maps. He sat there until the candles were burning low. If he was going to America then it would be as well if he learnt something about this new world into which Mr Pitt and his father were plunging him at such short notice.

Mr Pitt left for London early the following morning. His coach was a modest enough conveyance for a prominent member of the Government, at a time when a Minister of State could accumulate a considerable fortune. It was, as Alan knew, all the more remarkable in Mr Pitt's case, for his post as Paymaster was notorious for being the most lucrative in the Government. But Mr Pitt had announced, very loudly indeed, for he knew the worth of public opinion, that he did not intend to make a penny from the immense sums that passed through his hands. That fact alone had done much to make him such a popular figure in the country.

The Earl wrote letters busily all that morning after his guest had gone. He wrote letters to his bankers in London, instructions to his lawyers in Swansea, more letters to his agents in Boston, and finally, instructions to shipping firms in Bristol. Alan watched all this activity with a mixture of amusement and alarm, for he had seen his father in this mood before, swift, decisive, the trained staff officer and soldier who had earned the approval of a general who had demanded a higher standard than any the British Army had produced before in its long history.

Later that afternoon Alan strolled down to the village, where he was greeted with delight by the landlord of the Carey Arms, and the half-dozen or so men in the front parlour of the inn. Alan was a popular figure in the district, not only because he was prepared to be friendly to everyone, but mainly on account of his skill as a boxer and wrestler. There was not a man in Llanstephan who would not have backed him against any wrestler in Carmarthenshire.

'Finished with Cambridge, Mr Carey, so I hear,' the landlord said, as he handed Alan a tankard of beer.

'Yes, I'm going to North America, Morgan,' Alan said, and smiled somewhat wryly. The news spread quickly, he thought. From the servants at the Hall, of course, who had passed it on to villagers eager to hear any gossip about the Carey family; their houses, their cottages and farms were all owned by the Earl, and much of their future, probably their whole livelihood, was in his hands.

'America!' The landlord whistled. 'That's a mighty long way from Llanstephan, Mr Carey.'

Alan nodded and held out his tankard to be refilled. He was about to ask them all to drink with him when he heard from outside the crack of a whip and the loud squeal of a horse in pain.

'Hullo, what's that?' he asked quickly.

The landlord exchanged glances with the others. 'That's Dai Bowen, I expect, Mr Carey.'

Alan was at the window by this time. 'Bowen?' he said.

' You wouldn't know him, Mr Alan,' one of the men said.
' He's from Llandilo way. Married Blodwen Rees of Pentyrch
Farm, he did, last month. Helping her father with the farm,
he is.'

Alan could see for himself now what was happening outside.
A black horse was rearing and struggling wildly between the
shafts of a farm wagon. Lashing at the poor brute was a
burly, thickset fellow armed with a short whip.

Alan scowled, and strode to the door. ' I'm going to stop
this,' he said.

' Careful, Mr Alan,' the landlord said quickly. ' Dai Bowen
has been in the professional ring. Nasty-tempered brute, he
is.'

Alan barely paused on his way out. Beer mugs clattered
down on tables as the parlour emptied rapidly. Even Morgan,
the landlord, deserted his bar, and pushed his way through
the door.

Alan crossed the street towards the wagon. The whip
swung back again, and Alan's long arm shot out. He caught
the man's wrist, wrenched sharply, and the whip dropped to
the cobbles.

' That's enough, Bowen,' he said curtly.

Bowen swung round, his mouth open in surprise. He was
a swarthy, untidy looking fellow with a good deal of gipsy
blood in him, Alan thought, and a formidable figure with his
wide shoulders, great chest and long arms.

' And who might you be, Mister ? ' he asked, running his
hot, angry eyes up and down Alan's fashionably dressed figure.

' That's Mr Alan Carey, Dai,' one of the onlookers said.

' Yes, indeed, I've heard of you,' Bowen said. ' Know
how to use your hands, so they tell me, Mister Carey. Well,
you keep 'em off me, see.'

He bent quickly, picked up the whip, and turned his back
contemptuously. Alan stepped forward, caught him by the
shoulder, and whirled him round again.

' I said that was enough, Bowen,' he said quietly. ' Drop
that whip.'

Bowen raised the whip. But Alan had been watching him

M.V.—4

intently. He jumped in, grabbed the whip with his left hand, and locked his right foot behind Bowen's ankle. Then he pushed in one quick heave of his body. Bowen reeled back with a crash against the wheel of his wagon. Alan tossed the whip to one of the small crowd, but never took his eyes off Bowen.

Bowen rolled up his sleeves with exaggerated care, revealing thick, muscular forearms covered with black, curling hair. Alan shrugged himself out of his long coat, while eager hands helped him. Then silence fell on the whole group.

Bowen spat loudly on his hands, and shuffled forward, head low down between his great shoulders, two big fists

weaving in and out. He had certainly fought in the ring,
Alan thought, and a dangerous customer he looked, too. A
tingling sensation ran down his back, and his heart began to
thump.

But he was given no time to decide whether he was afraid
or not. He could not run away from this, even if he wanted
to. Up went his own hands as Bowen slid forward a foot and
his left hand flickered out. Just in time Alan blocked the
punch. It caught him on the forearm with a thud that sent
a swift stab of hot, burning pain up to his shoulder. The
man could punch.

He stepped back to make the most of his longer reach ; it would be fatal to hammer this out at close quarters. Bowen came after him relentlessly, swinging viciously with each hand, grunting loudly as his huge brown fists thudded home on Alan's guard or whistled harmlessly over his head. Alan ducked and slid out of danger, poking out with his long left, and slowing up Bowen.

He saw an opening, feinted with his left, and down came Bowen's guard. Alan swung his own formidable right in a swinging punch. But Bowen had not fought professionally for nothing. He half caught the blow on his arm, but Alan's fist cracked up against his forehead, and sent him staggering back.

There was a whoop from the crowd ; no doubt about which side they were on, Alan thought, and he leapt forward recklessly. He had him now. He swung again, left, then right, and his right went home over the heart. Bowen grunted, and went back again. Alan poised himself for the kill, and then in he went.

A terriffic blow caught him on the side of the jaw. The sunlight changed to red, darting flames ; a sledgehammer, so it seemed, smashed into his ribs, and down he went, the hard cobbles cracking up against the back of his head. Rough hands heaved him to his feet. He shook his head to clear his dazed brain. On his tongue was the sharp taste of blood ; one side of his face was numb, and a dull burning pain was shooting through his chest.

' See, Mister Carey,' Bowen said. ' Keep your hands off me.'

He rushed in again. He was intent on battering Alan to a pulp, that was clear, and threw off one hand that tried to restrain him. Alan poked out his left hand desperately. It went home on Bowen's face somewhere, but did little to check his rush. He was punching furiously with both hands, wild sweeping blows for a professional pugilist, but he was out to finish the fight quickly before his opponent recovered from that knock-down.

Alan retreated slowly, fighting it out, but another terrific

punch caught him on the side of the head. Once more the
red flames flared in front of his eyes, but he swivelled to one
side, still throwing out his left hand. But it needed more
than left jabs to keep off Bowen's bull-like rush and the torrent
of smashing fists that seemed to envelop Alan. He went down
again as another punch jerked his head back, followed by a
numbing blow in the ribs, and a final sweeping right that
bowled him off his feet.

But he was up in an instant. A flood of raging, uncontrollable temper engulfed him, such a violent urge to smash
and batter as had never possessed him before in his life. He
gave way to the feeling with a snarling growl that stripped
away the veneer of the fashionable gentleman, and leapt at
Bowen in a berserk fury.

Tough fighter though he was, Bowen gave way to the
tornado that descended upon him. Off his guard for a second,
he took a murderous right on his face, staggered, and then
Alan had wrapped his long arms around him. Up went
Bowen, with Alan's knee under his, and then Alan swung to
the left, putting all his strength into the throw, the ' Hype '
of the Cumberland style wrestler.

Bowen went sprawling on the cobbles with half the wind
knocked out of his body. But he was no coward, and there
was plenty of fight left in him. He heard the exultant yells
of the crowd, and, experienced boxer that he was, he lost
his temper, too, and jumped to his feet, hurling himself at
Alan.

Alan grabbed his wrist with his left hand, the upper part
of his arm with the other hand, turned his head, heaved down
and then upwards, all the bulging muscles of his six feet and
more exploding in one tremendous spasm of brute force and
skill. Bowen cartwheeled in the air, over Alan's back, and
then hit the cobbles with a thud, and a sharp crack as his
head went back. He quivered, and lay still, legs, arms, all
outstretched like a rag doll flung down on the ground.

Heavy hands thumped Alan on the back and shoulders,
and voices shouted in his ear in a mixture of Welsh and
English.

' As pretty a flying mare as ever I've seen, that last throw,'
Morgan said. ' Ah, Mr Alan bach, that'll teach Dai, indeed
it will ! '

Alan wiped the sweat from his face, while someone held
out his coat for him. He was breathing heavily as if he had
just finished a desperate race, and with every breath he could
feel the soreness of his ribs. He had never been hit so hard
before. He had been a fool, he realized, to rush into a fight
with a professional fighter like Bowen.

' How's Bowen ? ' he asked.

' Oh, he's all right, Mr Alan.' And indeed, Bowen was
already on his feet. ' Take more than that to keep him down
for long,' Morgan said. ' But you've . . .'

He broke off suddenly, mouth open, eyes staring over
Alan's shoulder. Alan swung round. Astride a horse a few
yards away was Lord Aubigny, surveying the scene before
him with placid interest.

He caught Alan's anxious glance, and one eyebrow lifted.
Did the firm mouth twitch, Alan wondered uneasily ? To
find his son brawling in the village street would hardly be to
the liking of the Earl.

' What's all this, Morgan ? ' the Earl asked.

The landlord explained hurriedly. The Earl listened without any comment until he had finished, and then turned to
Bowen, who was leaning against his wagon.

' I've no liking for men who ill-treat horses, Bowen,' the
Earl said. ' But you appear to have learnt a lesson, so I'll
let it pass this time.'

Bowen climbed on to the wagon, shook the reins, and the
crowd stood aside to let him pass. He said nothing, and kept
his eyes on the road ahead.

' You'd better see to that face of yours, Alan,' the Earl
said.

' Yes, sir.' Alan took his coat from Morgan. The innkeeper's left eye closed in a swift wink, and Alan grinned.
But the grin changed to a grimace of pain. His cheek must
be badly swollen, he thought, as he strode after his father,
who was already riding towards the lodge gates.

The Earl made no remark until they were inside the park. Then, ' Any damage ? ' he asked.

' No, sir. I'm . . . I'm sorry, sir. It must have looked bad to see me brawling with the villagers. But that fellow was half killing his horse.'

' Oh, there's no harm done,' the Earl said. ' There would have been if he'd thrashed you. But he didn't. You will discover that it does not really matter much what you do in this life, so long as you succeed. It's when you fail that people criticize.'

' I've discovered that already,' Alan said bitterly.

The Earl smiled, and glanced curiously at his son's swollen face. ' Did you know that Bowen had fought in the prize-ring ? ' he asked.

' Yes, they told me. Morgan warned me to keep clear of him.'

' Oh, I see.' The Earl smiled again, but Alan could not see what was amusing him. His face was much too sore for him to join in the joke.

Chapter Four

THE *HENRIETTA*

ALAN put down his candle on the dressing-table, and surveyed his bedroom with a feeling of utter depression. His boxes, securely locked and roped, stood by the door. The dressing-table had been swept bare ; so, too, were his wardrobes and all the drawers. Already the room had acquired an atmosphere of emptiness, almost of bleakness, as if it was no longer in use. Indeed, it would not be after tomorrow, for Alan was leaving Llanstephan in the morning.

His last day had been both delightful and gloomy. In the morning he had ridden along the coast road as far as Kidwelly, and in the afternoon he had walked down to the beach under the cliffs, and bathed.

He dived into the deep water from the rocks, and struck out into the bay. He loved swimming, and for his last bathe at Llanstephan the water was calm and warm ; a few white clouds drifted very slowly across a blue sky, the sun shone steadily on him as he turned on his back and floated luxuriously. To his left was the long line of the cliffs, dropping sharply to the estuary, and then rising again on the farther side in pleasantly wooded slopes of green. Between the trees down by the river he could see a corner of the red brickwork of the Hall, the windows flashing and sparkling in the sunlight. It was a familiar and comforting sight, his home, with many memories and a sense of solid security. He had been away regularly, to school and to Cambridge, but this time he was travelling many thousands of miles to an unknown and partly savage continent on the other side of the ocean.

A wave rippled over his face; he spluttered and started to swim back to the sands, driving himself through the water with an angry impatience; his last swim at Llanstephan for years, perhaps.

He walked slowly up the lane towards the Hall. By the gate to the church he saw Anne. She had left him alone very wisely all day, and she smiled sympathetically now as she saw his face.

' Don't wait for me, Anne,' he said. ' I'm going into the church.'

She hesitated, and then turned away. There was little she could do to help him, she realized.

The old church was dark and cool and very quiet after the bright sunshine outside and the dull rumble of the sea on the rocks. Alan's shoes clattered loudly on the stone floor as he walked up the nave, past the great family pew, and into the side-chapel beyond.

It was a peaceful spot, filled with the memorials and tombs of the Careys, and the Aubignys from whom they were descended. Alan strolled around, reading the inscriptions which he knew so well, for this was a favourite place which he visited frequently.

At one tomb he stopped. On the huge block of stone, raised from the floor, was a stone effigy of a knight in armour, mailed head resting on a stone pillow, feet crossed to show that he had been on Crusade to the Holy Land. His eyes were shut, and he lay there relaxed and at peace, the sun throwing patterns of red and blue and green on his armour from the stained glass window above.

Cut deep into the stone of his shield, much chipped and  worn now with the passing of many centuries, Alan could pick out the outline of a bird with outstretched wings. He smiled and looked at the signet-ring on his hand, with the same device of the hawk.

For this was the tomb of the most notable of his early ancestors, Sir Philip d'Aubigny, Crusader, friend and companion of Richard Coeur de Lion, a soldier of almost legendary fame, and one of those resolute Barons who had faced a scowling and furious King John on Runnymede Island.

Alan sighed. He did not suppose that Sir Philip had ever played the coward. He turned away abruptly as if the great knight had raised a disapproving finger to point at his descendant who had disgraced the family name.

They left early the next morning in the Earl's coach. Alan's father would travel to Bristol with him, and then on to London, for already Mr Pitt was calling together his supporters.

Alan knew the road well, through Swansea and around the bay to Aberavon, following the old Roman road through the vale of Glamorgan to Cardiff, and then alongside the Severn until they reached Gloucester. They travelled fast, despite the poor roads, for the Earl was an impatient passenger.

Not until they reached Bristol did Alan's spirits revive. As

they drove along the busy quays he craned his head out of the
window, eyes upwards to the tall masts of the ships moored in
lines, and out in the harbour.

Even the comfortable inn at which they slept that night
had a tang of the sea about it, with its models of ships, the
coloured prints on the walls, and outside the windows a vista
of masts and rigging in bewildering profusion.

The Earl wasted no time next day. He summoned his
agent, questioned him briskly, and then set out to find Alan's
ship. They made their slow way through the piles of packing-
cases on the quays, past sweating and cursing men loading and
unloading ships, avoiding creaking wagons and teams of
horses. Alan found it all exhilarating ; his nose caught the
whiff of strange spices from scented bales ; he watched the
mahogany-faced sailors with their tarry pigtails and rolling
bandy-legged gait, their jaws moving steadily as they chewed
tobacco. After the calm of Llanstephan this busy, noisy port
was refreshing and challenging, and he forgot his reluctance
at leaving home and the depressing prospect of new faces and
strange towns, for Alan's shyness and lack of self-confidence
made him cling to everything that was familiar and friendly.

' Here she is, my lord,' the agent said. ' The *Henrietta*. A
fine ship, my lord.'

The Earl nodded. He, and Alan too, knew little about
ships. But the *Henrietta*, even to their landsmen's eyes, was a
graceful and lovely sight. Her sails were furled, and she was
tied up to the quay, but she was moving slightly on the gentle
swell from the sea, trembling like some great bird anxious
to spread her wings. Alan looked up at the tall masts and
sighed with delight. He was going to enjoy this voyage, he
decided.

He hurried after his father and the agent who had already
crossed the gang-plank. The *Henrietta*'s holds were still open,
and long lines of men, bent under heavy loads, were filing
aboard and down below. Officers were bellowing orders,
other men ran backwards and forwards as if this was an ants'
nest suddenly disturbed by a stick.

' Captain Trevethan ? ' the agent called.

'What is it now?' a deep voice growled. A huge, broad-shouldered man turned to face them.

'This is the Earl of Aubigny, Captain,' the agent said hastily. 'His son, Mr Alan Carey, is sailing with you to Boston.'

The Captain raised a hand to his three-cornered hat. 'Good morning to ye, my lord,' he said. He glanced up and down Alan's tall figure, and his hard blue eyes twinkled surprisingly. ''Tain't often I meet someone my size,' he said. He spoke quietly, with a pronounced west country burr that was pleasant to hear.

From behind him there came a crash and an oath. He whirled around to see a keg rolling across the deck, and his voice rose effortlessly to a tremendous bellow.

'You ham-fisted, lop-sided son of a bungling horse thief!' he trumpeted. 'If you stave one of those kegs, I'll hang your guts out on the nearest yard-arm!' He turned back to his visitors, and his voice dropped magically to the same conversational tones with which he had greeted them.

'I'll show you to your cabin, Mr Carey,' he said.

The cabin was not very large, and for a man of Alan's size it was tiny. But it was clean and tidy, or so he considered. Captain Trevethan thought otherwise, for he bellowed for the steward in a voice that filled the low-roofed cabin like a peal of thunder. The unfortunate man came at the run, and for two minutes listened to an account of his misdeeds and the future that lay before him if he neglected his duty again, all of it delivered without a pause by Captain Trevethan, and without the repetition of a single blistering adjective.

The Earl leaned on his stick, and took snuff with great enjoyment as he listened. 'I must congratulate you, Captain,' he said when the steward had vanished. 'I had a troop sergeant in my regiment with a fine voice and a large vocabulary. But he would have been speechless beside you.'

Trevethan chuckled. 'You need a good voice in a gale, my lord.' He left the cabin, and the agent followed him.

'Well, Alan,' the Earl said. 'This is good-bye. For a few years, at any rate.'

Alan nodded. For the first time in his life he would be entirely on his own, with no understanding father to listen to his problems.

' You are driving to London today, sir ? ' he asked.

' Only as far as Oxford. I am staying with the Tonbridges.'

' Oh, yes, of course, sir.'

An awkward silence fell. Alan fidgeted with the ruffles at his wrists. The Earl opened his snuff box. Their eyes met, and they smiled.

' Take care of yourself, Alan,' the Earl said. ' And remember that there is always a home for you at Llanstephan.'

' I know that, sir.'

' Good ! Then I must be on my way.' He pressed Alan's hand. ' And don't be afraid of being afraid. I watched you tackle that fellow, Bowen. Morgan told me there wasn't a man in Carmarthenshire who would have taken him on.'

He took a rapid pinch of snuff, sneezed violently, and went out of the cabin. Alan followed, and watched his father cross the gang-plank, and walk away with a swinging stride, back erect, striding out like a man half his age.

The *Henrietta* was threshing along under full sail. As Alan looked up at the astonishing mass of white sail above his head he wondered, not for the first time, how any seaman dared to clap on so much canvas. But the *Henrietta* was revelling in the steady wind and the long Atlantic swell. With her deck tilted under the pressure of wind and sail her sharp bows were slicing through the green water, rising and falling with a long regular pitch as each swell approached. Down slowly, a smack as her bows hit the wave, a cascade of brilliant white spray, up again, shaking herself like a dog, then down again, another shower of spray, and so on with monotonous regularity.

But Alan was enjoying it. He had been vilely sea-sick for the first few days, and had never known such misery. But he had found his sea legs now ; he was eating huge meals, and had earned Captain Trevethan's respect and liking for his eagerness to learn all that he could about the ship and the sea.

He was at ease with the officers and the crew. They did

not find his size an object of amusement, and they liked his shyness and his diffident manner. When he shed his London-made clothes, and scrambled up the rigging, they were pleased with his enthusiasm ; they taught him how to walk out from the mast with his feet on the line under the yard, and how to lean over the thick yard itself and claw up the sail, warning him not to look down at the heaving deck of the *Henrietta* far below, and the white, creamy water falling away from the bows.

One morning, as Alan was leaning on the poop rail talking to the mate, Captain Trevethan appeared from below. He looked around critically, but for once he found nothing to arouse his displeasure, and from the mate there came an audible sigh of relief that made Alan grin.

'We'll start gun drill this watch, Mr Lang.'

'Aye, aye, sir.'

'Gun drill !' Alan exclaimed in surprise.

'Yes, Mr Carey. Half the crew have never handled a gun yet.'

'But you're not expecting to be attacked, are you ? '

'There's always the chance of running into a French frigate.'

'But we're not at war with France,' Alan said.

Captain Trevethan laughed. 'Not officially, Mr Carey, but they snap up a British merchantman if they can catch one.'

Alan watched the crew fall in around the guns. The *Henrietta* was not heavily armed, but she carried ten guns a side. Alan was bored with standing still, and he had finished all the books in his cabin.

'Can I join a gun crew, Captain?' he asked.

'By all means, Mr Carey,' and the Captain gave Alan an approving glance. 'You'll get on well in the colonies.'

Alan was startled. 'Oh, why?'

'There's many sorts living in the colonies,' the Captain said. 'Some gentlemen of family like yourself, Mr Carey, in the towns. But it's a new country with new ideas, and a new outlook, you see. They respect a man for what he can do, not for his name.'

'But I can't do much,' Alan said.

'You're the first gentleman who's sailed with me who took

off his fine clothes and helped to shorten sail, Mr Carey. And now you want to join a gun crew.'

The Captain walked away to leave Alan digesting this in silence, for he had learnt to value the Captain's opinion. But he fell in beside the nearest gun, and for three hours wrestled with the ponderous weapon, learning how to load and ram and prime and sponge, and run the heavy gun up on the tackle.

Gun drill became a daily affair after that, a hot and tiring drill, too, as the *Henrietta* bore steadily to the south to pick up the trade winds. A longer route than the more direct one across the North Atlantic, the Captain explained, but one that gave better weather, and less chance of meeting French men-of-war.

Four weeks out of Bristol, and the *Henrietta* had changed course. She was beating up for the American coast now, six days from Boston, if the wind held. The day was overcast, with frequent patches of grey mist over the sea, and the regular routine of the watch was suddenly disturbed by a hail from the masthead.

' Sail ho ! '

Captain Trevethan sprang for the rigging, telescope in hand. But he shook his head. ' Too far to recognize her rig,' he said.

There was no reason to suspect the presence of a French warship, for now that they were close to the American coast they were likely to meet many other ships. But the Captain was uneasy. He inspected the strange sail at regular intervals as she closed on the *Henrietta*. Finally Alan heard him grunt and fold his telescope with a snap.

' Clear the ship for action, Mr Lang ! ' he said. ' She's French all right. Frigate of thirty-six guns.'

' Faster than the *Henrietta* ? ' Alan asked.

The Captain pursed his lips. ' Depends how long she's been at sea. But she can blow us out of the water with half a dozen broadsides if she gets close enough.'

The crew were streaming up from below. Alan threw off his coat and stock, and ran to his gun station. He had learnt

the drill so quickly that he acted as gun captain now, and he
barked out his orders with an assurance that would have
surprised his Cambridge friends.

A boy ran up from the magazine with the paper cartridges
containing the charges for the guns. Alan nodded. Down
the barrel went the first charge, followed by a circular wad
rammed hard against the paper, for otherwise much of the
force of the explosion would be lost. Alan watched critically,
and then nodded again. In went the cannon ball, rammed
home in the same way.

' Run her up ! ' Alan said.

Two men heaved on the side tackle ; the small wooden
wheels, or trucks, as Alan had learned to call them, squealed
shrilly as the heavy gun was moved forward until the muzzle
projected over the side. Alan took his priming iron, a long,
thin spike, and thrust it down the vent-hole, tearing the paper
of the charge, and exposing the powder within. Another man
poured fine priming powder down the hole until it spilt over
the barrel.

The gun was ready to fire now, whenever the order was
given from the poop, and all that Alan would have to do was
to ignite the priming powder with the linstock.

He bent down over the circular tub beside the gun ;
inside were several lengths of wick treated with a special
preparation to make them burn slowly. One was already
alight, and Alan wound it round a short bar of iron with a
forked end, so designed that it held the smouldering end of the
wick, the linstock. With the least possible delay Alan could
bring the linstock down on the vent-hole, and the gun would fire.

The ship was quiet now that the guns were loaded and
run up. From the bows came the ceaseless wash of the waves,
and the wind hummed steadily through the rigging. Alan
had time to look for the French frigate, but she was still two
miles away on the starboard bow. She disappeared in a wall
of mist, and they did not see her again for several minutes.
But when she came into view again, it was obvious that she
had closed the gap, and her bows were pointed to cut off the
Henrietta.

M.V.—5

Twice more the mist engulfed her, and then she was
bearing down fast. Alan saw a puff of white smoke, heard
a dull, flat boom, and a spout of white water shot up ahead of
the *Henrietta*. It was the traditional shot across her bows, and
the message was clear enough. Heave to !

Alan heard Captain Trevethan shout at the helmsman,
and the *Henrietta* dashed into another bank of damp, drifting
mist. But the wind was dropping, as even an inexperienced
sailor like Alan could see for himself. When they ran out of
the fog, all heads turned anxiously. The frigate was close
enough now for all to see her sharp bows, and the two white
waves on either side.

Suddenly she turned into the wind until Alan could see
her whole length, with the menacing portholes of her gun
decks. White smoke wreathed up, blotting out the picture ;
a rumble like distant thunder, and Alan clenched his fists.
Something screamed over his head. A tremendous blow struck
the *Henrietta*, and Alan staggered. A man was screaming on
the main deck, and a group had gathered round him.

' Tom Watts, sir,' one of his gun crew muttered. ' Splinters,
I expect.'

' Yes,' Alan said, but he did not say any more, for his
voice might have betrayed his fear. He was frightened now,
his heart thumping with the same familiar sensation, the same
dropping at the pit of his stomach. He had heard Trevethan
talk about the effects of cannon balls hitting a wooden ship,
and the jagged splinters of wood that flew about ; the frightful
wounds they inflicted, and . . . Alan bent over the gun. He
must find something to occupy his attention. That was what
the Earl had said during their long drive to Bristol. If you
are under fire, do something ; don't stand and listen to the
bullets, and imagine that the next one will hit you.

' Here she comes again,' one of the gun crew said.

Alan looked up. The French frigate had lost way in
firing that last broadside, but she was overhauling the *Henrietta*
again, heeling over in the breeze, a high bow wave curling
away from the bows, and an occasional shower of spray as
she butted into the choppy sea. She was a lovely sight, built

for speed with long graceful lines, a pyramid of white sail
overhead, the white flag of the Bourbons fluttering from her
poop.

Alan was saved by a shrill whistle from the mate, and a
roar of ' Fire ! '

He jabbed the linstock against the breech. The priming
powder flashed, and the gun went off. A long tongue of
orange flame spat out from the muzzle, a thick cloud of smoke,
white and acrid, billowed upwards and over the crew, making
Alan cough. The crash of the explosion rocked his head back.

But there was something to do, now. The gun had jumped
back viciously from the force of the explosion. As it came to
rest, held securely by the breeching ropes, Alan shouted his
orders. The first man pushed a soaking mop down the barrel
to extinguish any smouldering fragments of the charge ; as
he stepped back, the second man rammed in the next charge
and the wad, while a third was waiting with the round shot.
Alan had stopped the vent with a plug to prevent any wear
of the hole by escaping gas.

' Run her up,' he said, and went through the drill with
his priming iron, watched the powder being sprinkled over
the breech, and reached for the linstock. As the gun went
off again, he was just conscious of another violent crash as
the frigate fired another broadside, and he knew that the
Henrietta was being hit. A shroud parted with a twang close
by, the *Henrietta* seemed to stagger and roll. But Alan was
intent only on firing his gun ; the familiar routine of sponging
and ramming, the urgent necessity to keep on feeding his
ponderous gun with charges and roundshot, took all his attention. He was surrounded by a fog of smoke, and could have
seen nothing if he had found time to look around.

A long whistle from the poop ; the smoke cleared and Alan
saw his men dancing and waving their arms. He leant over
the rail. Where was the frigate ?

' Got her foremast, sir ! ' one of his crew yelled.

Alan could see the frigate now, and the man was right. Her
foremast was bending slowly, still held in place by braces and
stays. Then the whole of the upper part of the mast heeled

over in a chaos of whirling yards and fluttering canvas. The frigate yawed, and came up into the wind. She seemed to drop astern of the flying *Henrietta* with a bewildering speed.

Alan wiped his face. It was streaming with perspiration, and his skin was itching from the smoke. He was exhilarated and happy, for he had fought down the dreadful sensation of fear ; he had done his part without anyone realizing how terrified he had been.

' We shan't see her again, Mr Carey,' the Captain said, and thumped Alan on the back, his red face creased in smiles.

Part Two

AMERICA

Chapter Five

NEW ENGLAND

ALAN was wearing a suit of his best clothes. He had arranged his stock with care, chosen a new waistcoat and a pair of silk stockings from his boxes, and felt extremely overdressed and uncomfortable after five weeks at sea. He had grown used to the rough coat and breeches which he normally wore when he went out shooting at Llanstephan.

The *Henrietta* was gliding past one of the many islands that lay off the port of Boston, and Alan was absorbed in his first sight of America. Ahead lay the town itself, surprisingly large and well built, with many brick houses, several tall church spires, and a thick mass of ships and bare masts.

They edged into a vacant berth ; the crew swarmed aloft for the last time, ropes were flung down to the quay, and the *Henrietta* bumped gently alongside the wharf. Alan watched the Negroes tying the ropes. But for them he might have just arrived at any typical port in England.

' Where are you staying, Mr Carey ? ' the Captain asked.

' I don't know the names of any inns in Boston,' Alan confessed. In a few minutes he would have to leave the *Henrietta* with her familiar faces and the friends he had made, and plunge alone into this strange new world, with all the difficulties and problems that lay ahead of him. He felt desperately lonely. He had not a single acquaintance in Boston, or indeed, on the whole vast continent. Much of his newly discovered confidence ebbed away.

' Go to the Royal Exchange Inn,' the Captain said. ' The beds are clean there, which is more than I can say for any other inn in New England. Take your own bedding with you, Mr Carey, when you travel in the colonies.'

He bustled away to attend to the ship's papers. Alan's face creased with worry. He had no bedding. Still, he would leave that problem for the moment. A couple of Negroes from the wharf would carry his boxes to the Inn for him, the mate said, and Alan waited while three of the crew staggered up from below with his baggage.

He watched the crowd on the quay. One man, short and very fat, was already crossing the gang-plank. He was well dressed, with a bright yellow waistcoat that exaggerated his huge stomach, and he strutted along the deck, carrying that astonishing curve in front, distended like a sail of the *Henrietta* in a trade wind.

The man trotted up the poop steps, and paused, wiping his red face, and panting loudly. To Alan's surprise he came across to him, whipped off his three-cornered hat, and bowed politely.

'The Honourable Alan Carey?' he asked.

'Yes,' Alan said, and returned the bow.

'Josiah Brewster, at your service, Mr Carey.' Another sweeping bow. 'I am his lordship's banker and agent.'

'I'm very glad to meet you, Mr Brewster,' Alan said heartily. For here was one problem solved immediately. His father had spoken of Mr Brewster as reliable and honest, and Alan liked the look of him.

'I have two men on the wharf to take your boxes, Mr Carey.'

'Oh, thank you, Mr Brewster. I don't know how far it is to the Royal Exchange. Captain Trevethan recommended it.'

'An inn!' Mr Brewster was shocked. 'But I must insist, my dear Mr Carey. I shall be honoured if you would stay at my house. Yes, honoured, sir,' and he bowed again.

Alan smiled. He had taken a quick liking to Mr Brewster. 'That's very kind of you,' he said. 'Here are my boxes now.' He ran off to arrange a meeting with Captain Trevethan before the *Henrietta* returned to Bristol, and then followed the plump little figure of the banker on to the wharf. A couple of grinning Negroes hoisted the boxes on to a hand-cart, and cleared a way for Alan through the crowd.

'This is Griffin's Wharf,' Mr Brewster explained. 'We'll walk, I think, Mr Carey, unless you would prefer a carriage.'

'No, I would much rather walk,' Alan said. 'I want to stretch my legs after five weeks at sea.' And indeed, it was strange to stride out again on land which did not heave and pitch under his feet. 'Boston is a fine town, Mr Brewster.'

The banker beamed with delight. 'The largest in the colonies, Mr Carey. Thirty thousand inhabitants, and growing every year.'

They were walking down a wide street, stone paved, and flanked by three-storey houses of brick. Mr Brewster pointed out the chief buildings : Faneuil Hall, which any English city might have envied, Alan thought ; the pleasant little State House, rebuilt quite recently after a fire had completely gutted the original house ; the Royal Exchange Tavern where Alan had expected to spend the night ; and then down State Street.

'Ah, this is my little house, Mr Carey.' The banker waved a podgy arm, with a mixture of pride and humbleness, as if he expected his guest from England to turn up his aristocratic nose at so meagre a place.

The house was certainly not very large compared to fashionable town houses in London, but it was well built of red brick, with freshly painted windows and gleaming panes.

Mrs Brewster greeted Alan in the small hall. Where her husband was short and fat, she was tall and angular, but she greeted Alan with kindness. Her manner was somewhat anxious, too. She apologized, as her husband had done, for the size of the house, and spoke with awe of the probable vastness of Llanstephan Hall. Alan tried to reassure her, which was not difficult, for when she realized that he was even shyer than she was, she smiled at him in a motherly fashion, and her manner became more natural and easy. 'A nicely mannered boy,' Alan heard her say to Mr Brewster a few minutes later, when she thought Alan was out of earshot, 'with no high-faluting airs about him.' Alan grinned, and decided that he might enjoy his visit to Boston after all.

Dinner was a long meal, served by Negro servants. When Alan looked over his shoulder and saw a black face and a row of white teeth a few inches away, he nearly jumped in his seat. Mr Brewster enjoyed his food, that was clear, and so, too, was the reason for his ample stomach.

But as soon as the last course had been cleared from the table, he swept Alan away to his office, and produced a forbidding array of ledgers and papers. Alan examined them nervously. He knew nothing of business, but he need not have worried, for the banker poured out a stream of figures and facts. Alan did not interrupt him. In any case, his ignorance was such that he could not have put any intelligent questions.

But the Earl had told him not to worry about the normal details of the Ashwater estates. The fur trade was the only point that was of interest to him. When Mr Brewster had finished, and had pushed away the last document, Alan cleared his throat self-consciously.

' My father is worried about the fur trade from Ashwater,' he said. ' The figures are disappointing, he thinks.'

Mr Brewster leant back in his chair and folded plump hands over the curve of the yellow waistcoat. He took a pinch of snuff before he spoke, and then crossed his two short and fat little legs in their silk stockings.

' Disappointing is hardly the word I should use, Mr Carey,' he said. ' They are downright dishonest.'

Alan sat up with a jerk. ' Dishonest ! ' he said.

Mr Brewster's neatly wigged head nodded solemnly. ' Yes, Mr Carey. Dishonest.'

' Who is responsible, then ? '

' Mr Hepburn, your father's bailiff at Ashwater.'

' Are you certain of this, sir ? '

' Quite sure, Mr Carey. But what can we do ? '

Alan flushed. ' He can be dismissed ! ' he said.

' Exactly. You appoint another man in his place, and the same thing will happen again.' The banker leant forward and wagged one stumpy finger in Alan's face. ' The bailiff deals with everything at Ashwater, and sends me his accounts, and remits the moneys paid. If he chooses to trade privately on his own account in furs, who can stop him ? That's what Mr Hepburn is doing, and in the eyes of the law he is innocent of any crime. A rogue, perhaps, and an inefficient bailiff, but nothing else.'

'What do you suggest?' Alan asked. He felt extremely helpless.

'Go to Ashwater yourself, Mr Carey. Dismiss Hepburn, and either take charge of the estates, or try to find an honest man.'

'I intend to go to Ashwater in any case,' Alan said.

'Good! Now, I must find a reliable man to travel with you, Mr Carey.' The banker stood up, and pulled down his waistcoat. 'My wife and I have been invited to a reception this evening, Mr Carey. You are included in the invitation, of course.'

Alan nodded, but the prospect of being introduced into Boston society did not attract him. He would be invited to many houses, he knew, and he had never found himself at ease in fashionable society. He was too conscious of his height and size, he had no small talk, and he could never move without the long skirts of his coat knocking over some bric-à-brac.

For three days Mr and Mrs Brewster presented him at the houses of their friends, and extremely pleasant people Alan found them, though he suffered many agonies of shyness. Dressed in his finest clothes, made by a fashionable London tailor, he felt like a prize bullock as he was led round the reception-rooms by a strutting Mr Brewster, bowing mechanically to face after face, muttering the conventional remarks expected of him, and fingering his stock nervously, wondering how long it would be before he could plead a headache, and leave without appearing rude.

Meanwhile Mr Brewster was making inquiries about guides for Alan to the Mohawk. The most promising of these he passed on to Alan for his decision. The man was called Winter, so he said, and Alan interviewed him in Mrs Brewster's drawing-room.

Winter was a new type altogether to Alan, a backwoodsman, so the banker had said. Alan had seen them in the streets of Boston, in buckskin clothes, loose, shambling fellows, padding

silently over the pavements in their moccasins, very much out of their element in this busy town. But Alan had never spoken to one of them yet, and he examined Winter with great interest.

He was in his late twenties, perhaps, lean and loosely built, almost awkward and drooping. His face was as leathery as his clothes, as if he had spent all his life in the open, which was the case, so Alan learnt later.

'You're Winter?' Alan asked, as the man came into the room.

'Yeah, Mister Carey. Jacob Winter.'

He looked round the daintily furnished room, shuffled his feet on the fine carpet imported from England, and seemed as out of place as a tramp in a palace. His jaw was moving steadily, and a few seconds later he spat out a stream of liquid tobacco with great accuracy into the fire-place.

He saw the startled expression on Alan's face, and grinned

ruefully. ' Guess I shouldn't have done that, Mister Carey,'
he said apologetically. ' But I ain't used to these fancy carpets
and this expensive furniture.' He ran his brown hand over
the highly polished surface of a small table.

Alan smiled. He could sympathize with the man. How
often he had felt the same, though there was no excuse for
him ; he had been brought up in the most splendid surround-
ings. But he felt that he liked Mr Winter.

' Please sit down, Mr Winter,' he said.

The backwoodsman looked a trifle surprised at this
invitation. In his interview with Mr Brewster he had stood,
as Alan could well imagine. But he sat down awkwardly,
and then glanced round for the fire-place, his face screwed
up in perplexity.

' For goodness' sake, spit if you want to,' Alan said. ' It's
not my fire-place.'

' Thanks, Mister Carey,' and Winter spat again with great
violence. He regarded Alan with some curiosity ; this fine
gentleman from London was not quite what he had expected.
' Most folks call me Jake, Mister Carey,' he said after a pause,
as if he had summed Alan up, and had approved of him.

' All right, Jake,' Alan said. ' Do you know the Mohawk
Valley ? '

' Yeah. My uncle lives in Albany. I was brought up in
those parts. My dad was a settler round there.'

' Do you know Ashwater ? '

' Bin there once, Mister Carey. But I can take you there.'
He spoke with a calm confidence, his voice a drawling twang.
Mr Brewster had said that there was probably a faint dash of
Indian blood in him, like so many backwoodsmen, for the
early settlers had often married Indian women. Alan could
believe this, for Jake had the typical high cheek-bones and
broad nostrils of an Indian whom Alan had seen in the street
the previous day.

' What are you doing in Boston ? ' Alan asked.

Jake paused to think out his answer, his jaws moving slowly,
his eyes on Alan. ' I had an argument with a bad character
in Albany, Mister Carey,' he said.

' Oh, what happened to him ? ' Alan asked, hiding a smile.

' He got hurt real bad,' Jake confessed. ' Cheated me out of a fur deal.'

' But is it safe for you to go back ? '

' Yeah, I guess so. I brought some furs to sell in Boston, and it's a couple of months since I left.'

Alan felt satisfied that he had found what he wanted, but he hesitated for a fraction before he spoke again. Then he made up his mind.

' Will you come with me to Ashwater, Jake ? '

' Sure, Mister Carey. Suits me.'

They settled the matter of payment, and Alan asked for advice on what baggage he should take. Jake inspected his array of clothes with a sardonic eye, and chuckled.

' Reckon you won't wear much of that outfit in the Mohawk Valley, Mister Carey,' he said.

But he made a selection, and went off with Alan to buy horses. Here Alan found that he knew more than Jake, and they haggled happily for an hour until Alan was satisfied that he had three horses at a reasonable price, one each for himself and Jake, and the third for the saddlebags. The bulk of Alan's wardrobe was to be left with Mr Brewster, who would send it on to Ashwater by carrier.

They rode out of Boston two days later, with the prospect of a two-hundred-mile journey ahead of them. Alan's new acquaintances in Boston had told him something about the country through which he would pass. Inland, for a hundred miles or so, he would find a fairly thickly populated area, well cultivated, with farms and villages. But then he would reach the vague frontiers of the colonies ; the villages and settlements would be farther apart, the roads would become rough tracks, and then eventually he would reach the virgin forest itself, the backwoods, as the townspeople called them, inhabited by scattered Indian tribes, and a few hardy European settlers. He would find it a savage, empty, and untamed wilderness of trees and swamps, vast in extent, and as yet not even mapped.

Alan was curious to see this new world, but he was apprehensive, too. Even the new friends he had made in Boston

now seemed more desirable than this strange world into which
he was riding, where money and family influence were of little
value, he had been told bluntly ; the ability to shoot straight
with a gun, to rely on his wits and his strength, were all that
mattered in the backwoods and the forest.

But he enjoyed the first part of the journey. He was
delighted with the countryside of Massachusetts, the small,
compact towns with their wooden houses and pretty gardens :
the meeting-house, the church and the stocks and pillory ;
they were the same in every town through which he rode.

Outside the towns the land was still heavily wooded, but
the frequent farms were well kept ; the houses were small,
mostly of unpainted wood, one storey high, with roughly sawn
flatboard roofs, and in some cases, no windows at all. The
roads were good, surprisingly so, but the inns at which he slept
were worse than Captain Trevethan had predicted. They were
dirty, smelly, verminous, and but for the blankets and pillow
that Jake had advised him to buy, he did not think he would
have passed one pleasant night.

His fellow guests were a hard-drinking and quarrelsome
collection ; they spent the evenings in gambling, drinking and
squabbling, and Alan wisely kept well clear of them. Englishmen, he gathered, were not always too well liked. They were
inclined to patronize the Americans, but nothing was said to
Alan. One look at his height and shoulders, and the tough-
looking backwoodsman with him, saved Alan from several
fights.

Alan learnt a good deal about Jake in the long days when
they rode steadily across New England, and he soon realized
that he had been fortunate in finding such a guide. Jake's
attitude to people who might have been called his superiors
amused Alan. There was a sturdy independence about the
man that was attractive, typical, Alan discovered, of all those
he met. He treated Alan with an offhand politeness ; he
obviously regarded him as some fragile and strange piece of
furniture that had to be carried with extreme care on a long
and bumpy journey.

Bridges became scarce as they reached the frontiers of

Massachusetts ; the roads were now tracks. They used ferries when they met them, but more often than not Jake had to search for a ford. One morning they halted by a river in spate, swollen by the heavy rain of the previous night. Jake inspected the fast-running water, grunted, and spat bitterly.

' I think we can get across,' Alan said. It was not very often that he ventured an opinion, but he felt that he knew more about horses than Jake.

Jake cocked an eye at him, and shrugged his shoulders. He rode down the muddy bank, leading the spare horse.

'Better let me go first,' Alan said. He had chosen his horse with care in Boston, for he needed something out of the ordinary to carry his weight. The current was strong, but he splashed his way across, though the water rose to his knees in the centre of the river.

As his horse scrambled up the opposite bank, Alan turned to see how Jake was faring. The packhorse was giving trouble, nervous of the water swirling past him, and jerking at the rope as Jake tried to persuade him to move. Then his own horse reared, and Jake, not the best of riders, toppled from the saddle. He went down with a loud curse and a violent splash. The

two horses, without any hesitation, plunged through the river
and joined Alan on the far bank.

Alan laughed as he saw Jake splashing in the current. But
his amusement suddenly changed to alarm. For Jake was
being carried downstream into much deeper water, and Alan
saw from his wildly thrashing arms and legs that he could not
swim.

The river turned abruptly just below the ford, sweeping
round a bend with high banks, abrupt and precipitous. The
water there, as Alan realized, would be anything up to fifteen
feet deep, and the current would have been dangerous for a
good swimmer.

He flung off his coat, and wrestled with his long riding
boots. As he kicked off the second one he raced down the
bank. He saw Jake's head appear and a waving arm. Alan
put his feet together and dived. As he hurtled down, he
wondered if the water was deep enough ; he would soon
know, when his head hit the bottom with a crash, and he
tried to flatten his dive when he felt the water close over him.

But he was breaking the surface, shaking the water from
his face, and searching for some sign of Jake. He saw a brown
back rolling downstream, and he struck out furiously, letting
the current sweep him down and round the bend. He grabbed
Jake's shoulders and heaved him up and back.

' Don't struggle, you fool ! ' he shouted. ' Lie still ! '

He hardly expected Jake to take much notice ; drowning
men always flung themselves about like madmen, he had
noticed, but Jake kept his head, and let Alan tow him slowly
towards the bank. They were well round the bend now, and
the banks had shelved down again, so that Alan was able to
drag Jake's limp body ashore.

' All right ? ' he asked anxiously, bending over him.

Jake was spluttering and spitting out water, and Alan left
him to bring down the horses. Fortunately they had not
bolted, and were cropping the grass by the bank when Alan
reached the ford. Jake was sitting up when he returned. He
grinned at Alan, and shook himself like a dog.

' Guess we'd better make a fire and dry out,' he said.

'You got flint and tinder in the saddlebags, Mister Carey. Mine ain't no use after being in the river.'

Alan found his tinder box in his coat, and handed it to Jake. He had not the slightest idea of how to light a fire, and he watched the deft, assured actions of the backwoodsman. It was to be his first lesson in woodcraft.

'You get four big rocks, Mister Carey. I'll cut the wood.'

Alan fetched four large stones from the side of the river, and laid them out under Jake's directions. By this time Jake was cutting small branches from a dead tree lying on the bank. He was using a little axe that Alan had seen hanging from his belt. A tomahawk, he had heard it called, after the weapon used by the Indians.

'Dead leaves, Mister Carey,' Jake said over his shoulder. 'And small sticks. Pile 'em up between the stones.'

As Alan made a small heap of dry kindling, Jake was forming a tripod of sticks ; he had peeled the dead bark half-way down each stick, letting the dry curls of bark hang down.

'Reckon you can light it now,' Jake said.

Alan placed a small piece of oily rag on the twigs, held the striker in his left hand, and struck it sharply with the flint. The sparks dropped down on to the rag, and Alan paused as he saw a tiny glow. He went down on his hands and knees and puffed gently at the smouldering rag. A flame ran out ; another cautious puff, and a leaf began to smoke, then a twig, and Alan moved back. In a few seconds the kindling was burning cheerfully, the flames running up the tripod that Jake had built, catching at the hanging curls of bark. Alan smiled as he saw the breeze fanning the flames like a miniature blast furnace.

Jake was bringing larger branches now from the dead tree, arranging them across the rocks and over the blaze. He took out his knife, fetched a length of rope from the saddlebags, and rigged up a line on forked sticks. Alan began to strip off his clothes, and hung them carefully on the rope. The day was hot and sunny, and he found it no hardship to squat on the bank, watching the steam rise from their clothes.

'I've got a great deal to learn,' he said.

' Guess you have, Mister Carey,' Jake said. He was biting off a piece of the black tobacco he favoured, and then he leant back comfortably against a convenient rock. ' You got to fend for yourself in the forest.'

He chewed happily, watching the flames. ' You can swim mighty well,' he added after a long pause. Another pause. But Alan was used to Jake by this time. He liked to think out what he was going to say. ' Reckon you saved my life then, Mister Carey.'

' I swim a lot at home,' Alan said.

' Yeah. I can see that. But it needed some spunk to dive into that river. I'm mighty grateful, Mister Carey.'

He relapsed into a thoughtful silence again. ' You going to need me after you reach Ashwater ? ' he asked.

' I think so,' Alan said. ' Do you know why I'm going there, Jake ? '

' To deal with Elijah Hepburn, I reckon.'

Alan sat up, and looked down at Jake in surprise. ' Do you know him ? '

' Never met him, Mister Carey, but I've heard tell of him, sure enough. Trades furs with the French, so they say.'

' Is there anything wrong in that ? '

' Yeah, plenty wrong. It's illegal, Mister Carey.' Jake spat at the fire. ' He won't be kinda pleased to see you arrive. You might need some help.'

' Will you help ? ' Alan asked.

' Yeah, reckon I will, Mister Carey.' He held out his hand, and Alan took it.

They crossed the Hudson River near the little settlement of Troy, and then turned south towards Albany and New York State, following the line of the river. They reached Albany towards midday, and Alan was surprised to see how large the town was, for he had not expected anything on this scale so far to the west. But Albany, as Jake explained, was the last big outpost. Beyond was little but forest, hundreds of miles of it, perhaps thousands, the vast unexplored continent of America.

Albany, so Alan had been told, was a Dutch settlement,

though the majority of the inhabitants now were of English stock. Alan and Jake rode down the wide main street below the hill on which stood the old Dutch fort. On either side were the quaint little Dutch houses, each detached and standing in its own garden, screened by trees. At the front of all the houses were neat porches, and in them sat the Dutch, basking in the afternoon sun, and peacefully smoking their pipes.

Jake regarded them sourly, and spat, a sure sign of his feelings.

' Don't you like the Dutch ? ' Alan asked, smiling. He knew his Jake by this time.

' No, sir,' Jake said. ' Money's all they want to finger. And they know how to make it, too.'

They spent the night at Albany in an inn which was clean and comfortable. There was something to be said for the Dutch, Jake admitted grudgingly. Soon after dawn the next morning they set off again. Ashwater, so Jake said, was about sixty miles ahead, to the north of the Mohawk. Alan saw the river for the first time at the little settlement of Schenectady, where they crossed by the ferry.

The road vanished. In its place was a wide track that followed the winding river. To the north was forest, an endless prospect of dark green trees that merged with the horizon and the misty outlines of mountains. The Adirondacks, so Jake said. The view to the south was very similar, the same apparently limitless forest, and another range of hills, the Catskills. Alan began to appreciate the importance of the Mohawk Valley now, for the river was wide enough for reasonably large boats, and was the only practicable route from west to east. For here, in the backwoods, the rivers were the only roads.

There were few signs of human settlements now ; an occasional clearing among the trees, a few specks in the great forest where men were slowly hacking out a space in which to live and plant their crops. In time, perhaps, these patches would widen and join together, and the forest would have been pushed back for another few miles.

After an hour, Jake stopped and dismounted. He lifted his musket from the saddle, and proceeded to load it with great care. Alan watched him for a moment, and then did the same with the new and expensive rifle which he had bought in Boston. Always interested in firearms, he was delighted with this new weapon ; the additional range, compared with the smooth-barrelled musket, was enormous, and the few shots he had already fired with it had astonished him with their accuracy. There was only one disadvantage. The bullet was made to fit the barrel with far more precision than was the case with a musket, for otherwise it would not be gripped and twisted by the rifling. This made loading a slower business, for the ordinary ramrod unaided would not force the bullet home against the charge, and a small mallet was provided to tap the end of the rod.

' What are you afraid of, Jake ? ' he asked. ' I thought the Indians were friendly round here.'

' Yeah, that's right, Mister Carey. But you'll soon learn not to move far in the backwoods without a loaded gun.'

' Tell me about the Indians,' Alan said. ' The only ones I've seen so far were a few in Boston.'

Jake snorted. ' Settlement Indians,' he said. ' The forest ones are mighty different. They're Iroquois round these parts. That's the name of the Six Nations, as they call 'emselves. Six tribes.' He counted off the names on his fingers. ' Mohawks, Senecas, Oneidas, Onondagas, Cayugas, and the Tuscororas.'

' Are there many of them, then ? '

Jake shook his head. ' The villages I've seen are pretty small, I reckon.'

' Aren't they friendly ? ' Alan said. ' Mr Brewster was talking about the Iroquois. I remember the name, now.'

' The Iroquois are, I guess,' Jake said. ' They don't like the French, and we've always traded with 'em.'

' But there are Indian tribes on the side of the French, aren't there ? '

' Sure. The Lake tribes up north and to the east, like the

Abenakis—they're Algonkin Indians.' Jake spat again, with even more violence than usual, and Alan grinned.

' You don't like the Indians, Jake,' he said.

' Reckon I don't, Mister Carey. Some folks say they're fine people. But I call 'em filthy and cold-blooded savages ! '

He was scowling bitterly, with his normally good-natured face hard and bitter. ' A friend of mine was taken prisoner by a bunch of Abenakis couple of years back,' he said.

' Why, what happened ? ' Alan asked in surprise.

' The Indians take prisoners for only one reason, Mister Carey. So they can spend a long time torturing them to death. Yeah, they're pretty cute at that.'

' Oh, I see,' Alan said, and shivered.

' If you ever get caught by Indians on the war-path, Mister Carey, and you see a bear, you walk right up to the bear. He'll be mighty kind to you compared to a bunch of Abenakis whooping it up.'

Alan shifted uneasily in his saddle, and looked nervously over his shoulder. The silent forest around them seemed to have assumed a sinister and menacing appearance.

They travelled steadily all day, passing a clearing in the forest at intervals, a few groups of wooden houses and some cultivated land. Without Jake, Alan would have been quite hopelessly lost long before this. Signposts did not exist for the most part, and in the unbroken forest there were few natural features to be seen that might have acted as guides to direction.

Towards the late afternoon, Jake turned up another track that led them away from the river. Nailed to a tree was a board, and Alan glanced at it idly. What he saw was so astonishing that he jerked at the reins of his horse, and called out to Jake.

' Yeah, that's the Ashwater board,' Jake said.

Alan nodded. He had ridden close to the board, and was bending forward to read the letters cut deep in the wood. At the top was the word ' Ashwater ', but it was the sign below that had attracted his attention. Some amateur artist had cut a crude design of a bird with outstretched wings, the Hawk of the Aubignys. Alan smiled incredulously. He had sailed for five weeks across the Atlantic ; he had ridden through a strange continent for over two hundred miles, and here in the silent depths of the forest he was looking at his own family coat-of-arms. The land he was standing on was Carey land ;

he laughed again. Llanstephan seemed very far away at the moment.

Jake was anxious to reach Ashwater before the sun set, so Alan cantered after him up the track. The Mohawk River was out of sight, and below them now, and the forest seemed to close in on either side. Alan glanced to right and left, into the dark, sombre tangle of trees and undergrowth, still and silent, virgin forest, untamed and wild. He shuddered as he caught up with Jake, and asked him how far away Ashwater lay.

' 'Bout five miles, I reckon.' Jake grinned, his lean face creasing like the leather of his buckskin coat. ' Hepburn expecting you, Mister Carey ? '

' No. My father didn't write to him, and asked Mr Brewster not to let him know I had landed in America.'

Jake's grin extended into a broad smile. 'His face sure will be worth seeing,' he remarked, and then the smile vanished. 'You keep your hand close to that rifle of yours, Mister Carey.'

'But there's no danger, surely?' Alan said. He pulled up his horse and was staring at Jake in astonishment.

Jake eyed him curiously. 'You ain't in England now,' he said. 'No, sir. Nor in Boston or Albany.'

'But Hepburn won't try to shoot me at sight!' Alan said.

'Maybe not,' Jake said slowly. 'But I remember what my dad used to say. You start running when the tree begins to fall. You don't stand and wait until it hits you. See, Mister Carey? You hold on to that gun.'

He kicked his heels into his horse's sides, and they trotted up the path towards Ashwater.

Chapter Six

MR ELIJAH HEPBURN

THE track turned north, skirting a wide stretch of swampy ground, and then swung to the west again. Alan had seen a map of the Ashwater estate at Llanstephan before he left, but the Earl had not vouched for its accuracy. The estate was a very large one, though, typical of the lavish grants of land made so casually by the Crown to a few favoured families.

At the top of a slight rise Jake pointed ahead, and Alan saw smoke rising above the trees. Another mile, and they could see the settlement itself. By this time Alan knew what to expect ; a wide clearing in the forest, cultivated fields, some stock of cattle and sheep, and in the centre a tall stockade with a single gate.

They trotted inside. To the left was a line of outbuildings, and in the centre a long, low wooden house with a porch. A small boy ran up to take the horses as they dismounted, and a man who was sitting on the porch came leisurely down the steps to meet them. He wore a black coat and breeches, with dark-grey stockings and black shoes with a plain metal buckle. The only relief to this sombre background was the white stock at his throat.

' Mr Hepburn ? ' Alan asked.

' I am Elijah Hepburn, young man.' His voice matched his appearance, deep and harsh.

A pair of cold, unsmiling eyes stared back at Alan ; the grim-lipped mouth was turned down in a perpetual grimace of disapproval at the corners, with two deep lines running to the nose, so deeply marked that they might well have been scored by a knife.

' My name is Carey,' Alan said. ' My father is Lord Aubigny.'

The hard, grey eyes flickered. ' You have arrived recently in America, Mr Carey ? '

' I landed at Boston a few weeks ago.' Alan handed over a sealed packet. ' These are letters from my father.'

Hepburn did not look at the packet, but pushed it into the pocket of his black coat. ' You had a pleasant voyage, I trust ? ' he asked.

' Yes, thank you. We were chased by a French frigate, but beat her off.'

' The Lord has been good,' Hepburn intoned. He lifted his eyes to the sky, and clasped his hands together. ' The Almighty has preserved you from the perils of the deep.' The eyes dropped again to Alan's startled face. ' We shall sing Psalm One Hundred and Seven tonight.' Once more the hands were clasped and the head raised. ' They that go down to the sea in ships, that do business in great waters ; these see the works of the Lord and His wonders in the deep.'

The harsh voice broke off, and the cold eyes bored into Alan's. ' You will join us at our prayers, I hope, Mr Carey ? '

' Yes, of course, Mr Hepburn.' Alan tried to make his

voice sound normal and sincere, but he found it difficult to hide his surprise. He had never met this type of man before.

'We must show a devout example in this wilderness,' Hepburn added as he ushered them inside the house.

Alan found himself in a spacious room. It was roughly furnished to his eyes; the chairs and the long table had obviously been made locally. The walls and floor were covered here and there with superb skins, and facing the door was a wide fire-place of natural stone.

Mr Hepburn clapped his hands, and a Negro hurried in, rolling his eyes as he saw the visitors.

'Yes, Mr Hepburn, sah?' he asked, cringing visibly as he met that cold glance.

'Prepare a room for Mr Carey, Sam.'

'And my man here?' Alan said quickly. He had no intention of being separated from Jake. 'This is Jake Winter, Mr Hepburn.'

Hepburn gave Jake a short and wintry look. 'Sam will doubtless find a bed for you, Mr Winter,' he said curtly. 'Hurry, Sam!'

'Yes, sah, yes, sah!' The Negro rushed out from the room as if he was glad to leave it.

Jake brought in the saddlebags, and they went to the room which Mr Hepburn pointed out in one wing of the house. It was clean and reasonably comfortable, Alan decided. Jake closed the heavy door, and dropped the latch. He bent his head down to listen for footsteps outside, and then nodded, as if satisfied they could not be overheard.

'What do you think of Mr Elijah Hepburn, Jake?' Alan asked.

Jake, for once, did not stop to think out his answer. 'Ever seen a rattlesnake, Mister Carey?' he said. 'No, I guess you ain't. I'd rather be standing close to one of them than near Hepburn. You can always blow the head off a blamed snake.'

Alan sat down on the bed, and grinned. He had the same feeling about his father's bailiff. The comparison to a snake was a good one, he thought. Hepburn's eyes were as cold and expressionless as any snake's.

But the man was polite and respectful at supper that evening. His speech was still very Biblical. He intoned a long prayer before the meal began, and he quoted with great facility from the Psalms and the Old Testament. The intensity with which he did so made Alan uncomfortable and embarrassed. He did not like fanatics. But the meal was surprisingly good, with varied courses, and all of them well cooked.

The sun had nearly set by the time the meal was finished, and immediately the table was cleared by Sam, the Negro servant, the door leading to the porch was opened and a stream of people surged into the room.

They formed up in lines against the walls, and Hepburn conducted a short service. He referred to Alan by name, and heads turned towards him for a minute, and then back to Hepburn. Whether they were sincere in their attitude, or were merely obeying the orders of the man who employed them, Alan could not tell. There was a touch of fear about some of the faces as they watched Hepburn, he thought, but that might have been his imagination.

During the long prayers, intoned by Hepburn with a passionate intensity, Alan studied the workpeople. They were a rough-looking crowd, some in buckskins, but the majority wore clothes of a coarse, tough linen, which, as Jake told him afterwards, was called Ozenbrig, and was imported from Osnabrück in Germany. Their shoes were home-made by their appearance, double soled and of rawhide.

There were several nationalities represented in the group, some English, or so Alan assumed, and a few obvious Germans and Swedes. Probably indentured labourers, for Mr Brewster had explained how many immigrants from Europe answered advertisements in papers, were given a free passage across the Atlantic, and then sent to farms and settlements where there was work available ; they were then bound to work at these places until their debt was discharged. After that they were free to go where they wished.

The service ended with the Hundred and Seventh Psalm, as Hepburn had promised. Everyone joined in with him as he recited the rolling phrases, while Alan watched him, puzzled and uneasy. He could not understand this man, and anything he found unpredictable worried him.

The following morning he was taken on a tour of the estate. He presumed that Hepburn had read the Earl's letter by this time. No mention had been made, as Alan knew, about the trade figures for the fur depot. Alan was described as a curious traveller. All young Englishmen of sufficient wealth did the Grand Tour as part of their education, and the Earl had explained that owing to the threat of war in Europe, Alan was visiting America instead.

This might mislead Hepburn. Alan doubted it, but the man was extremely polite as he showed Alan the farms and the whole of the settlement. Ashwater was only part of the estate, Alan learnt. There were outlying farms as well, with tenant farmers paying rent to the Earl.

Finally they came to the sheds where the furs were stored and treated. This was a business about which Alan was completely ignorant, and he was glad to see Jake follow them inside.

' We send all furs down the Hudson to New York,' Hepburn explained.

' There doesn't seem to be much here,' Alan remarked. It was a natural thing to say, he hoped.

' This is not the season,' Hepburn said quickly.

' The trade has been small, my father thinks.'

Hepburn shrugged his shoulders. ' The Indians are very unsettled, Mr Carey. French agents have been among them.' This was true, as Alan had been told in Boston. ' They seek to destroy their friendship with us.'

' Will that mean trouble ? '

' It is very possible. The French have corrupted the heathen and have done abominable works.' Up went the hard eyes to the roof of the shed. ' Deliver me from the workers of iniquity, and save me from bloody men,' he added with fervour.

Alan nodded. There was little that one could say in face of these constant quotations from the Psalms. But he knew now of what Hepburn had reminded him ; the fanatical Welsh preachers he had heard in Carmarthenshire.

Later that day, when Hepburn had left him alone for a time, he questioned Jake about what they had seen.

' The farms seem well run,' Alan said. ' I do know something about that. But what do you think of the fur business, Jake ? '

' The Indians are unsettled, Mister Carey. I reckon that Hepburn is telling the truth about that, and the drop in the number of skins that are coming in. But I wouldn't trust Hepburn farther than I could push this stockade.'

They were sitting on a stump of a tree outside the stockade, overlooking the trail, and Alan's attention was distracted by a group of men who had just emerged from the forest.

' Indians,' Jake said.

There were five of them, walking in single file, and dressed in buckskins, the inevitable clothes of the man who lived in or near the forest, so Alan was beginning to realize. He had expected to see men with bright red skins, but these Indians were a dark brown, with long black hair and broad nostrils. Their cheek-bones were unusually high, and to Alan they seemed all alike.

Their leader saw the two white men, and raised his hand in a slow and stately salute as they padded past silently and gracefully. They were dignified and fine-looking men, and Alan thought that he had never seen such a smooth and easy walk before. Gliding, he thought, was the best way to describe how these Indians were covering the ground.

' Mohawks,' Jake said, and spat.

' That's one of the Iro . . . Iroquois nations, isn't it ? '

' Yeah, that's right. My dad used to say they were the most dangerous of the Six Nations. They're the smallest tribe, though.'

' And the biggest ? '

' The Senecas, I guess. They live up round Lake Erie way.'

' I thought they had red skins,' Alan said.

Jake laughed. ' Only when they're on the war-path,

Mister Carey. Then they paint themselves all colours. I've seen a chief with five different colours on him. But red usually.' He heaved himself off the stump, and picked up Alan's new rifle.

' Have you tried out this new gun, Mister Carey ? ' he asked.

' Yes, of course ! '

' Yeah, that's what you think. Do you know whether it throws high, or to the left or right ? '

Alan shook his head guiltily. ' I think it throws a fraction high, Jake,' he said.

' Let's see,' Jake said. He led Alan to the edge of the big clearing, and sliced a piece of bark from a tree, leaving a white mark on the trunk.

' Try it at fifty yards,' he said, and paced it out.

' But it will carry up to five hundred yards, Jake ! '

Jake spat derisively. ' You'll be blame lucky if you ever get as much as fifty yards for a clear shot in the forest,' he said.

Alan nodded obediently. He was always ready to learn, as Jake had discovered, otherwise it is doubtful if he would have wasted any time trying to teach Alan.

He watched him now as he took up a comfortable stance, feet apart, half turned to the target.

' You look like a blamed tree standing up there,' he said. ' Deer and Indians ain't blind, Mister Carey.'

Alan flushed, but he said nothing. He was becoming accustomed to these bluntly-spoken backwoodsmen. ' Tell me what to do, Jake,' he said after a pause.

' Lie down behind that trunk.'

Alan glanced down instinctively at his breeches and stockings. They were his oldest, but they would be torn and scratched.

' I must have buckskins made for me, Jake,' he said.

' Yeah, that's what you need, Mister Carey. They don't tear or catch in bushes, you see, and they're warm in the winter.'

' What about moccasins ? '

' Same with them. Comfortable, once you get used to 'em.
And they don't make no noise. You can put your feet down
quiet on dry twigs, and balance easy.'

Alan nodded, and then stretched himself out behind the
log. If he tore his clothes, then . . . He grinned, and then
Jake prodded him until he was satisfied with his position. At
last he was allowed to fire, and he started to scramble to his
feet. But a remorseless hand pushed him down.

' I must reload ! ' he protested.

' Sure ! ' Jake said. ' Stand up ! You're only just over
six feet high. Climb a tree ! Tell the whole forest where you
are ! The deer won't mind. They'll turn their backs and be
durned polite and not look while you reload.'

Alan gulped, his face red. This was like school again.

' How do I do it, Jake ? ' he asked humbly.

' Roll over on your side.'

Alan did so with a loud crackle from the dry twigs beneath
him. ' I suppose that would scare every deer near the Mohawk,
wouldn't it, Jake ? ' he said.

' Guess they'll have to be mighty deaf for a while, Mister
Carey. But you'll learn.'

And Alan did learn. For some time he struggled to reload
while still lying on the ground. The long ramrod was the
most awkward part of the business, and he despaired of ever
being able to force the bullet home. The little mallet made
a considerable noise, too. But as Jake pointed out to him,
after the first shot, the deer, unless he had been hit, would
have disappeared by that time, so noise would matter little.
If it was a question of Indians, they would know roughly
where he was by the white smoke. It was safer to crawl to
a different position, and load there.

Alan fired half a dozen shots, and then they went to inspect
the tree. Jake whistled. ' Reckon you can shoot, Mister
Carey,' he said. His fingers covered the six holes in the trunk,
for they were grouped in a tiny circle, a sure sign that Alan
had kept the same aim throughout.

' It does throw a little high,' Alan said. ' But I can allow
for that, now.'

M.V.—7

Jake took him back a hundred yards the next time, though as he repeated, it would not be often that Alan would have such a range in the depths of the forest.

'Aim dead on,' he advised. 'You ain't got much time to allow for the drop when you're shooting a running deer.'

Alan's shooting was impressive, and even Jake admitted that he might yet teach him to be useful in the forest.

'In a couple of years you might be safe,' he said.

'Two years !' Alan said.

'Yeah ! You only get one chance with an Indian, Mister Carey. And you don't have much time to aim. Up and shoot, my dad taught me. If you don't hit them, then it don't matter, for you'll be dead meat after that !'

They strolled back to the stockade. The sun was setting behind them, but the indentured labourers were still at work in the fields. Hepburn was standing by the gate, and as Alan saw those cold, watchful eyes, he shivered.

But he forced himself to make some casual remark. 'How long do these men work during the day ? ' he asked.

'Man goeth forth to his work and his labour until the evening,' Hepburn intoned.

'Oh, I see,' Alan said, floored as usual by this type of answer. 'Can I have some buckskin clothes made, Mr Hepburn ? And a pair of moccasins ? '

'Hans Fricker is our tailor, Mr Carey. I will set him to work in the morning. I would advise you to give him a present of money. The labourer . . .'

'Is worthy of his hire,' Jake cut in. 'Sure, Mr Hepburn.'

Hepburn said nothing, but the look he shot at Jake was one of suppressed fury.

But the evening passed without anything suspicious, and Alan wondered if Jake was an alarmist. The supper that night was as well cooked and served as on the previous day, and Hepburn showed the first real sign of pleasure that Alan had yet seen on his gloomy features when Alan praised the food. But no wine had been served, unusual at that time, and Alan made a comment on this.

Hepburn looked up from his plate with horror. 'Wine is

a mocker,' he said with great severity, ' strong drink is raging, and whosoever is deceived thereby is not wise.'

The rest of the meal passed in silence, much to Alan's relief.

Alan was measured for his buckskins the next morning. Fricker was a German, speaking broken English, but he seemed to know his work, and told Alan that he had been a tailor in Cologne. The clothes, he promised, would be finished by the following day.

Hepburn suggested a ride to one of the outlying farms that afternoon, and they set off up the track. Jake had nodded silently to Alan when the suggestion was made, and he rode close behind Alan. His eyes did not often leave Hepburn, Alan noticed.

The farm, when they arrived there, appeared to be well managed, though Alan thought that the tenant farmer, a man called Wilson, had little liking for Hepburn. He was extending the cultivated land, and Alan walked over to watch a couple of men felling a tree. Jake stayed for a moment to tether the horses.

The men, stripped to the waist, were using four-pound axes, swinging with an unhurried rhythm, bringing down the axe heads with what appeared to be an effortless ease, and always hitting exactly the same spot with a crack that sent the white chips of wood flying out to one side.

Hepburn joined Alan, standing just to his left, and looking up at the top of the tree. A loud crack came from the stem, and the woodmen stepped to one side. Alan put his head back to watch as the tree began to sway, slowly at first, and then with increasing speed as the topmost branches swept down in a graceful and majestic curve.

Someone shouted behind Alan. He heard the sound of running feet, and a hand caught him by the collar of his coat and dragged him violently to one side. It was Jake, but he was not looking at Alan ; his eyes were fixed on the tree.

Alan turned his head, too ; the highest branches came down with a crash and a loud crackling of wood, smashing their way through the foliage of another tree that was still standing. The check was momentary, but the effect was startling. The severed part whipped back from the stump, and the thick trunk lashed out savagely with a thrust like the last dying kick of some enraged monster, right over the spot where Alan had been standing.

Alan drew a deep breath. The tree lay on its side, inert and harmless now, but it required no imagination on Alan's part to realize that that dreadful weight would have smashed into him waist-high with all the annihilating force of a sledge-hammer coming down on a china cup.

' Never stand behind a falling tree, my dad used to tell me,' Jake said. ' Ain't that so, Mr Hepburn ? '

' Yes, yes, indeed that is so ! ' Hepburn's hands were fluttering as he turned towards Alan. ' We are so accustomed to felling trees, Mr Carey, and I had quite forgotten that all this is completely strange to you.'

' Remember seeing a man killed just like that,' Jake said, his dark eyes on Hepburn's face.

' The Lord has watched over you, Mr Carey,' Hepburn said. ' You must render thanks to Him tonight.'

' And to Jake,' Alan said.

' Yeah,' Jake said, but he was still watching Hepburn. ' But I reckon I'm just naturally watchful.'

Hepburn met his glance, and for a brief second there flashed from his eyes a glare of malignant hatred, passing so quickly that Alan thought he must have imagined it. For Hepburn's face was again that of the respectful and polite bailiff as he pointed to another field containing cattle, and suggested that Alan might care to inspect them.

Alan nodded, and turned to follow. As he did so, he saw Jake looking at him. One eye dropped in a wink. Alan half smiled, but he was still too shaken to feel amused. He walked slowly after Hepburn.

Chapter Seven

THE FOREST

THE buckskins were ready the next day, as the German tailor had promised, and Alan tried them on eagerly. Perhaps, he was thinking, he would feel more at ease in the dress of the backwoodsmen, for he was painfully conscious that his old shooting clothes, shabby though they might have appeared to English eyes, were conspicuous and ridiculously out of place in the forest.

Jake fussed over the fit of the moccasins. They felt extremely comfortable to Alan, but Jake insisted that they be altered, and told the tailor to cut a pair of bark soles to slip inside, until Alan's feet hardened, and he could walk over rough ground or stones in the moccasins without bruising the soles of his feet.

'Yeah, that's better,' Jake said, surveying Alan. 'I'll take you into the forest this morning, Mister Carey. They want some venison here.'

But he seemed in no hurry, and spent some time collecting all the various items of equipment which he said they would need, and made certain that Alan was carrying a similar load.

'Say, listen, Mister Carey,' he said. 'Never go into the forest without flint and tinder, a sheath knife, a tomahawk, and a water bottle. And your gun, powder flask, and bullets.'

Then he strapped a small pack on to Alan's broad shoulders. 'Bread, cold meat, a tin cup, and a can for boiling water,' he explained.

'A blanket, too?' Alan said. 'We're not going to spend the night in the forest, are we, Jake?'

'Not today,' Jake said. 'But it's plumb simple to walk into the forest. It's not so easy to walk out. That's what my dad told me when I was a kid.'

93

They set off from the stockade, but Alan had not taken more than a few long strides before Jake halted him.

'You won't get far at that pace, Mister Carey,' he said. 'We're going to cover about fifteen miles at least.'

'But I've often walked farther than that,' Alan said.

'Not in the forest,' Jake said flatly.

At the edge of the clearing he stopped and looked round slowly from one side to the other.

'What are you looking for?' Alan asked.

'My bearings. There ain't no signposts in the forest, 'cept the ones you make yourself.'

Apparently satisfied, he took a well-defined trail that led them to the west. He walked with a slight slouch, hips swinging, with a long, easy stride, toes pointing straight ahead.

'You walk like a townsman, Mister Carey,' he said.

'I daresay I do,' Alan confessed. 'What's wrong, Jake?'

'Everything! Walk kinda flat footed. Let your hips and knees go slack. Keep your toes straight, and step out easy like. Less likely to trip over stones, then. You watch an Indian walk. They learn it when they're babies.'

Alan plodded along behind Jake, watching his feet, and trying to imitate the other's easy shamble that covered the ground with such little effort, and yet a surprising speed. The trail climbed a steep slope, and Jake halted at the top.

'This is where you start to learn where you are in the forest,' he said. 'There's Ashwater, due east. See the hill behind the smoke? And the single clump of pines to the left? Then the ground falls away, gentle-like, to the Mohawk. There's your signposts home, Mister Carey.'

Alan stared dutifully, and when he had memorized the scene Jake swung him round, and made him do the same to the west.

'We'll make a sweep to the north,' Jake said. 'Far as that hill there. Then swing down south again, and hit this trail.'

They walked steadily for an hour, Jake coaching Alan patiently as they went, teaching him the names of the trees they passed, the various birds, showing him how to flex his knees as they went downhill, and at every few yards teaching him how to memorize the route they had followed.

It was this that astonished Alan most, for Jake had apparently made a mental note of every detail of importance since they had left the stockade.

'But there's so much to remember,' Alan said.

'Mighty little,' Jake said. 'You look out for anything that's unusual, Mister Carey. You'll soon learn,' he added confidently.

Alan hoped so. A few minutes later Jake stopped him again. 'Now, you pick the route,' he said. 'We're going to swing north for that bluff I showed you.'

'I can't see it from here,' Alan said.

'Sure. Get where you can see it.'

Alan turned off the trail, and made for a slight slope in the thickly wooded ground. He could just see the rocky bluff some miles ahead, and pointed to it triumphantly.

'Yeah, that's it,' Jake said. 'But I knew where it was without coming up here.'

'How?'

'Remember that last slope we came down? Well, I had a good look from the top of that.'

Alan nodded humbly. He felt like a small child learning to walk, and Jake grinned when he saw his downcast face.

'Ten minutes' halt, Mister Carey,' he said. 'That's a good rule in the forest. We got all day, too. You'll soon learn,' he added cheerfully.

Alan had heard that before, and he shook his head gloomily. 'I want a nurse,' he said.

'Say, listen, Mister Carey,' Jake said. 'I was born in the forest. My dad was a settler. We lived ten miles from our nearest neighbours. I had to start learning how to live in the forest.'

'But you started as a boy,' Alan said.

'Sure. It'll take you years, too, Mister Carey, before you're a real backwoodsman. But you're ready to learn, not like some townspeople I've met. By the end of the

summer I'll have taught you how to fend for yourself, and how to find your way about. After that you'll learn for yourself.'

Alan's spirits rose slightly. He had little confidence in himself, but he was intelligent enough to see that Jake was probably right. And when they set off again, leaving the trail, he was encouraged to take the lead. The going was more difficult now, for they were not following any track at all. The trees were very tall here, the lowest branches some

twenty feet off the ground, but there was practically no undergrowth, and Alan's moccasins sank easily and softly into the
carpet of dead leaves. It was cool and shadowy under the
trees, for the sun could not break through the thick screen of
foliage far overhead. This indeed, as Alan realized, was the
real forest, sombre, endless, and silent.

Jake whistled softly, and bent down to examine a faint
mark on the ground.

' Deer,' he said.

Alan joined him, and inspected the marks while Jake gave him a short lecture on spoor marks.

'Pretty fresh, too,' Jake said. 'Loaded? Well, don't cock your gun till I tell you. We'll work upwind of him. Now put your feet down quiet; that's what moccasins are for.'

They worked their way very slowly through the trees. It was not so difficult, Alan discovered, to walk noiselessly in moccasins on the pine needles and soft leaf mould. He kept an eye on Jake, slouching ahead, lean, brown face set, as if he was sniffing the track of the deer. Up went a hand in warning, and he slowed his pace, moving now from one tree to another, waiting and watching behind each one before he slipped to the next.

The sun broke through just ahead, a bright and startling contrast to the dark tunnels through which Alan and Jake were walking. Then they reached the clearing, and Jake went down full length, with great caution, so as not to make the slightest noise, and Alan lowered his six feet and more to the ground, fearful of the scornful look that would certainly come his way from Jake if he as much as disturbed a leaf.

Ahead of them was a circular clearing, and on the far side there ran a little stream, chattering cheerfully as it ran over the stones. Jake put his mouth against Alan's ear.

'See that balsam?' he whispered.

Alan narrowed his eyes in the sunlight, but he could see nothing. Then at the foot of the tree something moved, and there was the leaden grey shape of a deer, head down, drinking from the stream. Now that he was still again, Alan realized how his colouring blended with his background.

'Cock your gun,' Jake muttered. There was the faintest of clicks as the two flintlocks were pulled back. 'Aim just behind the shoulder. Third of a way up the body.'

Slowly Alan brought his rifle up to the aim. He closed one eye, and squinted down the long, dull barrel, until the foresight was dead on the point behind the shoulder as Jake had said. Slowly still he drew in his breath, held it, and squeezed gently on the trigger. A flash from the priming pan, a loud crack, and a spurt of dense white smoke from the muzzle, and the scene was blotted out for a second.

He saw the deer leap into the air, and dart across the stream. Another wild leap, and he was out of sight.

' Missed ! ' Alan groaned.

' Hit,' Jake said calmly, and jumped to his feet. But he did not move out into the glade as Alan had expected him to. His head was cocked to one side, and he was listening intently.

' Don't chase a deer when he's hit,' he said. ' He'll stop if he thinks there's no one after him.'

' But I didn't hit him,' Alan said.

' You did, Mister Carey. He showed his flag when he jumped. The white of his tail.'

They stayed there for perhaps five minutes before Jake slipped from behind his tree, and crossed to the stream. He pointed to a bush where some of the smaller branches had been broken off.

' Look for the lighter colour,' he said. ' If you bend a bush over, the light underside of the leaves shows up.'

Alan looked to the left. He could now see for himself the faint trail left by the deer through the bushes growing by the side of the stream, and they walked slowly and quietly along the line, through another belt of trees, and into another small clearing.

Jake stopped and pointed. ' There he is ! '

The deer was sprawled across the centre of the clearing, and he did not move as they went over.

' Through the heart,' Jake said, laying his finger on the glossy skin. ' I reckon you don't know how lucky you are, Mister Carey.'

Alan was quite used to any reproof from Jake by this time, and he merely grinned now where a few weeks ago he would have flushed with anger.

' Why, Jake ? The range was only about thirty yards.'

' All ranges are short in the forest. It's the time you have to aim that matters.'

He took out his knife, and began the messy business of stripping away the skin. Alan realized with a gulp that he would have to learn the same task before long, and he went down on his knees and gave Jake a hand.

' How do we get him home ? ' he asked.

' They'll come out from Ashwater,' Jake said. ' I'll make a cache of the meat, and mark it. You can lead me here.'

' I'll try,' Alan said. ' How long does venison hang before you can eat it ? '

' Few days, I reckon,' Jake said. ' Never eat fresh venison if you've got anything else handy. I did once when I was out of food. Tough and mighty tasteless it was, too, and turned my stomach.'

The skin they decided to take back with them, for the German tailor was in need of skins. Deer were used by the Indians in an amazing variety of ways, Jake told Alan, apart from the meat itself. The skin was made into clothing and shoes, the antlers for tool handles and arrow points ; even the hooves were useful for glue, and the sinews were invaluable for thread and bowstrings.

After they had buried the carcass at the foot of a tree, Jake sliced off a piece of bark as a blaze mark.

Alan was hungry after his exertions, and Jake told him to make a fire, explaining that there were different types of fire, the small one for quick boiling of water, up to the large, long-burning fires of logs for warmth during a cold night.

' That's what your tomahawk's for,' he said. ' It'll cut all the small stuff you need.' He glanced at the sticks that Alan had collected. ' Too damp, Mister Carey. Stuff that lies on the ground's always like that. See that fallen tree ? Cut the small branches. They're dead and dry.'

He was whittling away at a small stick, and drove it into the ground. Then he picked the greenest branch he could find, notched it half-way down, and laid it carefully on the first stick, one end on the fork, and the other touching the ground. Underneath this he built the same pyramid of dry twigs that Alan had seen him make before. When the fire was red-hot he filled the tin can, which had a small wire handle, and hooked this over the notch in the green branch.

Alan enjoyed his meal, and particularly the hot tea that

Jake had made. The cold venison they had brought from Ashwater was delicious, and Alan ate hugely. He had a good deal to fill, as his Cambridge friends had often pointed out.

' What do Indians eat in the forest ? ' he asked.

' Jerked venison ; that's dried meat. Or else they go for hours on nocake.'

' What's that ? Nocake ? '

' Yeah. It's parched corn—maize—Mister Carey. You stir a spoonful of it in water ; it's beaten to a powder, you see, and then you just swallow.'

' Doesn't sound much of a meal,' Alan said, thinking of his own enormous appetite.

' You'd be surprised, Mister Carey,' Jake said. ' Three spoons a day keep an Indian going. I've done the same. Guess the stuff blows your stomach out, and you don't feel hungry.'

Alan hoped he would never be reduced to this meagre diet, but he would try it very soon, he decided.

' But Indians can find food anywhere,' Jake said. ' Wild berries, nuts, and roots. Reckon you'd better learn what the right kind look like, Mister Carey. You never know,' he added ominously.

He stamped out the fire with the greatest care, raking the earth away beneath the warm embers. ' Always do that,' he said. ' I was caught with my dad in a forest fire once.'

' Is your father still alive ? '

' Nope. Died five years ago. Great fellow, was my dad.'

Satisfied that the fire was harmless, Jake packed away the cooking tins, and turned to Alan. ' Now you take me back to the trail, Mister Carey,' he said, and grinned.

Alan stood up and looked around. They were in a bowl of trees, and he had not the slightest idea of the points of the compass. He did not even know where to begin.

' I'm lost,' he said.

Jake chuckled. ' You'll have to work it out for yourself one day, Mister Carey. Where does Ashwater lie from us ? '

' East.'

' And the sun ? '

Alan could not see the sun, but he suddenly realized that the shadows and the way they fell would show him the east and west.

' East's there,' he said, pointing over Jake's shoulder.

' Yeah. Now, think back the way we came after the deer.'

With some prompting Alan was surprised to find how much he had noticed and remembered.

' And this stream ? ' Jake asked. ' Where's it likely to run, Mister Carey ? '

' Oh, down to the Mohawk, of course.'

' Yeah, so if we follow it we should come out on the trail from Ashwater.'

Alan led the way. But walking in the forest, he was beginning to realize, was not only a matter of mere physical effort ; it demanded constant vigilance, the need to notice and memorize any item out of the ordinary, pools, fallen trunks, oddly shaped trees, any break in the endless march of the trees, anything unusual that might be of value if the need arose. Jake was a patient teacher, and Alan, thanks to an excellent memory, a good pupil.

But he was tired when they came in sight of the stockade of Ashwater. Jake was still slouching along in his casual manner ; he did not look like a man who had just walked over ten miles in the forest, and to Alan's envious eyes, he seemed quite capable of covering double that distance again.

They went out again the next day, and to Alan's delight, and the benefit of his growing self-confidence, he led Jake without a check to the spot where they had buried the venison.

But he was no nearer solving the problem of the fur trade, and the part played by Hepburn. No furs were coming in from the Indians. They, as Jake told him, were the main agents and traders with the tribes farther to the east of the Iroquois region.

' I guess I'll ride into Schenectady,' Jake said. ' My Uncle Pete lives there. He's in the fur business, and he'll know something about Elijah Hepburn.'

' I'll come with you,' Alan said.

Jake shook his head. ' Uncle Pete's a queer cuss,' he said.

' Don't like strangers. That's why I didn't stop there on the way out from Albany. But I'm plumb scared of leaving you here alone, mister Carey.'

Alan laughed. ' I'll be safe enough, Jake.'

Jake chewed reflectively, his leathery face screwed up in doubt. ' Reckon if you keeps your eyes open, you may be safe until I get back,' he said. ' But Hepburn's a mean cuss. You watch out, Mister Carey.'

But Alan missed Jake in the two days that followed. He had been warned not to go into the forest, certainly not by himself, and to be extremely careful with whom he did go if Hepburn suggested it. He rode over to the other farms on the estate which he had not yet seen, but by the third day he was bored, and the depressing company of Hepburn with his eternal quotations from the Psalms, and his repellent personality, was more than Alan could stand. Fricker, the tailor, a friendly little man, and an honest one, so Alan considered, suggested that he took one of the trappers out into the forest, a man called Isaac Lockett.

Alan was doubtful, but he could not see any possible danger. Lockett was half Indian, a swarthy looking fellow with the high cheek-bones of his Mohawk mother. About his knowledge of the forest there was no doubt ; he had spent his whole life there.

So they left the stockade just before midday. Alan told Lockett that he did not want to go far, and was expecting Jake back that evening, and wished to be home to meet him when he arrived. Lockett nodded with a flash of his white teeth. He was a vivacious and excitable little man, springy and agile, and he chattered volubly as they went down the trail above the river.

They had two shots at deer without any success ; the first time Alan missed, but the shot was a long one, and he had little time to come up to the aim. The second was Lockett's shot, and he missed hopelessly, much to Alan's surprise. After that they struck off to the north. There was a lake up there, Canada Lake, so Lockett said, and deer were plentiful. Alan let him take the lead, and as they pushed on rapidly, for

Lockett was setting a fast pace, he tried to make a note of their bearings, and any prominent landmarks. But without Jake's constant tuition he found it difficult, and after an hour he realized that he had little idea of where they were moving in relation to Ashwater.

They halted at one end of a narrow ravine, with a steep outcrop of rock on one side.

' How far are we from Ashwater, Isaac ? ' Alan asked.

' 'Bout ten miles, Mister Carey.'

' And in which direction ? '

Lockett pointed to the right without any hesitation. Alan looked for the sun to check for himself, but the sky was overcast, and the ravine shut them in on either side.

' Usually deer by that pool at the end,' Lockett said. ' Work round the rocks, and upwind.'

He set off up the rocks, with Alan at his heels, climbing above the floor of the ravine, and gaining a view over the surrounding trees. The sun broke through for a few minutes, and Alan glanced up casually. He hesitated, saw Lockett look round to see where he was, and went on again. But according to the sun the ravine ran east to west ; there was no doubt about it, even to the inexperienced Alan. But Lockett had said that Ashwater lay to the right. That was due north. Alan walked on slowly, not bothering to watch for deer. Lockett was a real backwoodsman, perhaps even more at home in the forest than Jake. He could not possibly have made such an elementary mistake.

Then there was something wrong, Alan's instinct told him. He watched Lockett's slight figure climbing nimbly over the rocks just ahead, and moved up close to him. Lockett stopped, and raised a hand.

' Deer,' he muttered, and crouched behind a boulder. ' Four, I think. You work to the right, Mister Carey. I'll go left.'

' You go first then,' Alan said. ' I might frighten them off.'

A flash of white teeth in the dark face, and Lockett vanished over the rocks. Alan crawled forward cautiously to watch. The trapper was out of sight already, hidden in a tangle of boulders and bushes, and so quietly was he moving that Alan could not hear a sound.

He looked for the deer, but there was no sign of them. A sudden wave of panic swept over him. He felt alone and very exposed. He would have given a very large sum of money then to have seen Jake's sardonic smile and slowly moving jaws close to him.

A gun cracked. The rock above Alan's head splintered ; the bullet whizzed away with a screech. With a gasp of fear Alan wriggled away from the spot, crouching low, expecting the next shot to smash into him. Fool, he thought, he's got to reload. I must get out of sight and range before he . . .

Feet scrabbled on the loose stones above and to the left. Alan rolled over. Hurtling down upon him was a small buckskinned figure, teeth flashing, one hand in the air brandishing a tomahawk. Alan kicked out savagely, heard a cry from Lockett, and then he was on his feet with the speed and agility of the trained wrestler. Lockett was on him like a whirling fury, all arms and legs. Alan shot out his long left arm, and caught the half-breed in the chest, sending him staggering back. Alan was on him instantly, and sent in a raking punch to the face that sent the little man reeling. The tomahawk clattered to the ground, and Alan leapt forward. He was doing something now in which he had ample confidence in his ability, and he moved with astonishing speed for a man of his size.

Lockett was on his feet, and when he saw the huge figure rushing at him he stepped back, threw up his arms and toppled over the edge of the outcrop. Alan leant over. He saw the trapper roll down in a crackle of broken bushes and twigs, and then bound to his feet and race down the ravine.

Alan snatched his rifle, thumb pulling back the cocking piece, left arm cradling the long barrel, and then the flying, crouching figure was in his sights. A deep breath, the faintest pressure on the trigger, and the curved cocking piece sprang forward and down. The spark from the flint, the flash in the pan and the sharp crack and jet of smoke from the muzzle seemed instantaneous. Alan peered through the drifting smoke.

Lockett had sprawled on his face, and all that could be seen
of him now was a patch of dull brown buckskin in the long
grass.

Alan rolled on his side and reloaded as Jake had taught
him. As he was tapping home the bullet he took a hasty
glance down the ravine. But Lockett had not moved.
Cautiously Alan crawled away from his firing position, working
round to the left and above the low ground below, until he
was opposite the spot where Lockett was lying. The man

might be shamming, he thought, but that was unlikely. He
was certain that he had hit him, and if the half-breed had any
sense, and had not been touched, he would have jumped to
his feet and bolted for the shelter of the trees when Alan was
reloading.

Alan watched the bundle of buckskin for five minutes.
But there was not the slightest sign of any movement. Alan
scrambled to his feet, and a sharp stab of pain shot through his
ankle and up his left leg. He bent down, and felt his ankle

gingerly. He must have turned it over during that brief
struggle on the loose stones and gravel. The damage was
slight, for there was no swelling, and he could walk, though
with a definite limp.

Suddenly the reaction after that short and bitter fight
swept over Alan. He had time to think again now, and he
realized his position. He was alone in the forest, ten miles at
least from Ashwater. Perhaps more, for if Lockett had lied
about the direction, he might well have misled Alan about the
distance, too.

Alan sat down. The memory of Jake's drawling voice
came to him, and what he had said about men lost in the forest.
They became panicky, rushed away on the line they thought
would bring them home, or to their camp, and the inevitable
happened. They began to move in a circle, their panic
increased, and then they were lost indeed. Sit down and think
it out, Jake had said.

So Alan sat and tried to fight down the sensation of fear
he knew so well. First of all, he thought he knew the line to
take, and he looked for the various landmarks, the patches of
high ground which would keep him from swinging to left or
right. Though it would not matter if he swerved to the south,
for then he was bound to strike the Mohawk. But that would
be miles off his course, and a waste of time.

The time ! That would be his chief danger. The sun
would be down in a few hours. If he was caught in the forest
in the dark, then his position would be hopeless. And there
was his ankle. The pain would almost certainly slow him up,
and the ankle would stiffen. And if he tripped, likely enough
when he was limping, he might break a bone. He shivered.
Jake had told him of backwoodsmen hunting by themselves
who had broken a leg in the forest. One man had blown his
brains out rather than wait for the slow and inevitable death.

There was only one sensible course of action open to him,
Alan realized. He must stay where he was for the night. He
had water and some cold venison. His ankle would be better
in the morning, and he could reach Ashwater in safety.

He had no blanket, though. He was in for a cold and

uncomfortable night, for Jake's lessons in woodcraft had stopped short of spending a night in the forest. Anyway, he could light a fire, he knew how to do that, and it would be interesting to see if he could do it himself without Jake's expert advice and running comments when he went wrong.

There was a dead trunk just behind him with ample fuel, dry and easy to cut. But was the top of the ravine the best place for the night ? He would be exposed to the cold night wind if he stayed where he was. Down in the sheltered ravine would be the best spot.

He limped down the steep slope, and selected a likely place, close to some bushes and a single tree. The fire started with surprising ease ; Jake had taught him well, and when he had a glowing mass of twigs and small branches burning, he laid some bigger logs across the centre. The wood was damp, and a dense white smoke cloud drifted up and was caught by the evening breeze.

Alan sat down, and foraged in his pack for cold meat and bread. He did not think he would sleep much that night ; he would have to keep the fire going most of the time, and when he had finished his meal, he limped off to cut more wood.

A gunshot sounded in the distance. Then another. Alan cocked his head to listen. Indians, perhaps, or fur trappers. He was not particularly worried, but as he brought back a fresh load of wood, and sat down by his fire, he began to feel the intense loneliness of his position.

Another shot ; a pause, and a fourth. Closer, Alan thought, and he reached for his own gun. It was loaded but not cocked. He laid it down by his side within easy reach. Two more shots, at regular intervals. Much too regular, they sounded, and Alan stood up. What was that, a whistle ? Yes, there it was again, and a long wailing cry.

Alan hesitated, then made for the rocks where he had fought with Lockett. He would have a good view around the area from there. The shots sounded again, one after the other, and once he heard the whistle. As quickly as he could he climbed to the top of the outcrop, and listened.

The calls were coming from the east. The shots must be signals ; they could not be anything else. He raised his rifle in the air and pulled the trigger. Almost immediately came two answering shots, flat bangs as if there was no bullet, and merely a light charge of powder in the barrel. Then a loud whistle, and two figures appeared at the end of the ravine.

Alan waved his arm and shouted. The two men stopped. Faintly Alan heard a cry, 'Mister Carey ! Hi ! Mister Carey ! '

Alan started to run down the slope, but his ankle was too painful, and he hobbled as quickly as he could to meet the approaching figures.

There was no doubt about the man in front. It was Jake.

Chapter Eight

THE MOHAWKS

'ALL right, Mister Carey?' Jake shouted. He saw Alan's limp. 'Hit in the leg?'

'No, just a sprain, Jake. But what's brought you here?'

'Just natural caution, Mister Carey.' He grinned at Alan with a certain amount of affection, an unusual display for his reserved temperament. 'Say, this is my cousin, Bless Winter, from Schenectady.'

Alan shook hands, though he was a little puzzled by the strange Christian name; but perhaps he had not heard Jake properly. Bless was a younger version of Jake, in the same well-worn and creased buckskins, the same leathery complexion and self-assured and reliant air, so typical of these backwoodsmen. But he was shorter and stockier than his cousin, and did

III

not appear to share Jake's somewhat sardonic view of life, for he grinned at Alan with the greatest friendliness and cheerfulness.

'Where's Lockett?' Jake demanded.

'Down there.' Jake swung round hastily, gun in hand.

'It's all right, Jake,' Alan said. 'I shot him an hour ago.'

Both Jake and Bless took little for granted, and they ran over to see for themselves. 'You shot him, Mister Carey?' Jake asked when he had returned.

Alan told them what had happened, and Jake chuckled. 'Reckon you're learning fast,' he said. 'But you were plumb crazy to come out with that half-breed, Mister Carey. I told you to be careful. He knew the forest better than you know the inside of the stockade. You ought to be dead by this time.'

'Yes, I was lucky,' Alan said. 'But how did you get here, Jake?'

'Bless and I got back to Ashwater an hour after you left, Mister Carey. Hepburn told me you had gone hunting with Lockett, but he didn't know where.' Jake spat with disgust. 'But that German, Fricker, he thought Lockett would take you north to Lake Canada. So we took a chance and came north, and then we saw your smoke.'

'Hepburn,' Alan said, frowning.

'Yeah, Hepburn,' Jake repeated with emphasis. 'He put Lockett on to this, Mister Carey.'

'But can we prove it?'

'Your dad gave you a free hand, didn't he, Mister Carey?' Alan nodded. 'Well, that's easy, then. Kick Hepburn out of Ashwater.'

Alan hesitated. He felt extremely helpless, and very young. Jake would deal with Hepburn if he asked him. Then he took a deep breath. He would do this himself.

'Yes, I'll dismiss him immediately we get back,' he said, hoping that his voice sounded more assured than he felt. But Jake nodded, and turned away, apparently quite satisfied.

'Guess we'd better spend the night here, Bless,' he said. 'Mister Carey's ankle ain't too good.'

'Yeah, Jake.' Bless brought a line and hook from his pocket. ' Some fish in that stream, I reckon,' he said. ' You make the fire and bedding, Jake.'

Jake walked up to the rocks, and looked around with satisfaction. ' This'll do,' he said.

' Up here? ' Alan exclaimed. ' I was going to spend the night in the ravine. It's more sheltered down there.'

' I reckon you would,' Jake said. ' But a valley catches all the damp air and mist at night. We'll be snug up here with the rocks as a wind break. Always look for a wind break, Mister Carey. A fallen tree's good enough, but rocks are even better. Light a fire in front of 'em, and you'll be warm enough.'

They started to collect wood for the night. When Alan limped back with an armful, Jake was lighting a small fire immediately below the rocks, and spreading out the red embers over the ground.

' Ground gets kinda damp and cold at night,' Jake said. ' This'll dry it out.'

He arranged a pile of stones for the bigger fire which would burn through the night, and then told Alan to collect all the small balsam sticks he could find. By the time Alan had done this, the small fire had been raked away, and the large one was burning cheerfully. Jake showed Alan how to lay out the balsam wood for bedding, until there was a layer on the still warm ground nearly two feet in thickness.

' Makes a comfortable bed that,' Jake remarked. ' Never use leaves and moss, Mister Carey. They spread out hard and flat under you.'

Bless came back with three fish, and Alan sat down to watch the two backwoodsmen cook the evening meal. They made him feel very useless, and he decided that he must learn to cook. He grinned. He thought of his father sitting down in the beautiful dining-room at Llanstephan, two liveried footmen behind his chair, an attentive butler by his side, facing an array of silver and a shining expanse of mahogany table. But perhaps the Earl had roughed it like this in his campaigns, though Alan doubted if he had ever washed up the dirty crockery and dishes afterwards.

The fresh fish were magnificent, and Alan thought he had never eaten such a delicious meal. He gave a hand with the cleaning of the few tin plates and mugs which they carried with them, and then lay back on the bed of balsam twigs. It was extremely comfortable, and the fire gave out a steady glow of heat.

The sun had set over the trees to the west, and the sky was clear. Alan lay back luxuriously, and watched the stars twinkling above him as he listened to Jake and Bless chatting quietly. He could smell the scent of pine and balsam, and hear the wind rustling ceaselessly in the trees below. A fox barked, and owls hooted incessantly. From the fire came an occasional spurt of flame, the rocks behind flickering redly in the darkness.

' Bless is a curious name,' Alan said.

The cousins laughed. ' That's my dad, Mister Carey. He's mighty fond of the Bible, you see, like Hepburn. He called all his kids after sentences from the Old Testament. I'm " Blessed be he that calls on the name of the Lord." '

' What ! ' Alan sat up.

' Sure, that's right,' Jake said. ' It's a mighty big mouthful, so we just calls him Bless.'

' But does your father use the whole name ? ' Alan asked.

' Depends how much gin he's got inside him, Mister Carey. After a bottle it's the whole name. After two we don't reckon he'll get much farther than Bless.'

Alan grinned. ' Hepburn talked about wine being a mocker,' he said.

' Oh, Dad ain't no mocker of a bottle of gin,' Bless said.

Alan listened to them talking. They had led a hard life, he thought. Perhaps as rough and squalid as the poor in England, and Alan had seen little of that, though he knew that the slums of the big towns, and of London in particular, were filled with overcrowded attics and cellars, surrounded by filth, disease and semi-starvation.

He had seen filth and squalor in the colonies, too, but there had never been any shortage of food. Perhaps that, and the empty forest and the huge spaces waiting to be filled had produced this breed of sturdy, independent people.

He closed his eyes, and the balsam bedding crackled softly as he turned on his side. He slept heavily, awakened several times by the fire and the necessity of replenishing it with logs. But he enjoyed his night in the forest. If it had not been for the prospect of facing Hepburn the next day, he would have felt happy and at ease. But he dreaded the coming interview with that cold, hard man.

The sun was just rising over the trees when Jake awoke him. He pointed down into the ravine ; below was a carpet of white mist, and Alan realized that he would have spent a cold and miserable night down there.

Alan's ankle was stiff, but the pain had gone. By the time they had left the ravine, he was walking quite easily and without any discomfort. Jake insisted that he should pick their route.

' What happens if there's no sun ? ' Alan asked. ' You can't sit down and wait for a break in the clouds all day.'

Jake unsheathed his knife, and held it, the tip of the blade down, on the dull shining barrel of his gun.

' See, Mister Carey,' he said. Even in the deep shadow of the trees overhead Alan could see the shadow thrown by the knife blade on the smooth barrel.

' There's always a shadow, even on a dull day,' Jake said.

' And there's other signs,' Bless said. ' Moss on the trees ; the Indians always say it's on the north side.'

The cousins argued about this, and agreed eventually that only on the tall, straight trees standing by themselves, was the moss to be found on the north side.

' More moisture there, I reckon,' Jake said. ' Watch the top branches of the pines, Mister Carey. Or hemlock. They usually point towards the rising sun, to the east, see ? '

They poured out their woodcraft into Alan's ears. Some they had learnt instinctively, and often they could give no reasons for the advice they put forward. But that did not matter to Alan. He tried to remember what was said ; much of it he would forget, he knew, but he could always ask again.

After a couple of hours they crossed a trail, and both men examined it.

'Indian trail,' Jake said, and Bless nodded his agreement.

'Reckon there's a village near,' he said. They both raised their, heads to sniff for wood smoke.

'Not so close as I thought,' Jake said. 'Wind's this way, too.'

Bless held up his hand. 'Saw something down there,' he said. 'Best get off the trail, Jake.'

They moved quietly up into the shelter of the trees, and stretched themselves out. Alan heard the clicks as the flint-locks were cocked, and he cocked his own.

'What is it?' he whispered.

'Indian hunting party, maybe,' Bless said.

'Will they attack us?'

Jake shook his head. 'But I never trust Mohawks,' he said. 'Specially now the French have been at 'em.'

Alan could see the Indians now, six of them in single file. They were in buckskin breeches, and were naked above the waist, finely built men, gliding silently along the track, as much part of the forest, Alan thought, as the deer themselves.

'Bunch of Mohawks all right,' Bless said.

'Yeah.' Jake stood up and eased back the cocking piece of his gun. 'Which way now, Mister Carey?'

'East and across the trail,' Alan said, not even hesitating before he answered. Jake nodded, and they plunged into the silent forest again.

'What do the Indians eat normally?' Alan asked.

'Oh, I guess they grow maize,' Jake said. 'But they eat a lot of meat. Venison, so they have to spend their time hunting like that bunch we saw. Their women look after the crops for them, and the men are out in the forest.'

'Say, Jake, hear something?' Bless asked.

They all stopped and listened. Alan heard a faint cry, and then it was repeated. 'Someone in trouble,' he said.

'Yeah,' Jake said. He cocked his gun, and Bless was doing the same. 'Never rush into anything in the forest,' Jake added. 'Take it easy, Mister Carey.'

They swerved to the north slightly and towards the cries, a regular succession of high-pitched calls.

'Round that way,' Bless said. 'There's a clearing there.'

He slouched forward, musket at the trail, and crouched down behind a tree. He turned his head, and beckoned the other two to come up to his side.

'Indian under a fallen tree,' Bless said.

Alan stepped forward, but Jake pulled him back. 'Your gun ain't cocked, Mister Carey,' he said. 'Take it easy now.'

With fingers on the trigger they crossed the glade. On the farther side a tree had fallen over the trail, and with both legs pinned underneath it was a young Indian. He looked up at them but showed no sign of fear or relief that someone had arrived to help him. He spoke rapidly to Jake, who nodded.

'Been here an hour,' Bless translated for Alan's benefit. 'Comes from a village on the other side of that hill,' and he gestured towards some high ground to the north.

'Are his legs broken?' Alan asked. He was examining the tree, trying to find a spot where he could put his arms underneath and lift.

'Reckon one's broke,' Jake said.

'I think I can lift here,' Alan said. 'Use your guns as levers there.'

Bless and Jake ran their eyes up and down Alan's huge figure. Then they pushed their musket barrels under the tree, and Alan bent down, his long arms under the thick trunk. He shouted to them to press down, and then he heaved. The trunk moved slightly, and Jake's musket slipped out. Alan let the trunk down slowly, and shifted his grip.

'Try again,' he said. Wrestling had taught him how to make the best use of his strength, and he thought he had found the right spot now. He planted his feet firmly in the soft leaf mould, and nodded to Jake.

'Now!' he said, and heaved upwards again, until he could feel the strain at the back of his legs and right down his shoulder muscles.

'He's clear!' Bless shouted, and Alan dropped the trunk with a gasp of relief.

Bless and Jake grinned at him as he stood there panting after the tremendous effort. ' Reckon you could wrestle a bear, Mister Carey,' Bless said.

' One leg broken,' Jake said.

' I think I can carry him on my back,' Alan said.

' But it's three miles, Mister Carey,' said Jake. ' He's only an Indian.'

Alan looked at Jake. But this casual, cold-blooded attitude towards the Indians was fairly common, he had learnt, among the white settlers. There was no charge of murder brought against a European who had killed an Indian.

' Cut a short splint for his leg, Bless,' Alan said. ' Tie it with that fishing line of yours.'

' Sure, Mister Carey.' Bless pulled out his tomahawk, and

hacked off a thick, straight branch from the fallen tree, trimming away the side shoots. He made two splints, and they tied them roughly to the Indian's leg. He must have suffered a considerable amount of pain from this crude surgery, but he lay perfectly still, and never uttered a sound. The break was below the knee, Alan saw, so that the boy would be able to bend his leg slightly, and that made it easier to carry him.

'Bless, you take my rifle,' Alan said curtly. 'Jake, lift him on to my back.'

In Alan's voice there was an entirely new note, one of brisk command, but he was quite unconscious of it. Jake had noticed it, though. The slightly cynical expression left his face, and his mouth twitched.

'Sure, Mister Carey,' he said. 'You say when.'

Alan knelt down, and they placed the boy's arms round his neck. Then he stood up, and balanced himself. Yes, he could walk fairly well, he decided, but the young Indian was heavy, and he would have to rest at intervals.

'Ask him to tell us the shortest way, Jake,' Alan said.

Alan stepped out, staggering a little until he became used to the load on his back. They had about two miles to cover, so Jake said after a short conversation with the Indian. But it was the longest two miles that Alan had ever experienced, and they were forced to stop and rest frequently. The boy could not have enjoyed the journey, either, but he said nothing, and not a single groan of pain came from him the whole time.

'Just over the brow, he says, Mister Carey,' Jake said after what seemed like many hours to Alan. His legs were aching, and all the muscles of his back were protesting violently at the strain of that heavy load. But he plodded on doggedly. His friends at school and at Cambridge had always told him that one of his many faults was an obstinate determination. Just like a mammoth, they said. But the obstinacy and the size, those of a mammoth or not, had been useful to him, Alan thought, as he staggered down a wide track, and between a row of bark-built huts. He was conscious of figures pressing round him, but it was impossible to look up while he was still carrying the boy.

'Drop him now, Mister Carey,' Jake said.

The boy unlocked his hands below Alan's chin, and slid to the ground. Alan straightened his back and stretched out his long arms luxuriously. For the first time he was able to look around at the Mohawk village.

He was not impressed with what he saw. The village was small ; a single lane of the bark huts, a small open space with growing crops, and a general atmosphere of filth and smells. He had stopped in front of a hut that was much larger than the others, and Jake was talking in the guttural Indian language to a tall and imposing looking man, the Mohawk chief, Bless whispered to him.

Apart from their size and age, and certain variations in

dress or ornament, the Indians all looked very much alike to Alan, with the same glossy black hair, treated with some form of grease, Alan thought, and the high cheek-bones and broad noses. The chief's hair was cut close to the sides of the head, leaving a kind of cock's-comb from the forehead to the back of the neck. The rest was carefully braided, and hung down like a pigtail at the back.

The men were all alike, too, in their bearing, silent, impassive, and very dignified. This was something of a carefully assumed pose, Alan learnt later when he came to know the Indians. Among themselves they were talkative and excitable, and this air of dignity was put on to impress strangers.

There were some children staring at the three white men. None of them wore anything, so far as Alan could see. At the back of the group around them were several women, with the same glossy hair as the men, but wearing it much longer, even down to the hips in some cases.

The guttural conversation came to an end, and Jake turned to Alan.

' This boy is the chief's son, Mister Carey,' he said. ' I reckon you've done a mighty good day's work.'

The chief said something, and made a sign with his hands, inviting them to sit down. A burning pipe was placed in Alan's hand.

' Take a few puffs and pass it on to me,' Jake said quickly. ' If an Indian offers you a pipe at his fire you're his guest, and he won't harm you, then.'

The pipe was passed round the circle of Indians, each puffing solemnly before passing it to his neighbour. Then women brought food on wooden platters, hot venison, vegetables, and maize, and this, too, was eaten in silence.

Only when the meal was finished did the chief speak, and he asked Jake a question, so Alan assumed.

' Wants to know where we come from,' Bless muttered. ' Say, that's surprised him ! '

For the chief was exchanging glances with the others, the first real sign of emotion that Alan had seen on their faces

M.V.—9

so far. Then he asked Jake more questions, and all the Indians stared at Alan.

He stirred uneasily. ' What's wrong, Jake ? ' he asked.

Jake was excited, too, so much so that his eyes were gleaming as he turned to Alan.

' Say, Mister Carey, listen to this ! ' he said. ' These Indians trade with Hepburn. The chief says that Hepburn offered him six good muskets if he would finish you off. Lockett was supposed to bring you here, or wound you, and then fetch the Indians. Indians will do anything for a new gun.'

' And now he's changed sides ? '

' Yeah, you bet he has ! I ain't much use for Indians, but they treat their children well, and you've saved his son's life.'

Alan stared at the chief who nodded at him, and then signalled to one of the women, and said something to her. She disappeared inside the hut, and emerged a few seconds later with a superb bearskin which the chief passed to Alan.

' Say, that's worth a pile,' Bless said. Alan nodded, and passed his hands over the lovely, glossy fur.

They left the Mohawk village soon after that, for Jake was anxious to reach Ashwater before the sun went down, and they had wasted a good deal of time carrying the Indian boy.

' You've got all the proof you want now, Mister Carey,' he said. ' This will put paid to Hepburn, I reckon.'

' Yes, it will,' Alan said. Oddly enough, the interview with Hepburn had lost many of its terrors now. He only hoped that this curious feeling of confidence would last until they reached Ashwater.

' How you going to handle him ? ' Jake asked.

' I don't know. I'd like to throttle him,' Alan said. ' Do you think there are any others at Ashwater who will support Hepburn ? '

' Maybe,' Jake said. ' Maybe. But we got three good guns here, Mister Carey.'

' But your dad owns Ashwater, don't he ? ' Bless asked. ' You're the boss there, Mister Carey. They know that, I guess.'

Alan smiled, and clenched his fists. ' If they don't, then it's time they learnt,' he said, and Jake looked at him again with that half smile on his face.

The gate of the stockade was open when they reached Ashwater. Alan paused, exchanged glances with Jake and Bless, and marched through the gate. As they crossed the yard, Hepburn's black-clad figure appeared on the porch. Alan saw him stop abruptly, and stare across at the three men walking towards him. But Alan was too far away to see the expression on the man's face. That sudden pause was significant, though, he thought grimly.

Hepburn came down the steps, and his bitter face creased in a smile of welcome. ' Your hunting was successful, Mr Carey ? ' he asked.

' Very,' Alan said shortly.

' And Lockett ? ' Hepburn asked, his eyes flickering from one set face to the other.

' He's dead,' Alan said. ' He tried to murder me, Mr Hepburn. On your orders.'

Hepburn stepped back, his white hands fluttering. ' Mr Carey . . .' He smiled again. ' I do not understand you.'

' We've been to the Mohawk village,' Alan said. ' The chief told us what arrangements you had made with him. Six new guns, wasn't it ? '

At this Hepburn paled. Alan watched the blood drain from his face.

' Mr Carey, you cannot possibly believe this,' Hepburn said earnestly. ' The word of a savage ! Mine enemies speak evil of me. All that hate me whisper together against me, and devise my hurt,' he gabbled.

' They sure do,' Bless muttered.

Hepburn snarled at him, and raised his hands as if in prayer, head back, and eyes upturned. ' Let them be ashamed and confounded that seek after my soul,' he intoned in his harsh, grating voice. ' Let them be turned backward and put to confusion that desire my hurt.'

Alan listened with growing disgust. ' You will be out of Ashwater in an hour,' he said. ' Bless, keep an eye on him.'

The news of what was happening flew around the settlement. The story, as Jake told Alan, had been exaggerated, and the rumours were increasing. As soon as Hepburn had gone, he suggested, Alan should explain to all the labourers why he had dismissed him.

Alan agreed. He waited until Bless reported that Hepburn had ridden off in the direction of the river. They were unlikely to see him again, Jake thought, and that was true enough. They heard later that the man had worked his way to the south, but after that nobody at Ashwater ever saw or heard of him again.

The sun was sinking as Alan came out on the porch and faced a curious crowd of the labourers and their families. He explained quietly what had happened. Heads nodded. Hepburn had been unpopular, he knew, but there were several there who must have worked with him in his fur business with the French. They were likely to cause trouble unless they were dealt with immediately.

Alan finished his story, and waited. A Dutchman, called Hendrik, pushed his way towards the steps. He was nearly as tall as Alan, with bulging arm muscles openly displayed now, for he was in his shirt sleeves.

Alan watched him warily. He saw Jake and Bless close up behind him.

'You have no right to dismiss Mr Hepburn,' Hendrik said.

Alan paused for a fraction of a second. He saw Jake shoot him an anxious glance, and then he walked slowly down the steps and up to the Dutchman.

'I have complete authority here, Hendrik,' he said.

'I say no, Mister.'

'Then you are dismissed, too.'

Hendrik shook his head vigorously. 'I take orders from Mr Hepburn only. I not go.'

Jake put his head close to Alan's ear. 'Guess you'll have to whip him, Mister Carey,' he muttered. 'Want any help? He's an awkward looking cuss.'

Alan shook his head, but he did not take his eyes off Hendrik. The superb feeling of confidence that had possessed him for the last few hours had suddenly vanished. Once again he felt that pounding of his heart and the shaking at his knees. But he knew one thing ; if he played the coward now, he would never have another chance.

' You will be out of Ashwater in half an hour, Hendrik,' he said. Even to his own ears his voice sounded firm and curt.

' You make me go, yes ? ' Hendrik asked.

Alan swung his right fist, with all his weight behind it. With a crisp smack it went home on Hendrik's chin, and the Dutchman staggered back. A shout went up from the crowd, and they surged around to watch.

Hendrik fingered his chin, his eyes smouldering. He rushed at Alan, arms swinging furiously. An amateur, Alan thought, and ducked and weaved his way out of danger, the huge fists whistling harmlessly over his head. He shot in a left that caught Hendrik in the stomach, and the fellow gasped as the wind was driven out of him. Another right crashed into his face, and he swayed on his feet. But it was like hitting a cliff, Alan thought. The man was immensely strong and tough.

He tried to rush Alan again, intent on putting his long, bear-like arms around him. Alan prodded him off, a punch to the heart, and another to the jaw. He must keep clear, he realized, good wrestler though he was. He slipped back to allow himself elbow-room. But he was too close to the steps of the porch. His feet touched them. Another step and he would trip over on his back.

With a bellow of triumph the Dutchman flung his arms round Alan, and heaved him off the ground. Alan let himself go, making no attempt to check the upward swing of the other's arms. But the pressure on his ribs was frightful. He wriggled one foot behind Hendrik's left leg, and fell forward, twisting sideways at the same time. If he fell with Hendrik's ponderous weight on top the fight would be as good as over.

They went down locked together, rolling over on the hard, dusty ground. Alan felt the crushing pressure on his ribs slacken. He saw one brown hand, fingers outstretched, coming for his throat. He rammed his fist into the scowling face so close to his, once, twice, in quick, stabbing punches. But they had no effect. The fingers gripped his windpipe and squeezed. Alan closed his eyes, writhed and struggled. A reddish mist flared in his eyes. He butted with his head, felt his forehead crack against Hendrik's, a bellow of pain, another frantic heave, and he was rolling free, gasping for breath.

He struggled to his feet with desperate haste, saw Hendrik coming for him, head and arms flailing. Coolly, Alan side-stepped, sent in a blow against Hendrik's ear that swung him round and up, and then Alan went for him in a ferocious berserk rage that startled even himself, a mixture of real fury, exaggerated by fear, desperation, and the urge to succeed and justify himself once and for all.

Hendrik took three punches that shook even his great strength, but he plunged in again, and this time Alan had all the room he needed. Just like that fight in Llanstephan with Bowen, he thought, as he seized Hendrik's arm in the flying mare of the west country style, turned his back and heaved. Hendrik went flying over his head, and Alan whipped round on his heels.

For the first time Alan heard the roars of the crowd, and had a brief vision of two jumping figures in buckskin, waving their arms in the air.

Hendrik had fallen awkwardly, and was slightly dazed. But he got to his feet, and then Alan hit him again, a perfectly timed punch, full on the point of the jaw. No man, whatever his strength, could have stood such a blow on that precise spot. Hendrik toppled back, flat on his back as if a four-pound axe from the forest had descended upon his head.

Alan stood over him, breathing heavily, his broad chest heaving. The Dutchman stirred, and opened his eyes. He sat up, one hand tenderly stroking his jaw.

' Going now ? ' Alan said.

Hendrik lumbered to his feet. The expression of sullen fury had cleared from his face, and he stared at Alan in astonishment.

' You knock me out ? ' he said slowly and in complete

bewilderment. He grinned sheepishly. 'I guess I stay, Mister, if you want me.'

Alan smiled. 'You can stay, Hendrik. But you take my orders.'

'Sure, sure, Mister Carey. You the boss now.' He nodded his head emphatically, turned, and pushed his way through the gaping spectators.

Alan went inside the house and sat down. His ribs were aching, and he was astonishingly thirsty. Bless and Jake had followed him, and were standing by the fire-place, watching him.

'You're a mighty dangerous guy when you start fighting, Mister Carey,' Jake remarked.

'Yeah,' Bless said. 'I'd have sooner wrestled a bear than that Dutchie.'

Alan grinned as Sam brought him a tankard of ale. He put his head back and let the cool beer flow down his parched throat.

'Aah! That's better,' he said. 'I want some help here now to run Ashwater. What about it, Jake?'

'Suits me, Mister Carey.'

'And you, Bless?'

'Yeah, sure thing.'

Jake chuckled and spat into the fire-place. 'Reckon Ashwater knows who's boss round here now,' he said.

Chapter Nine

HARRY NAPIER

ALAN and Hendrik were felling a tree. The two axes swung up and down in an unhurried, regular rhythm, the blades falling with a steady series of cracks on the tree like the tick-tock of a metronome. At each blow the great tree flinched, and high above them the topmost branches quivered and rustled softly.

Alan stood back a pace. 'Your side, Hendrik,' he said.

Hendrik nodded. He was a man of few words, and he knew exactly where to strike. His axe came down three times, and then he, too, looked up with Alan, and they backed away. The tree swayed with a rending crackle from the stump, and down it came, on the exact spot where they had planned to lay it.

Alan and Hendrik exchanged smiles of satisfaction. Tree felling was one of Alan's favourite forms of gruelling exercise, and after two years he was an expert now. But it was hot work on a warm spring day, and he wiped away the sweat from his face, leaving streaks of gritty dust on his cheeks and forehead. He wore buckskin trousers, and the sleeves of his coarse, thick shirt were rolled up above his elbows. The sun had scorched and tanned his face to a deep brown, and his black hair was tied loosely behind his head. There was little trace of the elegantly dressed and nervous young man of fashion who had boarded the *Henrietta* at Bristol two and a half years ago.

Hendrik was a big man, but he could not compare now with Alan as a physical specimen. Alan was fitter and stronger than he had ever been ; his strength and skill as a wrestler were proverbial along the settlements of the Mohawk ; many had challenged him, but nobody had put him on his back yet.

' That birch next,' Alan said, and they shouldered their axes as they crossed the clearing.

For Alan was biting slowly into the forest, and each year he was increasing the arable land at Ashwater. Settlers were pouring into the colonies, the frontiers were creeping westwards each year, and the towns were growing rapidly in size and in population. The demands for meat, for corn and vegetables were insatiable, and Ashwater was playing its part in satisfying the needs.

Jake and Bless were in charge of the fur business. Alan's friendship with the Mohawk chief had proved a profitable one, and ensured a regular flow of furs into Ashwater. From there they went to Albany, and then down the Hudson to New York for shipment to England. In Boston Mr Brewster sent encouraging letters to Alan as he pored over his neat ledgers.

But the financial side did not interest Alan greatly. He was happier and more contented than he had ever been in his life. By his own efforts he was creating at Ashwater something that would be permanent and worth-while in this wilderness of forest and swamp.

But of much greater importance, the work he was doing, the decisions he was forced to make each day, and the responsibility, had all given him a self-assurance that he had not possessed before. He was quite confident now of his ability to direct the labour of many other men ; he had mastered the details himself in those two years, and he had learnt the valuable lesson that if he knew his own job, then he need have no fears about telling others how to do it.

Hendrik laid his brown fist on the trunk of the birch, and glanced inquiringly at Alan. Without a word they swung up their axes. Both knew where they wanted the tree to fall, and they would put it there with a neat precision in a shorter time than any other pair at Ashwater.

Alan worked automatically, his thoughts far away. For there was one topic now that overshadowed all else in the colonies. The war. All Europe was aflame at last ; France, Russia, and Austria were at the throats of England and

Prussia, and the ripples from that tremendous struggle had spread across the Atlantic, as Mr Pitt had forecast.

But the English colonies were still hemmed in by the French on the north and the west, and in danger of constant attacks. The Iroquois had remained neutral, thanks to lavish gifts of guns and ammunition, and the skilful diplomacy of Sir William Johnson, one of the few white men who really understood the mind of the Indian.

Otherwise the war had gone badly. No important blow had yet been struck at the French line of forts. The Canadian Indians, the Algonkins from the Great Lakes, incited by the French, had swept down upon the isolated settlers all along the frontiers, leaving behind them such frightful evidence of their visits that even hardened backwoodsmen, long accustomed to Indian warfare, had turned white with horror.

Albany was walled : Ashwater was in a state of permanent vigilance, though the Algonkins had not attacked it so far.

Hendrik said something about the birch, and Alan paused to listen. Another ten minutes, he thought, and it would be down. He swung again, and his mind went back over the last two years.

He had been swept into the war. So had many of the colonists, reluctantly at first, but now they were raising money and troops. Alan had taken part in Colonel Bradstreet's expedition up the Mohawk to the French fort of Oswego, and he had come under fire for the first time on land. He had not enjoyed the experience, but he had not disgraced himself.

His knowledge of warfare was confined to the many conversations with his father on the subject. The Earl, he was sure, would not approve of these hastily trained levies, with their lack of discipline and training. Far more than amateur soldiers and casual expeditions would be needed to break the French stranglehold on the lakes and the rivers.

But Pitt was in power at last, and with complete authority over the direction of the war. The Earl had written enthusiastically from London. Great changes would be made, and Alan would soon see the effects in America.

The Earl had been right. Regular British regiments were

crossing the Atlantic ; some were stationed already at Albany :
a great expedition was trying to force the St Lawrence and
the approaches to Quebec. If the British soldiers were prepared to learn something of forest fighting, and if they could
combine their training and discipline with the better qualities
of the colonial regiments, and if Mr Pitt could find good
generals . . . Alan shook his head. There were still many
' ifs '.

' English soldiers, Mister Carey,' Hendrik said.

Alan looked at him in bewilderment. Had Hendrik been
reading his thoughts? But the Dutchman was staring
over Alan's shoulder, and there, marching up the track
from Schenectady, was a long column of scarlet-coated
soldiers.

Alan shrugged his shoulders, and turned back to the birch
tree. The soldiers were no concern of his. Not yet, at least,
for he was due to report at Albany in a month to form part
of the local levies for the summer campaign.

The axes swung up and down again. A few strokes, and
the tree would be down.

' Hi, you ! ' a voice roared from the track.

Alan smiled. The cry of an English drill-sergeant, he
thought. Some unfortunate private was having his name
taken for a trifling fault.

Hendrik stood back, and Alan chose very carefully the
exact spot for the last few strokes. The birch quivered. One
more, and down she would come.

A shadow fell across the grass. ' You deaf ? ' a voice
bellowed.

Alan swung for the last time, and stood quickly to one side.
A British Sergeant had suddenly appeared on the other side
of the tree, the side on which it would fall.

' Get out of the way, you fool ! ' Alan said curtly. ' Not
there ! To the right ! Quick ! '

But English sergeants with many years service were
accustomed to jumping smartly when an order was given in
that crisp tone of voice. He sprang to the right, looking up
in alarm as the tall tree crashed down.

'Well, what is it?' Alan asked. 'Was it you who was shouting at me a minute ago?'

The Sergeant eyed him doubtfully. He had indeed been bellowing at this huge and dust-streaked backwoodsman, in his shirt sleeves and creased buckskins. But in the Sergeant's experience, colonial labourers did not speak in the curt accents of English country gentlemen addressing their tenants.

'My Captain wants you,' he said.

'Tell him to come over here,' Alan said. 'I'm busy.'

He picked up his axe and shouted to two of his men to start trimming the side branches of the birch. There were several hours of work ahead before the thick trunk could be cut into small enough logs to be carried away. And there was still the stump, with its deep roots, to be prised out of the ground.

The Sergeant was still standing there. He had been given an order by his officer, and another by this odd person. He had an uneasy feeling that there would be trouble for him whichever he chose to obey. Hendrik chuckled, and the Sergeant's red face turned a deeper colour. There was little love lost between the British troops and the colonials; the British patronized the Americans, and the Americans regarded the British as nothing but dressed-up parade-ground soldiers.

Alan turned to find the Sergeant still there. His black brows crinkled in a quick frown. The two years of command and responsibility had given him a far more forceful personality than he realized he possessed, and he was not accustomed to finding his curt orders disobeyed.

Slowly the Sergeant's arm went up in a salute, though by the expression on his face he was faintly surprised to find himself acknowledging this person in such a manner.

'Er . . . yes . . . sir,' he said, and marched away, red coat-tails swinging, his stick tucked smartly under his left arm.

'Which tree next, Mister Carey?' Hendrik asked, grinning broadly at the stiff back of the retreating Sergeant. He was devoted to Alan now, and had been delighted at the discomfiture of the soldier.

'We'll make a start on that clump of balsam,' Alan said.

'Lay them down this way,' and he gestured with his wide, strong hands.

They walked through the undergrowth towards the trees. Have to burn all this, Alan thought. There were several small fires going now on the other side of the new clearing.

'English officer coming now, Mister Carey,' Hendrik said.

Followed by the Sergeant, a fairly short and extremely smartly uniformed officer was stalking towards them. Even at that distance Alan could appreciate the excellence of his coat, the cut of his breeches, and the careful arrangement of his white stock at the throat. But the general impression was not one of dandyism ; rather one of a precise neatness, confirmed by the brisk, swinging stride, and set of the shoulders, and . . .

Alan frowned, and put down his axe. That was very like . . . No, it couldn't possibly be . . . He swung round to take a closer look. But there was no doubt about it now. It was Harry Napier.

'Did you hear what my Sergeant said?' Harry demanded in a peremptory voice. 'I want to know about accommodation for my men tonight. You'll be paid a billeting fee, of course. And . . .'

He broke off abruptly and stared at Alan, his mouth open in astonishment.

'Good God ! It's Alan Carey ! '

Alan said nothing. He nodded, his hands clenching and unclenching on the grip of his axe.

'So, this is where you've hidden yourself ! ' Harry said. 'A regular backwoodsman, too, and more of a Mammoth than ever.' He looked slowly up and down Alan's rough and grimy clothes. 'I suppose an axe is more to your taste than a duelling pistol.'

Alan's face, dark enough already under the dirt and dust and sunburn, flushed, and his grey eyes blazed down at Harry with such fury that that immaculate young officer recoiled.

'If your men want accommodation, they can have it,' Alan said, controlling himself with an effort. 'But you're on my land now, and you'd better keep a civil tongue in your head, Harry.'

Harry shrugged his red-coated and epauletted shoulders, but his attitude had perceptibly changed. 'You'll see to it, then, will you ? Sergeant, ask Mr Vernon to march the men into the stockade.'

He wheeled round smartly, and marched away. Alan sighed and went slowly over to where Hendrik was waiting for him. But the pleasure had gone from the day for him. The warmth of the sun on his back and bare arms, the smell of burning wood, the feel of his axe in his hand, had all lost their flavour. He was seeing again the cold, accusing faces at Cambridge. Some of the confidence and assurance that he had built up were ebbing away.

He finished working much earlier than he had intended, and went back to the stockade. His steward had apparently satisfied the demands of the troops, for they were settling down in the outhouses and barns, and the stockade was filled with red coats and white breeches and the smell of cooking from camp fires.

Alan washed and changed. He supposed he would have to entertain Harry and his fellow officer, and he selected a coat and breeches that were more fashionable than his usual dress for the evening. Even so, he was plainly dressed in comparison with the two soldiers as he came into the main room of the house. They were resplendent in scarlet and white and gold, with snow-white wigs and much richness of lace at throat and sleeves. By their side Alan had almost a Puritanical appearance.

Harry formally introduced the other officer to Alan. 'The Honourable Alan Carey ; Mr Edward Vernon.'

Alan returned the bow. Vernon was a somewhat stupid-looking young man, with a receding chin and an air of extreme languor.

'Honoured to meet you, Mr Carey,' he said in a high-pitched and drawling voice, the vowels lengthened and exaggerated, the fashionable London accent, Alan remembered. 'I have the pleasure of knowing your brother George,' he added. 'Capital fellow, George.'

Alan bowed again and hid a smile. His brother took his duties as a Member of Parliament very seriously, and he was inclined to be pompous, but he had a brain as sharp as a razor blade, with a withering contempt for stupidity. His opinion of Mr Vernon would not have been a high one, and Alan doubted if George would permit this young fellow to address him so familiarly by his Christian name.

The Negro, Sam, brought drinks. Harry was looking around the room. There were not many changes since the time of Hepburn, but the place was lighter and more cheerful. Alan had not changed the heavy, home-made furniture, but he had added some magnificent skins to the floor and the walls ; the great bearskin that the Mohawk chief had given him was stretched out in front of the fire-place, and Sam had set a light to the logs there, for the spring evenings could be chilly at Ashwater.

Alan had grown fond of his home, but to Harry, no doubt, it was no more than a rude farmhouse in the colonies, far removed from the elegant and ornate houses to which he was accustomed.

They began dinner, but not before Mr Vernon had emptied his glass three times, and he drank steadily throughout the meal. One of these stupid and ignorant young officers, Alan thought wearily, with too much money and influence, knowing little about their professional duties, and very typical, unfortunately, of many officers from England at the moment.

' What's your regiment, Harry ? ' Alan asked.

' 55th Foot. Stationed at Albany.'

' What are you doing here, then ? '

' I've been ordered to make a reconnaissance along the north bank of the Mohawk,' Harry said, and there was a certain amount of enthusiasm in his voice. ' Useful training for the men in forest work, and I have to make contact with some of the blockhouses near the river.'

These blockhouses were an attempt to guard against the Algonkin raids. But they were too widely scattered in that enormous area to be really effective, and the Indians very wisely ignored them and attacked the defenceless settlements.

' I was told I would find guides here,' Harry said. ' I have

two men with me from Albany, but they don't know the ground
well after Ashwater.'

' I'll arrange that,' Alan said. Jake and Bless could go.
He would stay at Ashwater ; the less he saw of Harry the
better, though the evening was not passing so uncomfortably
as he had expected. That was probably due to Harry's
professional interest in his duties ; he took them seriously, that
was clear. Harry would make a good soldier, Alan thought, a
natural leader, and an intelligent one, too. But Alan did not
think he could ever be at his ease with him.

' Do you know the plans for this year's campaign ? ' Alan
asked.

Harry's face lit up, and he leant across the table. ' We're
going to take Ticonderoga,' he said. ' Do you know the country
round there, Alan ? '

' No.'

But this was good news, and a sure sign that Mr Pitt's plans
were being put into operation at last. For if the key to the
French power was Quebec, then the two possible routes there
were now being attacked, up the St Lawrence, and this southern
campaign, up the Hudson to Lake Champlain, and on by the
Richelieu River.

The French knew of this, of course, and they had built
forts along the lakes. Ticonderoga was the strongest, and that
would have to be taken before the British could advance any
farther.

They discussed the plans. Mr Vernon considered that it
would be easy, and could not imagine why the colonial
regiments had not finished the war long ago. Harry threw him
a glance of angry impatience, and turned his back on him.

' It's not going to be easy,' he said. His manner towards
Alan was stiff and distant, but the subject of the army was
obviously something very close to him, and he would have been
ready to discuss it with anyone. ' Lord Howe is not nearly so
optimistic as Abercromby.'

Alan knew that General Abercromby was the commander-
in-chief, but the other name was new to him. ' Howe ? ' he
said.

' Colonel of the 60th Foot. Only thirty,' Harry said, ' but he's the best man we have.'

' Howe ! ' Vernon hiccuped. ' Mad, my dear Harry. Goes off into the forest with that Ranger fellow, Rogers. Says we all ought to learn how to live in the forest for a month ! Cuts our baggage down, too. Even wants us to cut our hair short, wear buckskin breeches, paint the muskets a dull colour . . .' He filled his glass again.

Harry ignored him. ' Do you know the forest, Alan ? '

' Fairly well. But I've spent two years only here. You need a lifetime to know it.'

' Could you spend a month in the forest ? ' Harry persisted.

' I expect so. But we don't go out for more than a few days' hunting at a time,' Alan said.

For half an hour Harry asked questions. He was interested in nocake, when Alan mentioned it. Had he lived on the Indian food of crushed maize ? Alan had, and told him how it was made and eaten. Had he met Rogers ? Alan had, for Rogers came on the Oswego expedition.

' You must meet Lord Howe,' Harry said. ' Some of our officers had dinner with him a week ago. They sat down to pork and peas. Not quite what they had expected. And there weren't any knives or forks.' Harry chuckled. ' Howe said to them, " Gentlemen, is it possible that you have come on this campaign without providing yourselves with what is necessary ? " He had a knife and fork himself in his pocket, and he gave them little leather cases with a knife and fork each.'

A loud hiccup from the other end of the table made them look round. Mr Vernon was waving his fork. ' I got a fork,' he said. ' Can't find the knife.' He peered under the table, heeled over and fell flat on the floor.

Harry signalled to one of the soldier servants standing by the door, and Vernon's limp body was carried out.

' I apologize, Alan,' Harry said. ' We've got far too many officers like that. Are you coming with us into the forest ? '

' Yes, I will,' Alan said.

Alan, with Jake and Bless, spent two days preparing the

British soldiers for their march to the line of the blockhouses. Harry flushed with anger when he heard the comments of the two backwoodsmen on the uniform and equipment of his men. Alan watched him in amusement. He had suffered from Jake's blistering criticisms, and he wondered how Harry would take them. To Alan's surprise, Harry, after a short struggle with his temper and his pride, did as Jake suggested.

He could do nothing about the colour of the uniforms, conspicuous as they would be in the forest, but he supervised the dulling of all the musket barrels, and cut down the men's packs to a bare minimum.

He was dismayed at the complete absence of maps, for his training had taught him that no army could move without a set of maps.

' There aren't any of this area,' Alan said. ' Only the rough sketches we've made.'

' Can you keep direction and take us to the line of block-houses ? ' Harry asked. Jake and Alan laughed.

' Yes, we can do that,' Alan said.

' Good ! Then we march out at dawn.'

Chapter *Ten*

THE ALGONKINS

JAKE was in the lead, about ten yards ahead, walking with his tireless slouch. Behind him was Alan, with Harry Napier at his side. The main body of the hundred or so British infantry was behind them again, and two backwoodsmen from Albany brought up the rear.

They had been marching steadily since dawn, and the sun, when they could see it through the overhanging foliage, was practically overhead now. There had been no incidents, though Alan had not expected any, for the Algonkin raids had never penetrated so far to the east as this. But it was stupid to expect the Indians to be consistent, and the long column was prepared for attack at any moment.

Where possible, Jake or Bless went on half a mile ahead, and Bless was in front at the moment, with another fur trapper from Ashwater. Jake's experience of Indian fighting had taught him to expect an ambush. The Algonkins would be armed with French muskets, so he had warned Harry, and their shooting would be good. But no Indian could keep a musket in working order for long, and they had not the slightest idea of repairing the smallest fault with the flintlock.

They halted at midday for a long rest, and a meal. Mr Vernon was exhausted already. He was lolling against a tree, drinking thirstily from a flask. Harry was still on his feet, walking down the line of his men, looking at their rations, inspecting their boots, and chatting to them. Alan chewed his cold venison and remembered a remark of the Earl's. A good Dragoon officer considered his duty to be, ' The horses first, the men next, and yourself last.' By that standard, Harry was a good regimental officer.

A few miles farther on they reached the little clearing of a lonely settler and his family. They lived in a tiny log cabin, the chinks stuffed with moss. The man had made a crude chimney of clay, and had roofed the hut with birch bark. His wife was unkempt and lean with work, old in appearance and far beyond her real age. The four children, in their tattered clothes, stared with round eyes at the long column of red-uniformed men who had emerged so unexpectedly from the gloom of the forest.

Jake questioned the settler. ' Any sign of Indians ? '

' Not here, Mister. Never seen none.'

' Where's the nearest settler to you ? '

' Bill Mackenzie, I reckon. 'Bout five miles to the west.'

They gave him some powder and bullets, for his supplies were running short, and marched on.

' What a life ! ' Harry exclaimed.

' Why not ? ' Alan asked, for he knew these settlers, and admired them. ' He's free, and he's independent. And I would bet you a month's pay that he and his family eat more meat in a week than the average English farm labourer eats in a year.'

' I suppose so,' Harry said.   ' Are there many like that ? '

' They're all along the frontiers.   That's how this country is spreading.'

They reached the first blockhouse late in the afternoon, and spent the night there.   Alan had seen one of these small forts before, and he was prepared for the filth and squalor of the garrison.   Harry was horrified and furious.

' I'm not sleeping in that pigsty,' he told Alan.

' You needn't.   Sleep in the open.   Part of your forest training.'

It was pleasant for Alan to display his knowledge of the forest, and it helped him to regain much of his confidence when he was talking to Harry.   They showed the soldiers how to make their camp fires, collect bedding for the night, and how to pick spots sheltered from the wind.

Alan lay down on his bedding of balsam twigs, and rolled himself in his blanket.   He was tired, and ready to sleep.   He loved these nights in the forest, sleeping under the trees, with a fire glowing at his feet.

They left the blockhouse at dawn, and struck north.   They visited the next fort in the line, and then turned to the east, planning to work their way gradually down towards the river and the trail along which they had marched out from Ashwater.

The soldiers were marching well, better than Alan had expected, for the going was slow and tiring.   Well drilled and trained, he decided ;   probably the result of Harry's work. At midday, when they halted again, there were no stragglers, the one thing that Jake and Alan had feared, for their task would have been a hopeless one if the column had stretched out too far.

While they were eating their rations, Jake jumped to his feet.   Alan had heard the sounds, too.   Very faintly in the distance muskets were firing.

' South, Jake, isn't it ? '

' Yeah.   That's the direction of the settlement we passed yesterday.'   They exchanged glances, and Jake spat out a stream of tobacco.   Alan shivered.   If that gunfire came from the tiny clearing, and the Algonkins had attacked it, then it was better not to think of what might be happening to that bearded settler, his lean, overworked wife, and their brood of small children.

'Indians, Alan?' Harry asked.

'I expect so. We can't get there in time to help. But we might cut off the Algonkins if they're heading north. What do you think, Jake?'

'Yeah. Guess so, Mister Carey.'

'How many are there usually in these raiding bands?' Harry asked.

'Hundred perhaps. Maybe more, Captain.'

They moved on again half an hour later. Alan noticed that Jake was more on the alert now, his head jerking quickly towards the slightest sound in the trees, peering down at the faint trail they were following for any sign that Indians had passed along it recently.

Bless was ahead and out of sight. His danger signal was to be a soft whistle. The soldiers were marching with cocked muskets now, their heads turned to the dark tunnels of the forest on either side. Alan could sympathize with them. He had once felt this uncomfortable sensation of being shut in by the trees, and had yearned for the bright sunlight and open spaces.

From ahead came a whistle. Bless ran into view, padding silently in his moccasins.

'Indian trail ahead, Jake,' he said. 'Guess it's fresh, too. They went north to south, across our front.'

Jake bit off a piece of black tobacco, and chewed reflectively. 'What you think, Mister Carey?'

'They're the ones we heard firing, Jake. Will they come back on the same trail?'

'Reckon so.'

'Yeah,' Bless said confidently. 'And there's a mighty nice spot for an ambush just ahead, Mister Carey.'

Alan and Harry went forward with the two backwoodsmen to see for themselves. They halted on the crest of a shallow valley, lined on either side with trees. A small stream ran down the centre of the valley, and Alan could pick out the faint, winding trail.

' Suit you, Captain ? ' Jake asked.

Harry nodded, his dark eyes gleaming. ' It's ideal for an ambush,' he said.

He deployed his men amongst the trees on the slope, and when they were in position, Jake and Alan went down the hill to check their cover.

' Keep well above the trail, Mister Carey,' Jake said. ' These Indians can pick up signs better than a deer.'

But Alan knew that, and the uncanny gifts of Indian trackers who could detect the passage of a man or animal through the forest where a white man would notice nothing.

Harry had stationed his men well, and there was no sign of them from the bottom of the slope. They had been given orders not to open fire until either Jake or Alan fired the first shots. Jake had shaken his head when he heard Harry give these orders.

' This bunch of lobsters will blaze off as soon as the first Indian pokes his nose in sight,' he said pessimistically.

' Oh, no, they won't,' Alan said. ' There's one thing the British soldier will do. If he's given an order, he'll obey it. Their discipline is magnificent.'

' Maybe, maybe,' Jake said. ' Say, Mister Carey. These Indians may have scouts ahead. Let 'em go, and wait for the main body. Don't fire until the leaders are at the far end of the valley, and we've got a good bunch to shoot at.'

Alan settled down behind a convenient trunk that had fallen across the top of the slope. He laid out his cartridge case by his side, the flask of priming powder, his long ramrod and little mallet, and a handful of bullets. If he had learnt to reload quickly on his side, then here was the time to display his skill.

The time passed slowly. Occasional crackles of twigs showed that the soldiers were finding the wait a trying one. Jake's brooding eyes never left the trail, his jaws moving slowly and continuously.

An hour passed, and still there was no break in the sleepy

silence of the sun-filled valley below. Suddenly Jake hissed urgently. Alan saw a slight movement in the trees to the right. His grip tightened on his rifle, and he pushed it forward over the log.

A deer trotted daintily into the open. It paused at the stream for a second to drink, then flung up its head, and bounded down the valley. Jake cocked an eye at Alan, and they nodded to each other. They knew what that meant. Something farther up the trail had alarmed the deer.

Birds chattered in the trees, breaking the silence. Alan took a deep breath. One moment the valley was empty and still. Then three Indians were standing on the trail below, but they were unlike any Indians that Alan had ever seen before, and he knew that he was looking at the most dreaded sight in the forest of America, Indians, painted Indians on the war-path.

They were naked to the waist, and wore buckskin breeches below. Their bodies, their faces and foreheads were covered with fantastic patterns of colour, vivid reds and blacks and blues, hideous and utterly horrifying. They stood perfectly still for a moment, their shaven heads with the black cock's-comb on top turning slowly from side to side like a trio of evil snakes ready to strike.

Then they glided up the trail, soundless, menacing, a child's nightmare in the darkness, until they vanished again at the other end of the valley.

Alan let out his breath, and by his side Harry did the same. Their eyes met briefly, and they smiled at each other, a smile of relief that the tension was over for the moment.

Another deer leapt into view, crashing through the under-growth, bounding up the slope on the farther side. Alan stiffened, his eyes on the trees to the right. Then the whole valley was filled with Indians, a long line of gliding horrors, musket in hand, an endless file of painted savages like a coloured frieze on a wall, passing silently from right to left in front of Alan's staring, dilated eyes.

Jake's gun crashed out in a deafening roar and the little valley was filled with the reverberations of the explosion. Alan saw an Indian in his sights, and he pressed the trigger. His rifle kicked against his shoulder, but he did not pause to see where his shot had gone. He could not miss at that range. Already, before the last wisp of white smoke was trickling from the muzzle, he was ramming home another paper cartridge, then the bullet, then the priming powder in the pan, and pulling back the cocking piece. A heavy blow struck the log in front of him. A bullet screamed over his head. From the left came the thunderous roar of the disciplined volleys of the British soldiers, firing in two sections as they had been ordered.

White smoke wreathed up among the stately trees looking down upon this picture of death and destruction ; from below in the once beautiful little ravine came wild screams, and loud hysterical laughter, as if madmen from Bedlam were finding a perverted amusement in this dreadful scene.

Alan peered along his sights again. An Indian was bounding up the slope towards him. Alan saw his painted chest against the foresight, and fired. The Indian threw up his hands with a screech, and somersaulted backwards as if some invisible giant had flicked him down the hill.

The ramrod again, the bullet, the ramrod once more, the priming, the click as the flintlock went back, the flash of the pan, the kick on the shoulder, the crash, the familiar jet of smoke, and Alan snatched up another cartridge from the grass, rolled on his side and loaded and rammed, gasping loudly, muttering to himself in a dreadful delirium of haste and fear and disciplined movements of hands and arms.

Again the crash and the kick ; more screams from the valley, a mingled chaos of sound, the deep roars of the musket fire, that appalling high-pitched laughter again, and a blurred figure leapt over the log and across Alan's legs.

He dropped his rifle, snatched up his tomahawk, and whipped round on the Indian. He saw a hand go up with a tomahawk, gripped the wrist and twisted, brought down his own weapon, felt it sink into the soft ground, and then they were rolling over, snarling and shouting like two dogs. Alan heaved the half-naked figure clear, raised his arm and brought down his tomahawk again. The Indian screamed and yelled with that frightful laugh that Alan had heard, and then was still.

Alan half knelt, the breath coming from his mouth in harsh grunts. But everything was quiet now, except for the shrill laughter from below. The firing had ended, and Alan stood up, his knees trembling. Harry was staring at him, his face white. This ferocious hand-to-hand fighting was something he had never envisaged, perhaps, when he drilled his men on the parade ground, or when he drew himself up in accordance with the elegant etiquette of the duelling ground. This was jungle warfare, the fierce grappling of maddened animals at bay.

The smoke drifted over the valley, and the whole scene could be seen quite clearly now. The trail was littered with untidy, sprawling heaps of brown and red. More dead Indians lay on the slope leading up to the trees. Still there came to Alan's buzzing ears the sound of that maniacal laughter. Jake's gun boomed, and the sound was cut off abruptly.

'Keep down !' Jake yelled. 'Keep down ! Don't move until I say !'

His leathery face, lips clamped tightly, was peering over the trunk. Silence fell, and the last of the white smoke still clung to the topmost foliage of the trees.

'Guess it's safe to go down,' Jake said. 'Captain, keep your men here. Bless, Mister Carey, you coming ?'

They went slowly down the hill to the trail. Harry followed them.

'What was that awful laughing ?' he asked Alan.

Jake spat. 'Indian death laugh, Captain. They're trained not to show any sign of pain. So when they're hit or wounded, they laugh. Kinda gives you the creeps, I guess.'

He bent over a dead Indian and turned to Bless. 'What you say, Bless ? Abenakis, ain't they ?'

'Yeah. French missionary Indians, Mister Carey,' Bless said. 'They sure teach them a funny religion, don't they ?'

Harry had brought his men down now, and they were falling in on the trail. A Sergeant was counting the dead Indians.

' Seventy-four, sir,' he said.

Jake whistled. ' Mighty fine shooting, Captain,' he said, and clapped Harry on the back of his red coat. ' Reckon you were right, Mister Carey,' he added.

Harry grinned. Not even the familiarity of that rough hand on his aristocratic back had upset him. ' What about our casualties, Sergeant ? '

' Private Thomas, sir, Private Jenkinson, both killed. Two others slightly wounded.' He paused for a moment, and eyed Harry uneasily. ' Mr Vernon's missing, sir.'

' Missing ! '

' Yessir. I saw him run into the forest, sir.'

' Guess that's him up there,' Bless said.

They could see a red-coated figure among the trees. It was Vernon. He came limping down towards them, and halted in front of Harry.

' I've been chasing an Indian into the woods, Harry,' he said.

Harry stared at him in stony silence. ' Consider yourself under open arrest, Mr Vernon,' he said, and turned his back on him. ' What do you think, Alan ? Shall we make straight for that settlement ? '

' Yeah, guess so, Captain,' Bless said. ' But you won't like it.'

' Won't like . . . What do you mean ? '

' You won't like what this bunch of Abenakis have done. There's two of 'em here with fresh scalps.'

Alan had already seen them, and had looked away quickly. Harry gulped, and issued a string of orders to his sergeants. The two dead soldiers were hastily buried where they had fallen, and half an hour later the column was on the march again, heading south.

The British troops marched in silence as before. But they moved with a swing. They had been in action, and they had done well, and they carried themselves like men who knew now what they could do.

An hour or so later, Jake raised his hand, and the long, scarlet files halted. Alan was sniffing, and his nose crinkled

distastefully. For he could smell charred wood smouldering.
Jake spat loudly, and stepped out, the pace quickening as they
hurried on through the sombre forest.

The trees suddenly came to an end ; the smell of burning
wood was strong now, and they were in the little clearing
which they had visited a day ago.

The log cabin was a heap of blackened cinders, still glowing
redly in the gentle wind. The pitiful patch of corn had been
burnt, too, the fences smashed. Of the bearded settler and his
family there was no trace.

Harry stepped towards the remains of the cabin, but Jake
put out a long arm. ' Shouldn't, if I was you, Captain,' he
said.

But one of the Sergeants had run to the cabin, and he came
back, white-faced, his eyes staring.

' Reckon there's nothing we can do here,' Jake said. ' But
we've made that bunch pay for this,' and he looked around the
clearing.

They discussed the plans for the return march. The sun
would be down in two hours, and there was no hope of reaching
Ashwater before then. They would have to bivouac in the
forest, and Jake guided them to a spot by a stream where
he and Alan had often spent the night.

' There's a swamp to the north,' Alan said to Harry.
' That means you can easily cover all the likely approaches
with sentries.'

' Why, do you think there are more of these Abenakis
about ? '

' Could be,' Jake said. ' But you ain't taking any chances
after what we've seen here, Captain, are you ? '

' No,' Harry snapped. ' And the sooner we leave here the
better.' His face was strained and tired.

Once again the silent column set off. Nervous heads
watched the dark, threatening forest around them. Rough
though the British soldiers might be, hardened to poverty and
disease and filth as children, drilled and pounded into parade-
ground dummies by the ferocious discipline of the British
Army, and so inured and hardened, by many years of it, to

cruelty and violence, they had just witnessed an exhibition of savagery that had shaken them. They knew now the enemy they were fighting.

They camped for the night quietly and without fuss. They were becoming accustomed to these conditions now, and did not have to be told what to do. The wind was rising, and the trees swayed and rustled above the flickering camp fires.

Harry posted his sentries, and came back to the fire where Alan and the two backwoodsmen were sitting. But Jake was restless, and would not settle down.

' Kind of jumpy, ain't you, Jake ? ' Bless said.

' Yeah.' He jumped to his feet, and picked up his musket. ' I'm going round the sentries, Captain.'

' I'll come with you,' Harry said immediately, and Alan rose, too, to go with them.

They passed down the line of fires, and into the gloom of the forest beyond, speaking to each pair of sentries.

' Two more,' Harry said.

They were thirty yards, perhaps, from the nearest camp fire. Jake's uneasiness had infected Alan and Harry. Alan had his rifle in his hand, and Harry was carrying a cocked pistol.

' Where's that sentry ? ' Harry asked.

' Other end of his beat, I expect,' Alan said.

They walked slowly on for another ten yards. It was very dark now, and only an occasional red gleam on the trunk of a tree showed that there was a large camp a short distance away. The flickering light seemed to make the bushes move, and Alan twice brought up his rifle.

A twig rustled behind him. He half turned. A tremendous blow thudded down upon his head. He heard a startled cry, the crack of a pistol, and then another crushing blow fell on the back of his head. The dark shapes of the trees whirled around in a sickening dance, and he closed his eyes with a groan as he sank to the ground, his knees giving way beneath him, and he lost consciousness.

Chapter Eleven

RUNNING THE GAUNTLET

A DULL pain shot through Alan's chest and side ; then another, and another, as if he were being kicked brutally. He groaned and opened his eyes. He was being kicked, and a hand on his coat was tugging him to his feet. But it was still too dark to see where he was or to distinguish the figures standing around him. A blurred face, streaked with paint, pushed itself close to his, and he caught the acrid reek of sweating, unwashed flesh, and the smell of fish oil. It was an Indian smell, and Alan groaned again.

'Get up ! Walk ! ' a deep guttural voice said to him in French.

Another foot thudded into his ribs, and he scrambled awkwardly to his feet, for his hands were tied behind his back.

' All right, Alan ? ' Harry's voice came from the darkness.
' We're—— ' A thud and a groan, and Harry fell silent.

Alan was pushed forward ; a knife pricked his arm and
made him wince. He stumbled on, still dazed, his head aching
and buzzing, hardly aware of what was happening. How far
they walked, or for how long, he was never clear. If he
stopped to rest, a kick or the prick of the knife made him stagger
forward again.

At last he saw the red flickering glow of camp fires through
the trees, and they emerged into a clearing. A circle of painted,
half-naked Indians swarmed around them, and a chorus of
exultant cries went up. Alan swayed back, trying to press
away from those nightmare faces peering at him, and the
strong animal smell.

He was pushed to the ground. ' Stay there,' a voice said
in French. Alan was glad enough to lie down, and he put
his head back and tried to ease his bound hands.

' Harry ? ' he asked.

' Yes, I'm here. And Jake. One of my men, too, I
think.'

' Private Shaw, sir,' a new voice spoke up in the darkness.

' You were one of the sentries ? ' Harry asked.

' Yes, sir.'

There was silence for a moment, and then Jake began to
swear softly.

' All right, Jake ? ' Alan said.

' Yeah, I'm all right,' Jake growled. ' Me, Jake Winter,
caught behind my blamed back by a bunch of Indians ! '

Alan heard the familiar spit of disgust, and smiled, despite
his aching ribs and his despair at their position.

' I got off one shot,' Harry said. ' That would have given
them the alarm.'

' Mighty useful that will be at night,' Jake said. ' Even
Bless can't pick up our trail in the dark. He'll have to wait
until the sun's up.'

That was a comforting thought. They could not be more
than a few miles from the bivouac, and Bless would be after
them with a hundred soldiers in a few hours' time.

'Better try and sleep,' Jake said. 'We'll need all we've got in the morning.'

There was a long silence as they all digested this ominous remark. They had seen the burnt-out settlement, and Alan had told Harry something about Indian warfare and their treatment of prisoners. Alan shivered and felt sick. If he had any courage, and he was sure he had none at that moment, then he would indeed need it all, as Jake had said.

He dozed. But it was impossible to sleep for long intervals. The ground was hard and cold. The thongs around his wrists were painful, and he could not roll into a comfortable position. Overhead the wind roared through the trees, as if a gale was blowing, though in that clearing they were well sheltered. Trust the Indians to choose a good camping ground, Alan thought bitterly.

He must have slept, though, for when he awoke he saw the grey light of dawn, and the drifting smoke from the camp fires. The Indians were throwing on wood and were cooking venison. They seemed to be taking few precautions, for the smoke would show above the trees, and would help to guide Bless to the camp.

'Wind blowing up from the south,' Jake said. 'Bless won't smell or see the smoke.'

So Jake had had the same thought. Alan nodded dismally, and watched the Indians eat. Nothing was brought to the prisoners except some water, and Alan drank greedily.

'Here they come,' Jake said.

Three Indians walked towards the prisoners and stood looking down at them. Alan braced himself, his heart pounding, and his tongue licking his lips. He was hauled to his feet, and a knife slashed at the thongs at his wrists. But his hands were numb, and only after a few minutes did he feel the throbbing pain as the blood ran into his fingers, and he clasped them tightly under his arm-pits.

Another Indian came up. His face was a hideous mixture of black and red, a revolting mask that stared at the prisoners with a cold, passionless lack of emotion. The Abenaki chief, Alan assumed him to be, for when he raised his hand and pointed at Private Shaw, the other Indians seized the soldier and dragged him towards the fires.

' Captain Napier ! ' the man cried, turning his head in piteous appeal. ' What are they going to do to me ? What are they going to do ? '

Harry shook his head helplessly. The Indians were forming up in two long lines, facing inwards. Each man was brandishing a club or a stick, and they were shouting and dancing excitedly.

' What are they doing ? ' Harry muttered.

' They'll make him run the gauntlet,' Jake said. ' Favourite trick of the Abenakis.'

Alan glanced over his shoulder. But four Indians were watching them closely, muskets in hand. There was no hope of running even a few feet. A roar went up from the two lines. The terrified soldier, his red coat ripped from his back, was being pushed unwillingly towards the head of the lines. A club came down on his head, and Alan turned his head away and shut his eyes. He heard the frenzied screams of the Indians, like a pack of savage animals, rising and then falling, and then a fresh outbreak that lasted for several minutes. When it died away, Alan forced himself to look. A bundle of white breeches and stained white shirt was being dragged to one side, and the Indians were waving their clubs at the remaining prisoners.

The chief raised his hand and pointed at Alan. Two strong hands gripped him by the elbows, and pushed him forward. He saw Harry's white, unshaven face, haggard and despairing, Jake's long, lean jaw dropping, and then he was led away, making no resistance, his brain as numb as his hands had been during the night.

He was near the lines now. The two nearest Indians were watching him, their painted faces gloating with a frightful expectancy.

A sudden wave of fury boiled up inside Alan. He could not have controlled it had he wished, and it swept away all his numbness and paralysing fear. Was he going to let these filthy, naked savages batter him to pulp ? These smelly, dirty brutes, who murdered and scalped little children ?   He had never known such a searing rage, such a tearing, ripping passion of hatred and loathing before, and it transformed him into a growling giant, dangerous, as ferocious as the mammoth after which he had been named at school.

He whipped round on the two men holding him with the speed and suddenness of the skilled wrestler.   One flew over Alan's head with a shrill scream as his arm was snapped ; the second one went down as two huge fists battered in his face, and he never moved again.   Alan saw the Abenaki chief watching, and he leapt towards him with a hoarse roar.   A pair of Indians raced forward to cut off his rush.   Alan picked up a club on the ground, and swung it with murderous fury, raving, berserk mad, dashing them aside like two smashed dolls.

The chief tried to stop this raging monster that had suddenly sprung upon him, but a terrible punch caught him on the nose, a long arm like the hug of a bear crushed in his ribs, and his knife was snatched from his belt.

' Tell them to stand still ! ' Alan gasped.   He pricked the brown throat with the knife, and his blazing, half-demented eyes glared down at the Indian.   ' Stand still,' he shouted again in French.

The chief wriggled, but he was helpless, half stunned by that blow on his nose, the blood streaming from his face, and all he could see was this white, glaring face and madman's eyes.

He gasped out some words, and the rush from the fires halted.

' Get our guns, Jake,' Alan said.

' Got 'em, Mister Carey.'   Jake's voice was calm and firm.

' Bullets and powder ? '

' Still in our pouches.   What you aim to do, Mister Carey ? '

' I'll show you now,' Alan growled.   ' Can you make them understand ? '

' Guess so.   Near enough anyways.'

' Tell them we're taking their chief with us.   If anyone moves a step I'll cut his throat.'

' Yessir ! ' Jake broke into the guttural Indian language. Alan could understand some of the words, for he had picked up a small Indian vocabulary. The chief moved again, and Alan tightened his grip with a savage wrench. He shouted something to his men, and they fell back, their eyes on Alan, watching him with a superstitious awe.

' Jake, you lead the way. Harry, behind me. Pistol loaded ? '

' Yes, Alan.'

' South and into the wind, Jake,' Alan said. ' Take a smouldering stick from that fire.'

Jake hesitated. ' Do as I say, you fool ! ' Alan snapped. It was the first time he had ever spoken to Jake like that, and the backwoodsman snatched up a burning branch from the fire by his side.

Alan was already pushing the Indian chief towards the trees. They rushed along for a few minutes until the camp was out of sight.

' Fire that bush, Jake, quick ! ' Alan yelled.

' Yeah, I get you ! ' Jake said, and plunged the red-hot branch into the bushes. The high wind caught the sparks and whirled them forward in a puff of smoke that suddenly belched into life with a roar of flames.

Alan loosened his grip on the Indian chief, brought his fist down with a thud behind his ear, and left him lying on the ground.

' Make torches ! ' Alan shouted. ' Spread out ! '

Jake was yelling delightedly as he ran from side to side, increasing the width of the blaze. The dry pine cones spluttered and burst into flame, and Alan leapt on to the lowest branches of a tree with a flaring bough in his hand. The flames licked slowly up the trunk, then the foliage seemed to explode, and the rising gale carried the flames across to the next tree.

Already the fire was racing away from them and towards the Indian camp, the dense clouds of white smoke rolling ahead of the leaping flames.

' Spread out ! Spread out ! ' Alan shrieked.

Jake was imitating Alan, and setting light to the trees.

The driving wind did the rest, and as they ran, extended in line, they touched off each bush they passed. Behind they heard the roar of the flames, as the tinder-dry forest was transformed into a furnace of shooting flames that no Indian could penetrate.

' Got my rifle, Jake ? ' Alan asked.

' Yeah.' Jake handed it over, and grinned at Alan. ' Say, you're a great man, Mister Carey.'

They slowed their pace to a walk, still setting off isolated fires, for they knew that these would join up and spread out, driving back the Abenakis to the north. The front of the blaze was too wide to outflank by this time, and Alan realized that at last they were safe.

From the crest of a slope they saw the curtain of smoke drifting over the trees ; gouts of flames shot up into the air, with showers of sparks flying out on either side.

' That's a mighty nice fire,' Jake remarked with satisfaction. He had found some tobacco in his pouch and was chewing again happily. Alan gulped at his water bottle. His throat was parched, and he was streaming with perspiration, and trembling violently. The reaction, he supposed, after all that burst of savage violence.

They pushed on to the south until Jake estimated that they must be a few miles north of the bivouac. ' Fire a shot, Mister Carey,' he said, and as Alan fired, he waited for a few seconds, and fired his own musket in the air. They rammed in charges without bullets, and fired again, flat cracks that would carry well in the forest.

They listened, and then two shots sounded in the distance.

' That's Bless, I reckon,' Jake said. ' Down that ravine, Mister Carey. Keep to the trail. It'll lead us to the bivouac.'

Five minutes later Jake slipped behind a tree, and Alan and Harry did the same. The wind, still blowing hard from the south, brought with it the sounds of marching feet, not the soft moccasins of Indians, but the hobnailed boots of British soldiers.

' I never reckoned I'd like to hear those blamed boots

trampling in the forest,' Jake said. ' Beg pardon, Captain, but they do make an almighty noise.'

Harry grinned. ' All right, Jake,' he said. ' I don't mind.'

Jake threw up his head and shouted. ' Bless ! Oooooh ! Bless ! '

The tramping feet halted. Sharp orders were heard, and then the clear voice of Bless.

' That you, Jake ? ' and a buckskinned figure slipped into view, musket at the ready. Jake stepped from his tree, and waved his hand.

In a few minutes the entire column of troops had turned and were marching south, while Bless looked at the three escaped prisoners curiously. They were streaked with dirt and black soot marks from the fire they had raised, their faces were drawn with fatigue and strain, their eyes glaring, blood-shot and red rimmed. Alan and Jake's buckskins had not suffered from the journey, but Harry's uniform was in tatters, the coat ripped open, his breeches stained and filthy, and his long stockings hanging in shreds. He had long since lost his three-cornered hat and neat white wig.

' They got one of the sentries, too, Jake, didn't they ? ' Bless asked.

' Yeah. Made him run the gauntlet. Mister Carey got us away.' Jake spat and grinned. ' Say, Bless, you sure missed a treat,' he said. ' I guess there's a bunch of Abenakis up there who'll never come within ten miles of Mister Carey again.'

He told Bless the whole story as they marched towards Ashwater. Harry walked in silence. He was exhausted, and only his grim determination kept him on his feet. At each halt he slumped down, and dragged himself up again without a word, stumbling on by Alan's side.

But even Alan was glad to see the stockade of Ashwater. He was tired, and ravenously hungry. ' I'll have a hot bath ready for you, Harry,' he said.

' In half an hour, Alan. I must see to the men's dinner first.'

Alan watched the stocky figure limp away to inspect his men's food, barking orders to the sergeants, and squaring his drooping shoulders. Alan smiled, and wondered why he had ever disliked Harry Napier.

They met again an hour later, washed and shaved and in clean clothes. Vernon was confined by Harry's orders to his room, to Alan's relief. Harry was still limping, and he settled down with a sigh of relief in the chair facing Alan. Sam handed him a glass of wine, and they both drank in silence.

Harry refilled his glass, and stood by the fire, looking down at the smouldering logs. He glanced at Alan, coughed, and fiddled with his stock.

' Alan . . . I . . . er . . .' He took a deep breath. ' I want to apologize,' he said curtly. ' Will you shake hands with me ? '

Alan laughed. It was odd, he thought, he was quite at his ease with Harry now. They shook hands, and laughed at each other again. Harry raised his glass and toasted Alan.

' It wasn't you who marked those cards, was it ? ' he said.

' No. It was Hugh Goring. Didn't you guess ? '

' I did, afterwards. But it was too late to do anything then. Alan, I could eat a whole deer. I hope your cook knows that.'

They sat down at the table, and shouted for Sam to bring the first course.

Chapter Twelve

LORD HOWE

THE sound of a bugle brought back Alan's thoughts from the subject of next year's crops at Ashwater.

'Couple of miles to Lake George, Mister Carey,' Jake said.

But Alan could see the blue waters of the lake for himself now, with its scattered little islands of green. The ground rose gradually on either shore towards distant mountain ranges, the Adirondacks to the west, and the Green Mountains in the east. The heat haze rising on a hot July day gave an unreal and curiously softened atmosphere to the lovely view that filled Alan with delight.

'Yeah,' Jake said. 'It's a mighty fine country, this.'

'It is,' Alan said with conviction. He had grown to love the beautiful, empty, and unspoilt country. One day, he knew, it would be tamed and civilized, the forests cut back, the rivers bridged, the whole area covered with thriving towns and villages, connected by fine roads.

But Lake George had been awakened from its usual quiet. Even now, some five miles to the south, Alan saw the smoke from hundreds of camp fires, and the wind carried the sound of bugles and the roll of drums.

William Pitt, far away in Whitehall, had sent an army to Lake George. To the north, hundreds of miles distant, another British army, with a powerful fleet, were moving up the river towards Quebec. Pitt's object was to crush Quebec by a gigantic pincer movement, a thrust from Lake George and Lake Champlain, and a similar blow from the mouth of the St Lawrence.

Bless and Jake were both riding with Alan. They chatted excitedly for two such matter-of-fact men as they rode into the great camp, for there was much to see that was new to them. The blue of the American regiments and the red of the British were familiar enough, but they turned puzzled eyes to Alan as they heard an eerie wailing sound.

' Bagpipes,' Alan said. ' The 42nd Highland Regiment are here.'

Jake reined in his horse and pointed ; for once his steady chewing was checked in his surprise.

' Well, I'll be . . .' He turned to Bless. ' Kilts and all. Just look at them, Bless ! '

Alan questioned a soldier about the Headquarters of the 55th Foot, for he had promised to meet Harry there. Their tents were to the left, he was told, and a few minutes later he dismounted under the indifferent glances of a group of English officers.

But one of them ran forward. It was Harry. ' Alan ! I've been expecting you for several days. Hullo, Jake. And Bless, too ! '

' How do, Captain,' Jake said, grinning, and Bless greeted Harry with the same pleasure. They had made an exception of Harry in their general dislike of British officers.

' Sergeant White ! ' Harry shouted. ' You remember him at Ashwater, don't you, Jake ? He'll look after you and Bless.'

The Sergeant came running from a near-by tent. Alan heard him mutter something about a special brew of beer he had waiting for the two backwoodsmen, and they went off together, talking loudly. Alan smiled. He wished that relations between all British and colonial troops were as good as this. The skirmish with the Abenakis had taught one small section, at any rate, that each had much to learn from the other.

Harry led Alan inside the long tent that served the 55th Foot as an Officers' Mess. Heads were turned curiously as Alan entered. His exceptional height and size would have attracted attention at any time or place, but his dress of buckskin jacket and breeches made several eyebrows rise. Backwoodsmen were not the normal guests of an Officers' Mess.

Harry introduced him. The atmosphere changed quickly, with the references to Lord Aubigny and George Carey that Alan expected now. His response was curt and distant, though he had not intended it to be so. Three years ago he could have joined in the conversation about London society, but he was startled to discover how remote he seemed to be from these men. He was looking at them with the eyes of a colonial, resenting their patronizing opinions. How many of them, he was wondering, had seen any active service? How many knew anything at all about their profession?

He was introduced to Harry's Colonel, an elderly and dried-up man with an intelligent face and an air of competence.

'You've been teaching Harry and his company something of forest fighting,' he said to Alan. 'We've a great deal to learn.'

Alan changed his mind. Here was one British soldier who openly admitted that he had something to learn from the colonials.

'Take him along to Lord Howe, Sir Harry,' Colonel Elstow said. 'And I should be delighted if you would dine with us this evening, Mr Carey.'

Alan bowed, expressed his thanks, and went outside with Harry.

'The Colonel's a good soldier,' Harry said. 'So are some

of the others. And the men are magnificent. But you saw
that at Ashwater.'

'What about General Abercromby?' Alan asked.

'Old Mrs Nabbycromby?' Harry said with disgust.
'He's no good. Howe is our main hope.'

'But what's he want with me?'

'To ask you questions. He's always after information. I
had an hour with him about our fight with the Abenakis.
Here we are!'

Alan was ushered into another tent, a smaller one this time,
and furnished as an office. He found himself in a chair and
being inspected by a pair of blue eyes in a sunburnt face,
steady, unwavering eyes. Lord Howe was a young man, still
in his early thirties, with a long, sensitive nose, a pointed,
aggressive chin.

'It is a great pleasure to meet you, Mr Carey,' he said.
His voice was pleasant and crisp, without any of the affected
vowel sounds of so many British officers. 'I have met your
father. I was always told that he was the model of what a
regimental officer should be. A pity he left the Army so soon.
The Duke of Marlborough thought highly of him, I have
heard.'

Alan flushed with pleasure. Genuine praise of his father
had always delighted him. He realized that he was being
examined closely by a man who was accustomed to sum up his
visitors with a searching and penetrating inspection. And
then he was cross-examined, questions shooting at him like
volleys of musket fire, intelligent questions with rapid and
shrewd comments on everything he said in return.

He smiled when he was outside the tent again with Harry.
'I feel like a sponge that has been squeezed,' he said.

'Well, you made a good impression,' Harry said.

'How do you know that?'

'Howe would have told you pretty quickly if he thought
you a fool. He's no patience with fools, and he says so quite
openly.'

Alan had been attached by Lord Howe to the 55th Foot,
with Jake and Bless as their expert advisers on forest fighting,

and in the next two days he was given the details of the plans for capturing Ticonderoga. The army was to sail up the Hudson and the lake as far as possible. A large fleet of boats, a thousand at least, had been assembled on the lake under the command of Colonel Bradstreet, with whom Alan had served at Oswego.

He also met the New Hampshire Ranger, Rogers, a man with a legendary reputation by this time for his exploits against the French and the Indians. He was a rough-looking man with a battered face and a lop-sided nose, who had collected a couple of hundred backwoodsmen like himself, and formed them into a company of Rangers.

The army left the encampment on a glorious July morning, the boats pushing off at regular intervals, until the procession stretched for over six miles up the lake. The scene was one of extraordinary beauty, Alan thought, so much so that he found it difficult to realize that this was war, and that in a matter of hours he would be taking part in a violent attack on a strongly fortified stronghold.

He sat in his boat watching the regular dip of the oars in the sparkling water. Small islands glided past, the still warm air was filled with the fragrant scent of pine. Green-topped mountains rose on either side of the lake, their peaks clear and sharp against the blue skyline. Everywhere in the long procession of boats there was colour, flashing equipment and weapons, scarlet and blue uniforms, a picture-book scene from a child's nursery ; all moving slowly to the accompaniment of bugle calls, the beat of drums or the wailing of bagpipes.

Rogers and his Rangers led the fleet, for they had made several journeys up the lake as far as Ticonderoga, and were to act as guides. The main body, with whom Alan was travelling, consisted of the British regular troops under Lord Howe, the 55th Foot, the 42nd Highlanders, and also the three regiments of Royal Americans, the 27th, the 44th and the 46th.

In the rear were the heavier boats carrying guns and baggage, moving far more slowly, and falling behind the rest.

By five o'clock that afternoon the expedition had travelled nearly twenty-five miles, and had reached Sabbath Day Point, sufficient proof of the vital importance of a river route, for a force that size would not have covered half that distance in the forest.

Here the fleet came to a halt while the baggage train overhauled the van. The sun was setting behind the hills, but Lord Howe gave the order to advance. The light soon faded, and the stars appeared overhead, hard and bright in a clear sky. But the fleet moved on, the oars striking white showers of spray from the placid lake.

Alan dozed. Around him the British soldiers wrapped themselves as best they could in their coats, hunched up in the confined space, and shivering in the chilly night air. But it was a short night, and everyone welcomed the dawn and the warmth of the sun as it appeared over the mountains.

The lake narrowed. The trees came down to the edge of the water, so close and so densely grown that the boats were rowing through a tunnel of green.

The peace and beauty of the scene were suddenly broken. From ahead came the rattle of musketry, and the sound of cheers. An excited buzz went down the long line, with messages and reports of what had happened. The Rangers had driven off a small French force on the bank ; the army was to land, and to march from here to Ticonderoga.

Alan landed with the 55th, and stretched his long legs with relief after being cramped for so long in the boat. Officers roared orders, and gradually the long columns were drawn up on the banks of the river. Bugles were sounded, and the advance began.

There was little that Alan or Jake could do. The Rangers were acting as guides, for Rogers had detached several to bring up the main body. He, with the bulk of his men, had gone well forward to reconnoitre. But the plan was a simple one. They had reached the tip of Lake George, and the boats could go no farther, for the river was too narrow, running in dangerous rapids, and then turning sharply to the right, and then again in a left-handed sweep into the deep, wide waters of Lake Champlain.

The French had sited Ticonderoga at the very point where

the river met the lake, on high ground that could be approached only from the west, along the left bank and through the forest.

This was the route that Lord Howe had chosen, and his troops moved off in four columns. The ground was level at first, and open. But when the troops reached the Trout River, the forest closed in around them. The undergrowth was unusually thick and tangled, littered with fallen trees. The sunlight, so bright on the lake, hardly penetrated the foliage of the tall trees, and the orderly columns soon broke up into untidy formations and groups of men struggling through the clinging bushes, clambering over trunks of dead trees, quite unable to see where they were going, and not even certain that they were keeping to the right line of the advance.

Alan and Jake exchanged uneasy glances. What was Rogers thinking of when he led Lord Howe into such a tangle? Surely he must have realized that large numbers of troops could not possibly keep formation, or even direction in this sort of country.

' These Ranger guides are supposed to know this country,' Alan said.

' Maybe,' Jake said sceptically. ' They don't look as if they do.'

Lord Howe was just ahead of Alan and the leading files of the 55th. Well in front, Rogers was presumably covering the advance, so there was no danger of an ambush.

' *Qui vive !* '

The sharp, high-pitched cry rang out from the dense forest. Then again, ' *Qui vive !* '

' *Français !* ' yelled an English officer, and Alan took up the cry. ' *Français !* '

The forest exploded in a deafening volley ; white smoke billowed out from the trees. Bullets screeched overhead. Alan flung himself to the ground, as did Jake and Bless. They knew the rule of the forest. Do nothing when in doubt. Don't rush around like a frightened deer. Your enemy can probably see you, and you can't see him.

The firing slackened, and then stopped altogether. Alan

peered cautiously over his tree, but he could see nothing, not even the slightest movement in the trees.

' They must have fallen back,' he said.

' Rogers ought to cut 'em off,' Jake said.

As he spoke firing broke out again, but farther away this time, with loud shouts and screams. It was safe to move now, and Alan jumped to his feet. In front was a group of Rangers, a few British officers, all standing round a red-coated figure lying on the ground.

' Wounded ? ' Alan asked.

A British major turned to him with despair on his face.

' Killed,' he said.

' But who is it ? ' Alan asked in sudden alarm.

' Lord Howe. Shot through the chest.'

Chapter Thirteen

TICONDEROGA

THE army lay under arms in the forest all that night, nervously awaiting the next French attack. Captain Rogers came back with his Rangers to report that he had intercepted the French force, and had taken nearly fifty of them prisoners. But twice that number would have been poor compensation for the loss of Lord Howe, Alan thought, and he was not surprised when General Abercromby decided to fall back on the river, and begin the operation all over again.

Colonel Bradstreet moved up to the Saw Mills below the fort itself, and repaired the bridges there without any opposition from the French. The infantry could cross here, and avoid the flanking march through the forest. In readiness for the attack, the army marched up to the Saw Mills, and bivouacked there for the night. They would storm the fort on the following day.

But there was no chance of surprise now. The French were expecting an attack, and had ample time in which to prepare and strengthen their defences. The British knew the French numbers, about 6,000, hopelessly small, General Abercromby considered, compared with his 15,000. But Montcalm, the French commander, was expecting reinforcements, so the British were told, and Abercromby decided on an immediate attack, without considering the possibilities of approaching the fort from a different angle.

Few men slept throughout that night. Many sat up round the camp fires and talked and sang. Alan went with Harry to visit the 42nd Highlanders, where Harry had a friend, a Captain Mackenzie.

The Highland officers were sitting in a circle around a huge log fire. It was past midnight, but they showed no inclination to try and sleep, and they welcomed the arrival of Harry and Alan. They pressed drinks on them, and both sat down with their feet toasting in front of the fire.

Alan sipped his wine and listened to the conversation around him. These were good officers, he thought, and their men, from what he had seen of them, were well trained and eager to come to grips with the French.

An officer stepped into the firelight, and sat down by Alan's side. He nodded to Alan, and stared into the leaping flames, a man in his fifties, his face drawn and haggard, the eyes wide open and filled with horror, as if he had just awakened from a nightmare.

The conversation round the fire died away. ' Hullo, Duncan,' Captain Mackenzie said. ' I must introduce you to our guests. Sir Harry Napier of the 55th, and the Honourable Alan Carey. Mr Carey has estates on the Mohawk, and knows this country well. He will tell you that this is not Ticonderoga, but Fort George. Perhaps you will believe him ? Mr Carey, this is Duncan Campbell of Inverawe.'

Alan saw Mackenzie looking at him, one eye closing in a swift wink. But there was no gesture of fun in the warning, but rather one of urgency, and Alan nodded his head immediately, particularly when the Highland officer on his right nudged him with his elbow, and whispered, ' Say Fort George, for heaven's sake, Carey.'

' Yes, of course,' he said. ' Ticonderoga is several miles to the north of Lake Champlain.'

' Thank you, sir,' the Highland officer said dully. ' You are lying nobly, but I know this is Ticonderoga, and that I shall die tomorrow.'

Alan looked at him in bewilderment, and Duncan Campbell smiled sadly.

' No, I am quite sane, Mr Carey,' he said. ' I see you do not know my story. May I tell it to you ? '

' Yes, of course.'

' Some years ago,' Campbell said slowly, ' I was at dinner in my house at Inverawe. It was late, and the sun was down. My steward came to tell me that a man had just knocked at the front door. He craved shelter for the night, and protection from his enemies who were pursuing him, for he had killed a man in a duel that day, and these men were threatening to kill him in revenge.'

Campbell shook his head gloomily. ' I agreed, of course, and my servants brought him food and wine. Only when the meal was finished did he tell me the name of the man he had killed that morning. It was my cousin.'

' You turned him out ? ' Alan asked.

' No. I had given him my promise. But that night the ghost of my dead cousin came to me. He reproached me for sheltering his murderer. By the door he raised his hand in farewell, and said, " Farewell, until we meet at Ticonderoga." '

Alan nodded. He had heard of these Highland superstitions before. But this unfortunate man was accepting this ridiculous story with dreadful seriousness.

' It is perfectly true, Mr Carey,' another of the officers around the fire said, for he must have seen the doubt on Alan's face. ' Duncan told me this story three years ago. Neither of us had heard the name of Ticonderoga before. Nor had the other officers in the regiment.'

Several heads nodded.

' I bought a commission in the 42nd a year later,' Duncan Campbell said. ' We were ordered to America, and then I heard of Ticonderoga. We are storming it at dawn, and so I know I shall die today. It is past midnight.'

' But it's not Ticonderoga, Duncan ! ' Mackenzie insisted.

Campbell shook his head. ' My cousin came to my tent less than an hour ago,' he said. ' He held up his hand again, just as he did at Inverawe, and said that this was Ticonderoga, and that he would meet me again in a few hours.'

He stood up and walked away into the darkness.

' And what do you make of that, Harry ? ' Alan asked as they strolled back to their tent.

' Oh, I've heard that story before. There's no doubt about it, Alan.'

' Rubbish, Harry. Coincidence ! It's just the fact that Ticonderoga is an unusual name. He had a bad dream.'

M.V.—12

'Well, I hope so, for poor Duncan's sake. We'd better try and sleep, I suppose.'

The infantry marched up from the river just after dawn, the Rangers in front. Colonel Bradstreet and his armed boatmen followed, with the blue-uniformed American regiments, and the red column of the British troops in the centre.

They all halted in full view of the fort, and Alan clambered on to a log to see the position for himself. He was appalled by what he saw. Immediately in front of the fort the French had built a massive breastwork of trunks rising to a height of at least nine feet, he thought.

But that was not all. For over an area of several hundreds of yards in front of the breastwork they had felled every tree, until the ground was a littered tangle of branches and trunks. The work had been done quite recently, for the leaves of the fallen trees were just beginning to wither in the hot July sun. To Alan it seemed as if a hurricane had suddenly swept over that part of the forest, tearing up every tree in its path, and flinging them down like ninepins.

'We're not going to make a frontal attack through that?' he asked Harry.

'No time for anything else,' Harry said.

'But we could bring up the guns from the boats. Cannon balls will knock that breastwork over. Or why not try to work round to the north? The ground may be clear there.'

Harry shrugged his shoulders. 'General Abercromby is in charge now,' he said. 'Howe might have had different ideas. But we can do it, Alan. Nothing will stop the infantry. You'll see.'

There was little sign of life from the fort. The white flag of the French, with its fleurs-de-lis, fluttered from one corner of the breastwork, but Alan could see no troops on the parapet itself. An ominous silence hung over the formidable defences.

The bugles blew, the drums rolled, and the dense red lines of the British marched forward. They plunged into the maze of fallen trees. But all formation was hopelessly lost after a few yards. In groups, in file, in twos and threes, they struggled slowly forward, like a horde of red ants, worming through the gaps, swarming over the thick trunks of dead trees.

Alan was halfway to the breastwork when he saw a gush of white smoke, heard the sullen boom of cannon, and saw a ripple of fire run along the whole parapet. He dived behind a tree, and crouched down. Cannon balls crashed and thudded into the logs, musket balls ricocheted overhead with eerie screeches, or plonked into the trunks. A chorus of shouts and screams went up along the line of advancing infantry. Officers shouted, and the bugles blew again.

' Forward ! Forward ! Advance ! '

Alan wriggled his way onwards. Around him the British infantry cursed and yelled, tripped by branches, their coats catching in the foliage, stumbling over obstructions ; but they still tried to advance. Dead men hung in strange and horrible attitudes from the fallen trees, and still the merciless fire of cannon and muskets lashed them from the breastwork.

Alan found Harry by his side, crawling through a gap in two trees. He grinned at Alan, and they went forward together. But it was impossible to keep down under cover all the way. Every now and then Alan had to brace himself and leap to his feet, scrambling desperately over a tree, in full view of the French, his whole body shrinking, his skin tingling as he waited for the crushing impact of a cannon ball, or the numbing blow from a bullet.

Sweating and muttering, his face and hands torn and bleeding, he saw the breastwork looming above him at last. A wild cheer went up on either side, and a horde of British infantry, in a ragged line, made a mad rush over the last few yards to the foot of the breastwork. Alan pulled up suddenly as a deep ditch yawned at his feet. It was filled with sharpened stakes, covered by a withering cross-fire from each flank.

The bugles blew urgently. ' Fall back ! Fall back ! '

Alan turned and burrowed like a mole into the depths of the fallen trees once more, while the guns thundered from the fort, and the bullets screamed overhead. He was back in the forest again, forming up with the tattered survivors of the 55th, and he looked round anxiously for Harry and Jake and Bless.

But they were all there, and he reloaded his rifle, for he had fired just before he left the ditch.

The bugles blew. 'Advance! Advance!'

Alan went forward with the others, to the same nightmare of undergrowth, crawling, climbing, flinching, as the dreadful fire from the French beat down the slowly advancing infantry. He had little recollection of what really happened in the next two hours. By some miracle, or so it seemed, he was not hit. He was not even afraid, or was he so terrified and numbed with fear and exhaustion that he did not know how frightened he was?

Six times the bugle blew for the attack. On six occasions the British infantry flung themselves into the hopeless advance. Only iron discipline and training and immense courage sent

them forward again and again. The Highlanders, spurred on by the wail of bagpipes, leapt down into the ditch and tried to climb the high breastwork. But it was useless.

Alan, at some time during that inferno of smoke and fire and noise, found himself crouching near the breastwork, peering up for a target. He saw a blue, three-cornered hat, white-uniformed shoulders, and he pressed the trigger. A sprawling figure fell forward, dangling head downwards over the wall of logs, and Alan shouted exultantly as he reloaded.

The sun was sinking when at last orders were given to retreat. The American regiments on the flanks were firing heavy volleys in rapid succession to keep down the heads of the French on the breastwork while the British brought back their wounded.

Harry was still in front, Alan was told, and Alan plunged, for the last time, he hoped, into the shambles of the fallen trees. Scattered groups were making their way back, holding up or carrying badly wounded men. Alan saw Sergeant White, and called out to him.

'Where's Sir Harry, Sergeant?'

'In front, sir. Seeing to the last of the wounded.'

Yes, Harry would certainly be the last of the 55th to leave the breastwork, Alan thought. Well, if Harry could face that horror again, so could he, and he struggled on towards the fort. The musket fire had died away considerably, owing to the covering fire from the colonial troops, but an occasional cannon ball still hurtled into the maze of trees.

'Alan! Alan!'

Alan stood up cautiously on a sloping trunk, and looked around him. He ducked, as he had done so many times that day, as a cannon ball howled past him, and then he saw Harry, caught in the branches of a tree.

'Keep your head down,' Harry said as Alan reached him. 'They can see me.'

Blood was trickling from the sleeve of his coat, and his arm was hanging down limply. Alan pulled out his tomahawk and hacked away at the branches holding Harry.

'Bullet?' he asked.

'Yes. In the shoulder. Ah, that's done it!'

He stumbled forward and Alan put an arm round him. 'There's something to be said for a tomahawk, you see, Harry,' he said.

Harry grinned. 'And there's a lot to be said for a Mammoth to hold you up. You'd better put a pad on my shoulder, Alan.'

Alan took Harry's handkerchief, but it was far too small. 'Take your stock off, Harry,' he said, and opened Harry's coat.

They crouched down as a hail of bullets whizzed overhead, and Alan stuffed the thick white stock under Harry's coat. 'That ought to stop the bleeding,' he said. 'Come on, Harry. You're too heavy to carry.'

They crawled and wormed their way back, but it was a slow business, and twice Alan had to lift Harry bodily over the piled-up obstructions. But at last they were back in the forest where the survivors were assembling, lines of sullen angry men, scowling at the breastwork in the distance, still untouched and defiant.

Alan found a doctor for Harry, and saw him led away with the other wounded men. Jake and Bless were untouched, and Jake was sitting on the grass, his face gloomy and dispirited, but his jaws moving inevitably as he chewed his eternal tobacco. They marched back to the river with the others, while behind them the French cannon still boomed away, and the muskets crackled incessantly.

By the Saw Mills Alan saw the pitiful remnants of the 42nd

Highlanders, and he suddenly remembered that strange officer whom he had met by the camp fire in the night. He went over and saw Mackenzie, a grimy and blood-stained bandage over his head.

' Hullo, Carey. Harry Napier all right ? '

' Yes. Slightly wounded, that's all. Is Duncan Campbell safe ? '

Mackenzie shook his bandaged head. ' He died ten minutes ago of his wounds,' he said.

Part Three

QUEBEC

Chapter Fourteen

LETTERS FROM ENGLAND

JAKE had just ridden in from Albany where he had taken a large consignment of furs. He had brought back with him letters from Boston and New York, dealing with the Ashwater trading accounts, and also a letter from England.

Alan opened the letter eagerly, and spread out the thick paper on the table. He smiled as he saw his father's vigorous hand. The Earl was in London, for the address was that of his brother, George.

'I read with interest your account of the affair at

Ticonderoga,' the Earl wrote. 'I do not know what surprises me most, the courage of the troops, or the stupidity of your general. To launch infantry in a frontal attack on a strongly fortified position without adequate artillery support or any previous reconnaissance . . .' There followed a thick dash of ink, as if the Earl's emotions had been too much for his pen, and Alan grinned. 'We managed affairs better under the Duke.' And Alan grinned again.

'I have shown your letter to William Pitt. He was bitterly disappointed over the failure of the expedition, but he read your comments with some interest. He noted your references to Sir Harry Napier. Good regimental officers are scarce, I understand, but then they always were.'

Alan turned over the page. 'Pitt has great confidence in the Quebec expedition, and the general in command, young Wolfe, of whom I have heard good accounts.'

There followed references to George Carey, now holding a post in the Government, news of Anne's first season in London society, all very remote, so it seemed to Alan. But he read with interest the Earl's remarks about his other brother, Rupert, fighting with the East India Company's army in India.

He pushed away the other letters, and strolled outside to talk to Jake and Bless. Spring had come again to the Mohawk Valley after a long, hard winter, and there was much to be done, more land to be cleared, more acreage to be ploughed and sown. But Alan was afraid that he would have to leave it again. He held the rank of Captain now in an American regiment, but like so many other landowners he served during the summer only.

No advance had been made after the disaster at Ticonderoga. Abercromby had been recalled, and a new commander, Amherst, had just arrived from England. Bradstreet had captured Fort Frontenac, and the British now controlled Lake Ontario.

Fresh plans had been made by Pitt for the summer. Amherst was to attack Ticonderoga again, and attempt to reach Montreal. Another large expedition was to move by boat up the Mohawk Valley and take Fort Niagara, and so distract the French, and leave Wolfe free to launch the main attack at Quebec.

Alan supposed he would serve at Ticonderoga or Niagara. The latter, he hoped, but he wished he could join the St Lawrence expedition. He liked the sound of this young general, Wolfe, and he had mentioned this casually in his last letter to his father.

Three weeks later he was in the fur warehouse talking to Jake and Bless when he heard horses on the trail, trotting up from the river. He went out to see who they were, for visitors were a welcome change in that lonely place.

' Alan ! ' The leading horseman, a British officer, was waving to him. It was Harry Napier.

He dismounted and came running across the stockade. Alan went to meet him. ' How's the shoulder ? ' he asked.

' Oh, that's all right ! ' Harry said impatiently. ' Alan, read this ! ' and from the pocket of his long-skirted red coat he produced an official looking document. ' Orders from London. What have you been saying about me ? '

' Nothing,' Alan said. ' I write to my father fairly regularly.' He led the way inside and shouted to Sam for food and wine. ' What's happened, Harry ? '

Harry smiled at Alan's bewildered face. ' You seem to forget on this desert island of yours what influence can do in England,' he said. ' Your father has Pitt's ear. And Pitt is supreme. You and I have been ordered to the St Lawrence ! '

Alan snatched the document. But there it was in the clear copperplate hand of a clerk at the Horse Guards. Captain Sir Harry Napier of the 55th Foot, and Captain the Honourable Alan Carey of the 46th American Regiment were to proceed immediately to the St Lawrence and there report to General Wolfe's Headquarters.

With the order was a covering letter from the Earl. It was short and to the point. The orders were indeed prompted by Mr Pitt himself. Wolfe had asked for two A.D.C.s from the army in the south ; their experience there might be useful to the army on the St Lawrence.

' When will you be ready to start ? ' Harry asked, eating

busily, for he was hungry after his ride. ' The campaign will
be over in a month, I expect. What's the best route ? Sail
from New York ? Boston might be better, wouldn't it ? Will
you take Jake and Bless ? '

Alan laughed. ' I can't leave Ashwater at a minute's
notice, Harry,' he said.

' Can you ride back with me to Albany tomorrow, then ? '

' Oh, I expect I can do that,' Alan said. It was difficult to
withstand Harry when he was in this mood.

He sent for Jake and Bless, and they greeted Harry like
old friends. It did not take Alan long to arrange with them
the plans for Ashwater in the next few months, and packing
was no longer any problem for him. He was accustomed to
travelling with the minimum of clothing, and two large
saddlebags took all that he would need for the journey.

They were in Boston ten days later and at the mouth of
the St Lawrence by the end of June. They had been fortunate,
for lying off the wharf at Boston Alan had seen the *Henrietta*,
bound for Quebec with supplies for the army, and Captain
Trevethan had an empty cabin which Alan and Harry had
shared.

The *Henrietta* laboriously tacked her way up the great river,
and Alan took his first look at French Canada, a neat and
pleasant countryside, with compact little farmhouses of stone,
occasional churches, windmills, and every sign of a hard-
working and prosperous colony.

But the traffic on the river was entirely British now. A
graceful frigate swept past them on the first day, and they met
many more ships returning to Boston for supplies. Then the
river turned, and far ahead lay Quebec. Alan and Harry
leapt for the rigging, and peered eagerly through telescopes
lent to them by Captain Trevethan.

In the centre of the river was the Isle of Orleans, and
around it rose a mass of masts, tall and sharp against the sky.
After a few minutes it was possible to distinguish the ships
themselves, the transports and supply ships, small gun-boats,
a few frigates, and the long line of ponderous British battleships,
with tall sides and long rows of gun ports.

To the right rose the precipitous cliffs of Quebec with its sloping roofs and slender church spires, an impregnable fortress, to Alan's eyes. And now he could hear the sounds which were becoming so familiar, the bugles, the drums, the boom of cannon.

But there did not seem to be a great deal of activity. As the *Henrietta* glided up the river, the encampments of the two armies came into view, orderly lines of white tents, the zig-zagging lines of the entrenchments, moving specks of men in white and scarlet and blue. A cloud of smoke drifted lazily away from the ramparts of the citadel, and a gun banged out dully. More guns replied from the Isle of Orleans, and the gentle breeze pushed the white smoke low over the water.

Captain Trevethan sent them ashore in a boat, and at the jetty a Sergeant of the guard saluted them as they stepped ashore.

' 28th Foot,' Harry said, eyeing the Sergeant's facings with professional interest. ' Sergeant, we want General Wolfe's Headquarters.'

' That white farmhouse up the track, sir. I'll get two of my men to bring up your baggage.'

More sentries stopped them outside the farmhouse, and a bored-looking staff officer took their names inside. He glanced at them curiously, but made no comment except to ask them to wait a few minutes while he told the General that they had arrived.

Harry paced up and down restlessly ; he disliked waiting, even when it was a high-ranking officer who was the cause. Alan sat down on a wooden settle by the whitewashed wall ; hours of crouching patiently in the forest for a shot at a deer had taught him the gift of relaxing and he crossed his arms and sat back patiently.

An officer clattered down the stairs, whistling softly. He glanced at the two men as he crossed the hall, and then halted with a loud exclamation of surprise.

' Harry Napier ! Where on earth did you spring from ? I heard you were on the Hudson with Amherst.'

Alan sat up as he heard that pleasant, clear voice. It was

Hugh Goring, in the uniform of a Lieutenant of the 38th Foot.

Harry shook hands, and explained his sudden arrival. Alan, who knew his Harry well now, recognized the slight note of reserve in his voice and the stiffness of his manner. But Hugh noticed nothing amiss, apparently, for he chattered excitedly, ignoring the buckskinned backwoodsman on the settle until Harry jerked his head in warning.

Hugh turned. He recognized Alan then, and he stepped back a pace, the blood draining from his face.

' Alan ! ' he gasped. ' Alan Carey ! '

' Yes, it's Alan,' Harry said grimly.

But Hugh had pulled himself together with all the quickness of his mind and the smoothness of manner that had made so many valuable friends for him. He shook Alan warmly by the hand, but his eyes flickered from side to side as he spoke to him.

' Stephen Rawle is here, Harry,' he said. ' He transferred from the Dragoons to the infantry. Not much chance for cavalry out here. And James Dundas and Edward Rankin are in the 58th too.'

' Quite a collection of Cambridge men,' Harry said dryly. For there were six of them now on the St Lawrence, six of those who had played cards in Hugh's rooms that night. ' Almost enough for a card party,' Harry added.

Hugh stared at Harry's coldly-set face and the accusing expression in his eyes. He stammered, recovered again swiftly, and smiled, the charming smile that had seldom failed him. But it did this time. Harry bowed, and hoped they would see each other again soon.

Hugh's countenance was saved by the arrival of the staff officer who said that General Wolfe was ready to see the two arrivals at once. They were shown into the main room of the farmhouse, transformed into an office, with a desk, a table, some chairs, and a profusion of maps and parade states pinned to the walls.

The General was by the window, looking up the river towards the citadel of Quebec, and he was in profile to Alan, who stared at him in amazement. For this odd and insignificant little man could surely not be the general on whom the great Mr Pitt rested all his hopes.

The General's untidy red hair was tied behind his head. His face was an extraordinary shape, that of a triangle, with a receding forehead that ran out sharply to a thin, tilted nose, and then dropped again to a weak mouth and a chin that simply did not exist, so much did it fall away. There was nothing impressive about his figure, either ; the scarlet coat and heavy gold epaulettes could not disguise his thin, sloping shoulders ; his silk stockings revealed in all their shame his spindly legs and large, awkward feet.

General Wolfe sighed, and turned towards the two young officers. In a flash his whole face was transformed for them as they met his eyes, alive, compelling, and searching, the most remarkable pair of eyes that Alan had ever faced. He could not have believed that a man's eyes could so dominate his whole appearance, or have such an extraordinary effect upon those who met him.

' I am very glad to see you, Captain Napier,' he said, ' and you, Captain Carey.' He shook hands with them both, and asked them to sit down.

He stood in the centre of the room, his long coat falling to his thin knees, his pointed nose sniffing at them, so Alan imagined.

' Mr Pitt himself recommended you both to me,' he said. ' For the moment you will be attached to my staff.' Then he questioned them about their experiences on the Hudson and the Mohawk in the same shrewd, intelligent manner that Alan had experienced with Lord Howe. Mr Pitt, he thought, knew how to select great commanders.

During the next few days they learnt much of the difficulties that were holding back the British force. For so far the French had beaten back all the attacks made on their lines. Their commander, the same Montcalm who had smashed Abercromby's wild attack on Ticonderoga, was a fine general, probably a great and inspired soldier, and not even the British hold on the Isle of Orleans and Point Lévis, facing the citadel on the other bank of the river, the greater numbers of the

British, nor their command of the river, had made him waver in his determination to hold out.

The only practicable route to the citadel was along the northern bank, and that was covered by three lines of defence, the deep ravine of the Montmorency, the Beauport River, and finally the River St Charles. Even after those obstacles, the British would still have to climb the steep ascent to the town, and storm the walls at the top.

A Major Jackson of Wolfe's staff took them up the river in a boat to see the position for themselves. They lay in the sunshine on the heights of Point Lévis, and looked across the river to the battered and half ruined citadel on the other side. The daily artillery duel was in progress, but it was clear to Alan that if the British demolished every house in Quebec, they would still not be any the better for that.

'If Montcalm holds out for another two months, he's safe,' Jackson said.

'Why two months?' Harry demanded.

'The St Lawrence will be solid ice all winter. Our ships will have to sail down river at the end of September to be safe.'

On the 31st July, Wolfe made a determined attack on the northern bank. The landing place was the wide strand of mud left bare by the tide when it ebbed. The French had built redoubts to guard this strip, but Wolfe hoped to surprise them.

The main attack would be made by the Royal Americans and the Grenadiers. Various other groups would help if necessary, and both Alan and Harry might find themselves in the battle if all went well. The assaulting troops embarked in boats during the night. At dawn many of the British vessels sailed up and down the river to mislead the French ; artillery opened up with a roar from the falls of the Montmorency ; warships bombarded different spots all along the northern bank. From the French point of view the attack might come at any place, and they could not risk concentrating their much smaller forces for fear of going to the wrong position.

Alan, on board a small gun-boat, watched the mud strand gradually widen as the tide ebbed. By the late afternoon there would be sufficient room for the assaulting troops to land and deploy. The sky was dull, with the promise of rain, but that should not affect the success of the plan, everyone hoped.

The sixty-four-gun battleship, the *Centurion*, glided slowly past ; her starboard gun ports were open. Blue-coated officers stood quietly on her quarterdeck ; the only sound was the ripple of water from under her bows, and the chanting of the man sounding as he whirled the long line around his head and let it drop into the river. She was a beautiful and stately ship, and Alan watched her in respectful awe, the first battleship he had ever seen at such close quarters.

A shrill whistle came from the quarterdeck. Long gouts of flame belched from the open ports ; the *Centurion* heeled as her sides vanished in a cloud of smoke, and her whole broadside went off with a frightful crash that made Alan flinch and clap his hands to his ears.

Dust and stones flew up around the French redoubts. Again and again the *Centurion's* broadsides hammered away at regular intervals, like the slamming of gigantic doors, the waves of sound echoing over the river, and the heavy clouds of smoke covering the water and obscuring the banks.

The British artillery had opened up from all sides now, rising to a crescendo of noise such as the quiet St Lawrence and the lovely countryside had never heard before. The assault was about to take place.

Lines of rowing boats were pulling for the mud strand. Waves of red and blue-coated figures raced towards the redoubts, and then the rain swept over the hills and hissed and splashed on the water, blotting out the whole scene as Alan ducked for shelter.

From the shore came the rattle of musketry, the shouts and yells of the hand-to-hand fighting that was still in progress. The rain eased, and it was now possible to see what was happening. The British and American regiments were falling back from the redoubts ; they had captured them but could advance no farther, and General Wolfe had decided to cut his losses. Five hundred of his best troops had been killed or wounded in that short fight.

Dinner that night in the Headquarters Mess was a silent and depressing meal. Alan was rising from the table when Harry touched his arm.

'It's Hugh Goring,' he said. 'He was badly wounded this afternoon, and has sent for us.'

They followed a guide down the muddy path to the hospital, one of the barns belonging to the farm. Candles and oil lanterns hung from the bare walls. Lines of cots lay on the floor in the uncertain light, doctors moved about amidst the grim scene, while badly wounded men tossed on their beds, or lay still, staring up at the roof. Alan shuddered, while Harry asked for news of Hugh, and where he could be found.

'In the small ward at the end,' a doctor said. 'Are you friends of his?'

'Yes. Is he seriously wounded?'

'He won't last the night,' the doctor said bluntly, and moved away.

The small ward was at the far end of the barn, and three other British officers, their red coats covered by long cloaks, were standing under the light of a lantern. Alan recognized them with a start of surprise. He saw the freckled face of Stephen Rawle, the dark, usually cheerful Dundas, and the snub nose of Rankin.

'Hullo, Harry,' Stephen said in low tones. 'Hugh's sent for you, too, has he?'

'Yes, and for Alan, too,' Harry said.

'Alan?' Stephen said. 'Do you mean Alan Carey? But he's not here!'

They saw Alan's huge figure looming in the poor light, and Stephen came forward quickly, and then checked abruptly.

'I wouldn't be here,' Harry said curtly, 'if it wasn't for Alan. He's saved my life twice in the last year.'

A medical orderly opened the door behind them. 'Are you the officers to see Lieutenant Goring?' he asked.

'Yes, how is he?' Harry said.

'Pretty bad, sir. You'd better come in now.'

They filed into the small room. In the corner, Hugh was lying on a mattress, the blankets drawn up to his chin. His face was a chalky white, and his cheeks had fallen in until the bones seemed to be bursting through the skin. He was breathing in hoarse gasps, but his eyes were open, and he managed a vestige of a smile as he saw the group around him.

' Thank you for coming,' he said.

' That's nothing, Hugh,' Stephen said. ' Is there anything we can do for you ? '

Hugh shook his head. ' Is Alan here ? ' he asked.

' Yes, Hugh.' His tall figure threw an enormous shadow on the wall.

' Listen, all of you,' Hugh said, but they were forced to bend down to catch his words. ' It wasn't Alan who marked those cards. I did.'

There was silence in the room except for Hugh's laboured breathing. But all heads turned to Alan.

' I'm sorry, Alan,' Hugh whispered.

Alan knelt down by the mattress. ' Don't worry, Hugh,' he said. ' I knew all along that it was you. It hasn't done me any harm, you know.' He took Hugh's limp hand as if he could inject into that dying form some of his own enormous strength.

Hugh smiled, still the same charming and winning smile. ' It would have ruined me,' he said. ' But that doesn't matter now. I'm glad I've told you all.'

He closed his eyes, as if the effort had drained what little life there was left. They watched him for a few minutes, but he did not stir again or open his eyes. Harry looked up, and they followed him quietly out of the room and into the darkness.

' Our mess is just over there,' Stephen said. ' Come and have a drink, Harry. And you, Alan, too.'

They found a quiet corner of the mess tent, and glasses were filled. Harry looked at them, and his face had that determined expression so familiar to Alan.

' Listen to me,' Harry said. ' I've got a lot to tell you, too.' They had so often followed Harry's lead, and deferred to his natural leadership, that Alan grinned as they listened intently and with growing surprise to his account of the fight with the Abenakis and the attack at Ticonderoga.

When he had finished, three embarrassed faces turned to Alan, and Stephen shuffled his feet. ' Will you forgive me, Alan ? ' he said at last.

' Yes, of course, you silly fool,' Alan said without any heat. ' Anything to stop Harry talking.'

They laughed, and the tension was eased immediately. Harry held up his glass.

' To Hugh,' he said, and they drank the toast.

Chapter Fifteen

THE PATH

ALAN hitched the pack on his back to a more comfortable position, and trudged on up the track. He was a disreputable sight with his unwashed and unshaven face, but the man with him was even dirtier, and their creased buckskin breeches and coats looked as if they had been dragged through the mud of a swamp. Both were carrying muskets slung over their back, French guns made in Paris.

To the south-west lay the St Lawrence, out of sight now below the cliffs, but Alan could see the lines of white tents marking the French and British lines, and the walls of Quebec were straight ahead. They must be stopped by sentries soon, he was thinking. He dreaded the thought, but in some ways it would be a relief to put their story to the test.

' Sentries, I think, Mister Carey,' the man by his side muttered.

' Yes, I can see them. Don't speak English again, Tom.'

' *Oui, oui, Pierre,*' the other said, and laughed.

Alan grunted. He disliked this business intensely, and was badly scared. What a fool he had been to volunteer for such a desperate plan. Just because he was always trying to prove to his own satisfaction that he was not a coward, he had pushed himself forward when there was no need for him to have said a word.

Five days ago General Wolfe had asked for volunteers to make their way inside the citadel as spies. The chances of picking up really important information were remote, but Wolfe was desperate ; all his plans had failed ; in a few weeks at the most he would have to raise the siege and retreat to the sea. Any scrap of news, anything at all at which he could clutch as a last resort to save the situation even now, might give him the fortress. His health, never strong, had given way

completely under the strain. For several days a fever had
kept him to his bed, and his staff, devoted though they were
to him, and so completely under the spell of his extraordinary
personality, were convinced that he was dying.

The volunteers had come forward, all Rangers who could
speak a reasonable amount of French, and they had been
interviewed by the General. But he was not very optimistic
of their chances ; their French was not fluent enough, and he
doubted if they would know what to look out for inside the
citadel.

It was then that Alan had spoken up so rashly. His French
was good, so good that he might be taken for a Frenchman,
and coaching from the staff officers would soon teach him
what details to watch in Quebec. So here he was, together
with one Ranger, Tom Hoskins, a New Englander, and Quebec
was a mile away.

' *Halte !* '

A white-uniformed French sentry stepped into the centre
of the track, and pointed his musket at them, the long, needle-
sharp bayonet barring the way.

Alan slouched up to the man, but inwardly he was tense
and frightened, his heart thumping, and his stomach turning
over with a spasm of sheer nausea. A Sergeant came out of
the tent under the trees, and ran his eyes up and down the
two men.

' Where from ? ' he demanded.

' Pont Auxerre, Sergeant,' Alan said. ' Trappers,' and
he opened the pack on his back to show the beaver skins
inside.

' You won't sell many of those,' the Sergeant said. ' The
town's half empty. Names ? '

' Pierre Michelot,' Alan said.

' François Guidon,' Hoskins mumbled in his role of the
surly trapper who resented questions, and was a man of few
words. He was to leave the talking to Alan, in case his French
aroused suspicion.

The Sergeant poked about idly in the pack, and handed it
back to Alan.

' Know of a good inn ? ' Alan asked. ' Not too expensive, and with some respectable wine ? '

' Try the Three Bears. It's as good as any.' The Sergeant walked away.

Alan sighed quietly, and nudged Hoskins. They humped the packs on to their backs again, and set off.

' Easier than I thought,' Hoskins said when they were out of earshot.

' We're not inside Quebec yet,' Alan said. ' Nor out of it again.'

They were stopped at the main gate, and here the cross-examination was more thorough, and they were searched. But there was no danger of the sentries discovering any suspicious articles on them, for they were well equipped to stand a worse test than this perfunctory search of their belongings. Their guns, pouches and powder, and bullets were all French, taken from prisoners and deserters. Their money was French, their knives and tomahawks, even the buckskins that Hoskins was wearing. But no prisoner had been found large enough to cover Alan's great height.

Pont Auxerre was a real settlement, thirty miles to the north-west of Quebec, and they had been landed high up the river, well above Pointe-aux-Trembles. From there they had taken a wide sweep to the north, and had approached Quebec by the River St Charles. Alan kept repeating all this to himself as they watched the French sentries rifle their packs. Despite his fears, he knew well enough that there was little danger if he kept his head ; trappers did come frequently into Quebec to sell their furs, so deserters had told him when he had interrogated them, and no one paid much attention to them.

The Three Bears was a ramshackle and grimy place, but Alan paid for a room for the night, and they were given an indifferent supper, sure proof of the effectiveness of the British blockade of the river.

The main room of the inn was full that evening, mainly with soldiers from the garrison or from regiments stationed close outside the town. There were few townspeople, which

was not surprising. Most of the houses had been damaged by
the incessant gun-fire from the British batteries, and there had
been several outbreaks of fire.

Alan and Hoskins found a corner, and listened to the
conversation around them. Morale was not high amongst the
French, apparently, but General Wolfe knew that already.
Shortage of food and sickness had depressed the French, and
the news of the loss of Ticonderoga, which had fallen at last,
had reached Quebec. Few in the inn thought that the British
would capture Quebec that summer, but they seemed to think
it was inevitable in the following year.

Alan and Hoskins sold their furs the next day. They had
been told by deserters the prices that were considered reasonable
in Quebec, and so did not attract attention by quoting
ridiculous figures. But information was scarce, except what
they could see for themselves. Alan did not think that would
be of much value to Wolfe.

They decided to spend one more night at the Three Bears.
Alan sat in his corner again, and a French soldier, who had
been drinking heavily, got into conversation with him. The
man was inclined to be quarrelsome ; too much wine, as he
admitted quite frankly, usually led him into a fight. Alan
hastily bought him more wine. The sooner the fellow was
under the table the better ; he was in no position to become
involved in a tavern brawl.

The Frenchman started to grumble about his duties outside
the citadel. He was part of a small detachment on the east,
on the Heights of Abraham, as they were called. Alan
wondered why the French kept troops on guard there, for the
cliffs were far too precipitous to be climbed.

' The English will never attack on that side,' he remarked,
filling the man's tankard again.

' Never, m'sieur ! ' The soldier hiccupped loudly, and
tried to focus his eyes on Alan. ' Only a path up the cliff.
Room for one monkey at a time, m'sieur. No army could
climb there,' and he drained his tankard. He closed his eyes,
and went peacefully to sleep, head down on the table, snoring
happily.

Alan winked at the soldier who had come in with the
fellow, and asked him to have a drink ; he was interested in
this mention of a path, but he still had no idea of where it
was. The second man was not so drunk, and was quite ready
to talk to this friendly trapper who had had a good day selling
his beaver skins. By the time another four tankards had been
emptied, Alan had an approximate idea of the site of the path.
Here, at least, was something that might be of use to the
General.

They had no difficulty in leaving Quebec. They walked
all that morning, and then worked round to the south, hitting
the river about ten miles above Quebec, and there they were
picked up by the boat that had landed them three days before.

Alan reported to Wolfe that night. The General was still
in bed, and Alan was alarmed by his appearance. But his
eyes were as keen and alive as ever, and he cross-examined
Alan for an hour.

' This path, Captain Carey,' he said, as his orderly put
another pillow behind his head, ' could you find it ? '

Alan shook his head.   ' I'm a strong swimmer, sir,' he said.
' Could a boat from one of the ships of the line take me up-
river ? I could float down with the current. A boat would be
spotted close in, but not a swimmer.'

' Tomorrow night,' the General said. ' Fetch Jackson,
will you, please? He can make arrangements with the
Admiral.'

A long boat from the *Sutherland*, the Admiral's flagship,
took Alan up the river that night. The tide was turning, and
the current was running downstream, at about four knots, the
naval Lieutenant estimated. They kept well to the southern
bank, in case French sentries saw them. But the night was
dark and there was no moon, and conditions could not have
been better for Alan.

The boat turned about two miles above the citadel, and
Alan stripped, until he was wearing nothing more than a pair
of cotton drawers and his moccasins. He buckled a belt and
knife around his waist, and slipped into the water. Harry
Napier was in the boat, for he was finding his duties as a staff

officer extremely boring, and this would be more interesting than writing up long lists of parade states.

He bent over the gunwale. ' Cold, Alan ? ' he asked.

' Yes,' Alan said, ' but it will be all right when I am moving.'

' I've got a full flask of brandy in my pocket,' Harry said. ' You'll need it after this.'

' A tot of navy rum will be better still,' the Lieutenant said. ' We'll drop down river, Captain Carey. Make for the *Sutherland.* You'll see her lights.'

Alan pushed off, and swam easily down the river, letting the current do most of the work for him. The water was cold, as he had said, although it was August, but there were warm patches here and there. After a few minutes he saw the cliffs of the Heights of Abraham towering above him in the darkness. He kept about twenty yards out in the stream, for he was afraid of hitting rocks near the surface.

There seemed to be no breaks in the wall of rock, and he wondered how far down river he had come. From what the French soldiers had said the path was in a small cove ; he should be able to see that, even in this darkness, and his eyes were accustomed to the bad light by this time. He trod water, staring to the south, trying to pick out the lights of the British position on Point Lévis. But he could see nothing, and he swung in again towards the foot of the cliff.

He swam slowly and as quietly as possible for another few minutes, and then at last he saw the flicker of lights high up on Point Lévis. If the Frenchman was correct, then the cove must be close at hand.

The cliffs turned inwards, and Alan followed them. This could be called a cove, he thought, and then his moccasined feet touched ground, and he scrambled over some rocks to a tiny, sandy beach. He took his time ; there might be a sentry posted at the foot of the path, and if so, his white breeches would show up clearly even in the darkness.

But the beach was deserted. Alan moved on, glad that he need wait no longer, for the night breeze was cold on his bare shoulders and back. His feet kicked up loose pebbles,

and he flinched as he heard the noise. But he would not be
heard above the ripple of the current over the rocks, and he
could see the path now, a narrow-winding track, zigzagging
up into the darkness above.

Was it a practicable route for soldiers? That was the
only question the General would ask him, and there was
only one way to find the answer. He would have to climb it
himself.

He climbed quickly, and then fell into a trench dug right
across the path. He had cut his knees, he thought, as he
muttered under his breath, and clambered out again. If
there was one trench, there would be others, and he went
more slowly.

There were trenches at fairly regular intervals, but he
thought that the British troops could cross them. In any case,

once the top was held, other men with spades could level the path.

He was near the top, and his pace dropped to a crawl. He saw the dark grey line of the sky against the crest of the cliff, and he went down on hands and knees, wincing as the sharp stones cut into his knees, and he put his weight gingerly on the sore places where he had cut himself in the first trench.

He was on the top now, and he lay in the grass, panting a little after his painful crawl. Ahead, about twenty yards distant, perhaps, were some white tents with lanterns hanging inside. He heard voices singing, and a sentry was pacing up and down. He would be passing Alan in another ten yards, and Alan ducked down and wriggled himself backwards until he was well under the overhang of the path. What if the man stopped to look down the path? He must see Alan's white skin in the night. There would be a flash, a report, and the smashing blow from a bullet, or, and Alan writhed in anticipation, the white-hot, searing stab of that long bayonet.

He crouched down, pressing himself into the ground, ignoring the sharp pain from a stone that was cutting into his leg, drawing in his breath, afraid even to breathe, sure that the thump-thump of his heart must sound like the clang of a smith's hammer on the anvil.

The slowly pacing feet went by; there was no pause, and Alan let out his breath in a gasp of relief such as he had not experienced since the last charge at Ticonderoga. He stood up and hurried down the path, suddenly conscious again of his cold, shivering body. He jumped over the trenches, and ran down the little beach, wading out quickly into the water, shuddering as he plunged in, and struck out furiously, anything to warm himself.

There was no point now in keeping to the north bank; he could find that little cove again easily; he could lead the entire British army there in a fog, he decided exultantly, and he nearly started to sing, so great was his relief and the reaction from those long frightful seconds waiting for the sentry to pass.

He could see the lines of camp fires on the bank now, and the lights from the Isle of Orleans. The *Sutherland* was berthed just above the island, below a frigate. And there was the frigate. Alan swam past her, and the great bulk of the battleship loomed ahead, with lights streaming from the stern windows in long, quivering lines on the water.

He floated down the starboard side until he saw the rope ladder hanging down, and he trod water, arms outstretched.

'That you, Alan?' a voice called from above. It was Harry.

'Yes.' Alan clambered upwards, tired now, and very cold. Helping hands pulled him aboard, and a coat was thrown over his shoulders. He was led below into a cabin that was blissfully warm and snug after the chill night breeze. The naval Lieutenant held a tin mug under his nose.

'Put that inside you,' he said, and Alan gulped down the rum, coughing as he did so, and feeling the wonderful sensation of warmth run through him.

Vigorous hands rubbed him with towels, and he winced as they touched the cuts and scratches from his scramble up the path. Harry had brought spare clothes for him from their billet, and Alan dressed hastily, for the Admiral was waiting to ask him questions, and Admirals, to judge by the anxious face of the Lieutenant, were not people to be kept waiting.

Alan bent down to fasten the buckles of his shoes, and as he stood up again his head hit the low roof with a crash that made him blink and curse.

'You'd find it worse on a sloop,' the Lieutenant said, laughing. 'I know a tall Lieutenant on the *Eagle* down the river who has to open his skylight when he shaves. He stands in the cabin, pokes his head through the skylight, and props his shaving mirror on deck.'

'I'm glad I'm not in the Navy, then,' said Alan. 'You'd have to rebuild the fleet for me.'

He followed the Lieutenant along a passageway and into the Admiral's cabin in the stern, wide and spacious, with hanging lanterns, silver candlesticks on the table, carpets on the floor, and only the breech of two huge guns to remind Alan that he was still on board a line-of-battle ship.

Sitting round the table were several officers, most of them

in the blue and white of the Navy, and the others resplendent in the scarlet and gold of the Army.   One of the soldiers jumped to his feet, and hurried across to Alan.   With a start of surprise he recognized General Wolfe, white and haggard, his eyes burning like those of a man with a fever, which he probably was, for he looked a sick man.

'You were successful, Captain Carey?'

'I think so, sir,' Alan said cautiously.   His mood of wild exhilaration had vanished now.   On what he said might depend the future of the Quebec expedition.

'Good!   Good!   Come and sit down,' the General said briskly.   'You must be tired.'

Everyone drew up chairs to the long table by the round stern windows, and the wigged heads turned towards Alan, the weather-beaten sailors, the sunburnt soldiers.   Alan took a deep breath, and told his story.   He was not interrupted, and when he had finished, the General turned a flushed and glowing face to the Admiral at the head of the table.

'Well, Admiral?' he exclaimed triumphantly.

Admiral Saunders rubbed his double chins, the fingers rasping loudly over the grey stubble of his chin, and his heavily lidded eyes rested for a moment on Alan, and then on the General.

'What are your plans, General?' he asked.

'A diversion towards the mud strands as we did last time, artillery from the Montmorency, and the main landing tomorrow night in this cove that Captain Carey has discovered.'

Admiral Saunders shook his head doubtfully.   'It's a gamble,' he said.

'Of course!' Wolfe said.   'But it is our last chance, Admiral.   We have tried everything else.'

One of the soldiers spoke.   It was Brigadier Townshend. 'You realize, sir,' he said slowly, 'that if you take the landing force to the Heights of Abraham by this cliff path, then there can be no retreat for them once they are up.   They will be fighting with the cliff at their backs.'

'Yes,' Wolfe said calmly.

Another Brigadier leant forward. ' And the number you can land and send up this path in the darkness will be limited, sir. Five thousand at the most.'

' Yes,' Wolfe said again. ' And you, Monckton, have you any comment ? '

The third Brigadier shook his head. ' It's a frightful risk, sir.'

Wolfe's calm suddenly deserted him. His cheeks flamed, and he banged the table with a thump that made everyone stiffen. For all there knew and feared his sudden and rare outbursts of temper.

' I am going to land at this cove,' he said, ' and I shall go up with the leading troops. And if Montcalm attacks us with every man he has, and he will outnumber us up there by three to one, then I shall stand and fight, and blast him off the Heights of Abraham ! '

There was silence in the cabin, broken by the gentle rasping of the Admiral's fingers on his chin. Only he could oppose the General's decision, for the others were of junior rank.

' We can land your men in small boats,' he said. ' Cook, you know the river better than any of us. What do you think ? '

At the end of the table sat a man of about thirty, in the uniform of a Master in the Navy. He had a big face, a big nose, and a massive chin, but what impressed Alan most was the air of unshakeable composure that seemed to envelop the man ; he radiated calm efficiency. You felt that anything he said would be carefully considered, and that anything he said he could do he would carry out without any possibility of doubt.

' I have sounded all the river, as you know, sir,' he said. ' I should not advise taking the larger ships up the river for this attack. Send the troops up in daylight, and they can be rowed down with the ebb-tide in the night.'

The Admiral grunted. He still had to make his own decision, even though his chief expert said it could be done as far as the landing was concerned. He turned his hard, strong face towards Alan.

' You can take the boats to this cove at night, Captain Carey ? ' he asked.

' Yes, sir,' Alan heard himself saying. He was appalled at his own rashness. Could he guide all the boats ? What if he made a mistake ? The effects would be disastrous. He saw the calm, steady eyes of Cook watching him, and the firm lips smiled. ' Yes, I can do that, sir,' he said.

He was thinking, too, of the letters from England that had just arrived, the grim urgency that lay behind his father's last letter. Ticonderoga had fallen ; so had Crown Point and Niagara. The British had broken through the iron ring of the French forts, and if Quebec fell this summer, the whole fabric of French power in America would be smashed to pieces. And behind his father's words must have been the passionate driving force of Mr Pitt, that wild, unbalanced genius. What had he said ? ' I know that I can save the country, and that I alone can ! '

' I know that Mr Pitt is determined to have Quebec this year,' he said slowly, forgetting for a moment to whom he was talking. ' He told my father so just as he was writing to me.'

' Your father ! ' Admiral Saunders exclaimed sharply. ' Who is your father, Captain Carey ? '

' Lord Aubigny, sir. He is a friend of Mr Pitt's.'

' Yes, I know,' the Admiral said slowly. He grunted and cleared his throat noisily. He glanced around the table. The mention of that one name, Pitt, seemed to affect every man in the cabin, as if they could hear that tremendous voice, see for themselves his flashing eyes and theatrical gestures, and feel sweeping over them his astonishing power of making his hearers believe that nothing, nothing at all in the world, could stand against them, or resist the power of Britain.

' I am quite ready to give you all the help you need from the Navy, General,' the Admiral said.

Wolfe smiled, and spread out on the table a large plan of Quebec. The wigged heads drew closer together, and Alan stretched out his long legs and sighed deeply. He had opened his mouth again. Instead of sitting back, he had thrust himself into danger once more, and the terrifying responsibility of

leading this desperate and forlorn hope in the dark to that
tiny beach beneath the cliffs of Quebec.

Cook nodded at him. Well, if that quiet and capable man
thought it could be done, then he would do it. Alan smiled,
and his confidence began to return. He listened to the
General's decisive voice as he outlined his plan, and the three
Brigadiers scribbled notes of their orders.

Chapter Sixteen

THE HEIGHTS OF ABRAHAM

HUDDLED under the shelter of waterproofs, Alan and Harry watched the rain sweep over the hills and across the river, pattering on the decks of the *Sutherland*, and flecking the green waters of the St Lawrence with thousands of tiny splashes that vanished, and then appeared again and again.

High up on its impregnable cliffs Quebec was wreathed in clouds of black smoke from the houses that were still burning from the British bombardment. Up river the lines of battleships were hammering the French positions on Cap Rouge. More guns were firing from Point Lévis into the deserted streets of the citadel, and by the Isle of Orleans still more warships were sending broadside after broadside into the redoubts above the mud strands. The rain seemed to dull the sound of the explosions, reducing them to a continuous rumble of sound, rising occasionally to a thundering roar as all the British guns seemed to go off at the same moment, and then descending in the scale again to the rolling of many hundreds of gigantic drums.

The white smoke was drifting across the water, beaten down by the rain, and the whole of the river, the encampments of the two armies, the great ships on the river, the entire panorama was wreathed in a thick, white mist, clearing here and there for a few seconds to reveal the orange flashes of the guns, and then closing in once more to hide that particular spot; and then the curtain would roll up farther away, with the same flashes, the same furious din, the same gout of flame and jet of smoke drifting over the rain-flecked water.

General Wolfe had withdrawn all his men from the Montmorency; he could not conceal that movement from Montcalm, nor could he hide the fact that he was about to attack again. But he could conceal the exact point where that attack would come.

So he had arranged a series of feint attacks, one far up the river at Cap Rouge, a general threat along the whole line of the mud strand opposite the French redoubts, with all his guns in action, and all his warships in motion, while Montcalm waited for the British to strike. Only then could he concentrate his troops at the critical position.

Wolfe was on board the *Sutherland*. Like a gambler who had seen his pile of counters dwindle away, he had inspected his hand, and now with set lips and a confident face he was hurling down on the table his last stake. Either he would win everything, or else he was ruined. There were to be no half measures this time.

But the torrential rain had upset all his careful planning. His landing force was still cooped up on the flatboats above the citadel. They should have landed the previous night, and were cramped on the boats in considerable discomfort, hungry, cold, and wet.

This morning, Wednesday, 12th September of 1759, he would strike. The clouds were lifting, and by nightfall, the sailors hoped, the sky would be clear. Five thousand men, all that Wolfe could spare for this blow, were ready.

'Blue sky!' Harry exclaimed, and pointed to the north.

Alan looked up. Tonight, then. No more waiting, he hoped.

A midshipman touched his arm. 'Would you come to the Admiral's cabin, please, sir?'

Alan hurried below. Admiral Saunders and General Wolfe were sitting at the table, and facing them was a man in buckskins, standing between two British Marines.

'This is a deserter from the French colonial troops, Captain Carey,' the General said. 'He speaks no English. Would you question him, please?'

'Any particular questions, sir?'

'Future French moves, and what do they think we are about to do.'

Alan broke into his fluent French, and the deserter's face cleared when he heard his own language. He spoke readily, but his knowledge of the French plans was as vague as Alan had expected.

'Anything else?' Alan asked.

'A convoy of stores is coming down the river in the night, m'sieur. For the citadel.'

'What time? How many boats?'

But the man did not know, and Alan interpreted to the General and Admiral Saunders. The General's quick brain seized on the importance of the convoy.

'That may help us,' he said. 'The French sentries on the river will be expecting rowing boats tonight. They'll take us for the convoy. Thank you, Captain Carey.'

The troops embarked again that evening, for they had been landed to take on fresh rations, and to dry out their uniforms. Twenty-four men, picked to climb the path with Alan, boarded the *Sutherland*, and down below on the gundeck Alan spoke to them. They were volunteers from the Light Infantry regiment and their Colonel, the brother of Colonel Howe who had been killed at Ticonderoga, introduced Alan to them as their guide.

'Captain Carey swam down the river and climbed the

path two nights ago,' Colonel Howe said. ' He will explain the plan.'

Alan inspected the volunteers. They were a tough-looking group of men, he thought, hard and fit. He wanted no stragglers for that first wave up the cliff.

' We shall land first,' he said. ' No one else will land until we have reached the top, and have dealt with the French sentries up there. The path is filled with trenches, so be careful. Muskets loaded and slung, but you must not cock your muskets or fix bayonets, until I give the word. And no man must fire until I say. When we reach the top, get into line quickly, and fix bayonets. You'll see some tents about twenty yards away. Charge when I say, and you can make as much noise as you like then.'

The sunburnt faces grinned at him confidently. There was one he recognized, too. It was Stephen Rawle, watching him curiously, as if he were seeing Alan for the first time.

' I want a runner to go back down the path to let the General know immediately we have cleared the top,' Alan said. ' Somebody used to mountains and paths like this.'

' I will, sir.' The speaker was a bandy-legged little fellow with a dark face and a quick, lilting voice that made Alan's heart jump.

' You're Welsh,' he said.

' Yes, Mr Carey, that's right.' The little man grinned at him. ' You're from Llanstephan, sir, aren't you ? '

Alan nodded. ' And you ? '

' Llandilo, sir. Gareth Rees is my name, sir.'

' Right, Rees, you'll move behind me. It'll be Wales for ever tonight. We'll show them how to climb a cliff.'

Alan turned away, smiling. He had no worries now. How long will this mood last, he wondered ? In an hour I shall be as nervous as ever.

Stephen Rawle was standing by his side. ' Are you the officer who went into Quebec, Alan, and who swam down the river to find this path ? '

Alan nodded, and flushed as he heard a sardonic chuckle from Harry who was listening to the conversation.

'You needn't worry, Stephen,' Harry said. 'I'm coming, too, and if I had to make a pick of the Army here to take us to the top of the cliffs, I'd pick Alan every time.'

'I'm not worrying,' Stephen said. 'I'm glad Alan is leading us.'

They went to the wardroom of the battleship to eat supper, and to pick up rations for the night and the next day, for there would be no room on this expedition for supply parties.

When they came on deck again the sun was down, and the rain had stopped. Alan decided to stay on deck from then on, so that his eyes would become accustomed to the dark. But there was a good deal to watch, for the whole of the British fleet was in action. Every gun that could be brought to bear was firing. All down the river he could see the sudden flashes, the single row that indicated a small gun-boat, the two long lines of a battleship, while high in the dark sky there soared signal rockets of many colours. They were not in fact indicating any particular message, as Alan knew, but they gave the French the impression that a tremendous assault would sweep over the redoubts at any moment. No movement had yet been made by the French, and their main forces were still concentrated above the redoubts and facing the Montmorency.

Not far away a battleship was firing regular broadsides ; each time the big guns exploded, their flashes lit up the tall sides of the ship, and silhouetted her slender masts ; then she vanished into the night, and reappeared for a brief second as her guns roared out their defiance. It was a comforting sight, Alan thought, this concentration of the power of the Navy. He would not be alone when he climbed that path in a few hours.

'Surely it's time we started,' Harry said.

'Not until the tide turns,' Alan said calmly, though he was as impatient to start as Harry. Still, it was pleasant to know that Harry could become jumpy, too. He was not the only one whose nerves played uncomfortable tricks on him.

Nailed boots clattered on to the deck from below ; lanterns were being hoisted into the maintop shrouds of the flagship, the signal that the assault troops were to embark. The tide had turned at last.

General Wolfe's pointed features came close to Alan. 'Good luck, Captain Carey. I have complete confidence in you.'

'Thank you, sir,' and Alan went over the side. If Wolfe thought he could lead the boats to the cove and up the path, then he could do it, he thought, as a sailor took his arm and helped him into the boat.

'All present,' came Stephen's voice from the second boat. Alan grinned. Stephen was jumpy, too, to judge from his voice.

'Harry?' Alan asked. 'Private Rees?'

They both answered. 'Shove off,' Alan said to the Lieutenant in command of the two boats.

The oars rose and fell, and they glided away from the towering sides of the *Sutherland*. Alan thought he could see the other boats farther up the river, and the guns were still thundering away below the citadel, the low clouds reflecting the continual flashes.

'Keep well into the north bank,' Alan muttered to the Lieutenant.

Already they were slipping past the cliffs looming up above them, grim and silent and somewhat forbidding. Alan tried to estimate their position, but he could not see the lights from Point Lévis yet. As soon as they came into view, he must slow down the pace, for the cove was just around the next bend then.

They were moving fast with the tide carrying them down, and the sailors were pulling steadily and quietly. A man laughed in the boat astern.

'Quiet, you fool,' came Stephen's growl, and there was instant silence.

Alan smiled. They need not worry with that infernal din from the battleships, but it was just as well to make the men realize that there must be no unnecessary noise, especially when they were climbing the path. He peered ahead for the lights of Point Lévis; a wave of doubt swept over him, and he clenched his hands, until he could feel the nails cutting into his palms. Behind were five thousand men all waiting for him to lead them to one spot. If he made a mistake . . .

' *Qui vive !* '

Alan sat rigidly on the thwart. A hiss of breath came from Harry and the naval officer at the tiller.

' *Qui vive !* ' The clear, high-pitched call sounded again from the wall of rock and forest high up on the left. Alan shivered. The last time he had heard that shout was in the gloomy forest below Ticonderoga, and a volley of bullets had followed, killing Lord Howe and ruining the entire attack. Would the same thing happen now ?

' *Qui vive !* '

Alan raised his head. They had been seen, so there was no point in pretending to ignore the challenge. Could he make the sentry believe they were the convoy for the citadel ?

' *France !* ' he shouted.

' *A quel régiment ?* '

' *De la Reine !* ' Alan cried, his voice shrill with tension. There was such a regiment farther up the river under the command of Bougainville, so a prisoner had said during his interrogation.

The sailors had stopped rowing and the boat drifted down on the tide. Harry and the Lieutenant were holding pistols, and the click as the cocking pieces were pulled back sounded clearly above the ripple of water over the rocks to their left.

' Don't fire ! ' Alan whispered.

Feet clattered on loose stones, and a larger stone dropped with a splash into the river. Alan saw a white-uniformed figure scrambling down the rock, swinging from bushes like a monkey.

' *Quel régiment ?* ' he shouted again, and he was standing on a rock now, level with the boats.

' *De la Reine, imbécile !* ' Alan said in the curt accents of a French gentleman rebuking a stupid private of his regiment. ' Provision boats. Don't make such a noise.'

' *Pardon, m'sieur,* ' the sentry said apologetically. ' Are you the convoy for the citadel ? '

' Yes, you fool ! Do you want the English to hear us ?
The other boats are astern. Don't challenge them ! '

' *Oui, m'sieur.* '

The sentry started to clamber up the steep rock again, and
the tension relaxed in the boat.

' Give way,' Alan whispered.

The oars dipped silently, the cliff slid past again, and Alan
felt the cold sweat on his forehead. They must be close to
the cove, and yes, there were the twinkling lights on Point
Lévis and the flash of the batteries still firing across the river
into the citadel.

' Pull in,' Alan said. ' There, there ! ' his voice cracking
with relief as he saw the tiny beach.

Clumsily he rose to his feet in that confined space and
stumbled as the boat grounded with a sudden jar. He jumped
over the side, felt the cold water on his moccasins, and splashed
ashore.

' All out, and in single file ! ' he said. The second boat
was gliding in. ' Stephen ! '

' Here, Alan,' and Stephen Rawle splashed ashore.

' Get your men in single file. Tell them to remember the
trenches across the path. Private Rees ? '

' Yess, Captain bach ! ' and a small, bow-legged figure
stepped towards Alan.

Alan turned, and started up the path. Immediately behind
him was Rees, and Harry next. Alan's rifle was slung over
his shoulder, and so, too, were all the muskets of the men in
the first party, for they would need both hands to climb
quietly. But they were Light Infantrymen, trained to move
independently, and freed from the rigid drill movements of
the barrack square.

Alan stopped. Ten yards to go. He looked down. The
white blurs of Harry and Rees peered up at him.

' Crawl ! ' he whispered. ' Sentry at the top, I expect.
Wait for me to grab him.'

He went down on hands and knees. Much more
comfortable in buckskin breeches, he thought, remembering
the sharp stones that had cut his bare knees two nights ago.

Below and to the right, he could hear the thunder of the guns and the leaping flashes ; it might be a summer storm of sheet lightning. The sentry would hear nothing with that continuous rumble of noise, but he would be more alert.

Alan's head rose slowly above the crest. There were the tents and the lights inside, and the singing of the French soldiers. They would be singing a different tune in a minute, and Alan's teeth showed as he grimaced nervously.

Where was that sentry ? Yes, there he was, just turning

at the end of his beat. Thirty yards to cover, and he would be past Alan, and his back exposed. Alan felt the knife in his belt. No, he couldn't stab the man in cold blood. It might be that drunken fool whom he had plied with cheap wine in the Three Bears. Hurry, man, march faster! But the fellow was pacing slowly, and he had stopped. Had he seen them on the path, or heard some sound? But all was quiet below. The orders had been to stop when the man in front halted, and the Light Infantrymen must be crouching down now, waiting for Alan. And General Wolfe would be waiting, too, down there in his boat, his pointed, triangular face tilted upwards ; another hour or so for him, and he would be a famous soldier, his name a roar of voices in the streets of London, printed on popular ballads ; or else disgraced, on half pay, the rash fool who had led a British army to death and destruction on a precipice in North America.

Would that sentry never move ? A distant blast of sound from the distance. That must be a battleship firing her whole broadside. Alan shifted his weight cautiously ; no shower of stones must roll down the cliff now. Again the roar of a broadside, and the rolling rumble of more guns. It reminded Alan of the time when he had been taken behind the scenes at Drury Lane, just before the curtain went up, with the hum of the audience, and the last crashing chords from the orchestra, with the actors standing still, tense and strained. He knew what they felt like now, and he . . .

The sentry was walking past. A distant gun flash twinkled briefly on the brass of his equipment, and his back was towards Alan.

Alan crawled slowly on to the grass, rose to his feet, and tiptoed on soft moccasins after the unsuspecting figure, arms hanging loose, crouched like a great bear.

Now ! He jumped, arms outflung. One huge hand closed round the man's windpipe, the other pulled him back and brought him crashing to the ground. Alan bent over him, flicked out his knife, and waved it under the fellow's bulging eyes.

' Silence ! ' Alan hissed. ' One sound and I cut your windpipe out ! '

He relaxed his grip on the throat, and the sentry gasped for breath. ' Don't, m'sieur, don't, m'sieur,' he whispered.

' Stand up, then,' Alan said. ' Over here ! '

He pushed the man towards the top of the path. ' Harry ! Bring the men up.'

A head appeared against the grey skyline, then another, and two black figures stood on the edge of the cliff. Then more, until a long line was spreading quickly out, cocking pieces were clicking back, bayonets snapping into place.

' Alan ? ' It was Stephen.

' Yes. All your men up ? '

' All ready.'

Alan unslung his long rifle, cocked it, and stepped forward.

' Advance,' he muttered and the word ran down the line in soft whispers. Boots rustled in the grass, the gun-fire caught the slender gleam of the bayonets.

Alan raised his rifle, aimed at a shadow inside a tent, and pressed the trigger.

' Fire ! ' he yelled.

Muskets flashed out, a ripple of flame in the darkness, a crash of sound, and Alan leapt forward.

' Charge ! Charge ! '

The whole line rushed forward with him with exultant yells after the long silence. One tent went down with a flare of flame from the lantern. Black figures stumbled into the open ; Alan swung at one with the butt of his rifle, felt the jar of the blow up his arm, and the brief skirmish was over as a group of frightened, chattering prisoners were herded together.

' Rees ! ' Alan called. ' Down the path, and say the top is held ! '

Rees bounded downwards like a mountain goat, and Alan walked past the tents. But it was too dark to distinguish anything. There were no other French troops in sight, though, and Stephen Rawle was already spreading out his men to cover any sudden attack.

Alan wiped his forehead. His job was over now. He watched, feeling oddly detached as a stream of men poured over the top of the cliff, line after line forming up, and marching away into the night.

A thin, spindly-legged figure in a long cloak came up to him. It was General Wolfe, and he clasped Alan's hand.

' I owe you a great debt, Captain Carey,' he said. ' I shall not forget it,' and he hurried away, shouting orders.

Still men swarmed up the path. Alan wondered how many had arrived. The sun would be up in a few hours, and the entire force must be in position by then before the French counter-attacked.

Dawn came at last, a grey misty morning with a threat of rain from low clouds. The ground was level, and covered with grass, rising steadily in front of the British position and hiding the walls of Quebec. To the left were cornfields, but the whole area was not more than a mile in width, with the cliffs and the 300 feet drop to the St Lawrence on the right, and the winding course of the St Charles to the left.

General Wolfe and his Brigadiers were drawing up the long lines of red-coated infantry. The Royal Americans were still guarding the landing beach, for that was the only line of retreat, and all that Wolfe could muster on the Heights was a bare 5,000 men, not even sufficient to cover the full width of the plateau.

The General was everywhere, driving his sick, exhausted body to the limit of his endurance. Townshend's brigade, two battalions strong, was posted at an angle to guard the dangerous gap on the left towards the cornfields, and then the army was still, waiting for the French.

Wolfe could do no more now. He had brought his tiny force into position. A gambler's throw it had been, and more than that. He had put his last stake on the table, and now he had exposed his cards for all to see. It was for Montcalm to show his hand next.

Alan found himself in the centre with Harry and Stephen and the rest of the Light Infantry. To the right he saw the waving tartans of the Highlanders, and heard the wailing of the bagpipes. Ahead was the level turf, empty and peaceful.

Muskets crackled on the left. Puffs of smoke appeared in the bushes there and then came the deeper boom of small cannon. An extended line of skirmishers moved out from Townshend's brigade. Alan saw red-uniformed figures stagger and fall, and then the threat was over, and the plateau fell silent again.

A shower of rain hissed over the grass, and then the warm sun broke through. But the British lines never moved, still waiting for the French. They could hear bugle calls now from over the brow of the hill, the roll of drums, and the shouted orders.

A single horseman galloped over the hill, and pulled up with a jerk, silhouetted against the skyline, a blue-coated figure on a black horse.

' Montcalm himself,' an officer near Alan said. ' Sergeant, stand the men up.'

All down the line the orders were passed. Officers and sergeants bellowed hoarsely, the men shuffling into perfect dressing as if they were on a parade ground. Alan smiled as he thought of what Jake would have said about this careful drill. This was no forest skirmish, but a set-piece battle in the open. Two European armies, trained and drilled for this very type of ground, were ready to fight it out with the grim preciseness of ordered volleys, of steady commands, rigid lines, until one side broke and ran.

Alan looked over his shoulder. The British could not run. They must fight and die where they stood, or sweep the French back into the town.

A deep murmur ran down the red lines. The ridge in front was no longer empty. A horde of white-uniformed men was swarming over the crest, covering the entire front of the British. Two small cannon that had been dragged up the cliff bellowed out from Alan's left. They were firing grape-shot, and Alan gasped as he saw men tossed aside and hurled to the ground in the steady ranks of the French.

But the gaps closed up. The standards waved overhead, the drums beat out the wild rhythm of the ' Pas de Charge ', and the French came on, their faces to the British.

Alan set his teeth. He glanced at the tense faces on either side, the firmly closed lips, the half closed eyes. Ticonderoga would be a child's skirmish to this murderous storm that would break in a minute over the Heights of Abraham.

High-pitched, screamed orders ran down the British line. Five thousand muskets came up to the aim. But the French never faltered as they saw that menacing sight. The drums still beat, their officers ran ahead, waving swords, and the white breeches and black boots rose and fell in quick step as the dense columns advanced.

The British were silent again, waiting. The French were barely sixty yards away now. Alan could distinguish the faces, the features. Surely they must fire at them now ? This was madness to wait. The French were firing. Bullets cracked overhead, smoke billowed over the leading French ranks. A man on Alan's left fell forward ; screams came from behind.

Alan gulped. His sights were on a French officer. Fifty yards ! This was lunacy. He must fire soon.

' Three paces forward ! MARCH ! '

The whole British line stepped forward, a delicate, precise drill movement.

' Fire ! ' The bugles blared and screamed, and Alan pressed his trigger.

He saw the familiar spurt of flame and the gush of smoke, and then his ears, his whole brain reeled and throbbed as five thousand muskets exploded in one single and appalling crash.

The French columns vanished in the billowing smoke cloud. Fresh orders were being howled. Five thousand ramrods worked as one in the swift, jerky drill that had been pounded into these red-coated infantry. Alan was reloading with the rest. Up to the aim again. What was happening to the French ? He could see nothing but white smoke.

' Fire ! '

Again that bellowing crash. More orders, more ramrods up in the air.

' Fire ! '

The crash was not so sharp this time, for each man was firing as soon as he had reloaded ; the din was continuous, an incessant roll of dull explosions in the distance, sharper and louder by Alan's side.

The bugles sounded again. Then blessed silence, and slowly the great fog of smoke lifted, the gentle breeze over the cliffs shredding its way over the cornfields.

In front was a howling, shrieking and disorganized mass of men, their ranks in shreds, their columns blown to pieces by those frightful volleys from the British infantry. But they were given no chance to recover. Alan saw a long-legged figure run to the front, hat in hand, red hair glowing in the sunlight, and his sword pointing towards the French.

The bugles clamoured, a roar of cheering went up from the British lines as they saw their General, and they rushed forward, no longer in the neat, straight drill formation, but in an uneven, irresistible rush.

The bagpipes screamed on the right wing, the Highlanders drew their broadswords, and down went the points of the English bayonets. Alan charged with the rest, all fear banished, drawn into the infectious fury of this wild stampede, waving his rifle like a flail, for he had no bayonet. He saw a red-faced, black-moustached Frenchman howling at him, a row of white teeth, and then the vision had gone, and Alan was laying about him in his berserk rage, shouting and cursing, until there were no more yelling faces, only white backs running over the grass, and he knew that the battle was won, Quebec was won, and the French dominions in America had been won, too.

'Better find Headquarters,' Harry said. He grinned at Alan, and they both started laughing, the high-pitched hysterical laughter of men whose nerves have been strung and stretched to the breaking point.

They made their way back through the British lines. Officers were re-forming their men before the advance was continued to the walls of Quebec. Alan saw the Headquarters flag, and Major Jackson standing there, his face a mask of grief and horror.

'What is it, Jackson?' Alan asked, and clapped him on the back. 'We've won, man, we've won!'

'Yes, I know, Carey. But it's the General. He's dead.'

'Dead!'

'Yes, he was wounded twice, but he refused to go to the rear. Then he was shot through the chest, and he died in my arms a few minutes ago.'

Alan felt the exultation drain away, and his great shoulders drooped.

' Did he know the battle was won ? '

' Yes, he knew. We told him.' Major Jackson turned his head away as if ashamed of the tears trickling down his cheeks. ' He said, " Then God be praised. I die in peace." '

A group of officers came up. Among them was Brigadier Townshend. He acknowledged their salutes in silence, and stared away into the distance before he straightened his shoulders.

' Captain Carey, will you report back to Admiral Saunders on board the *Sutherland*. Tell him I am advancing to the citadel. And tell him that . . . that General Wolfe is dead.'

Alan saluted, and walked back to the cliff.

Chapter Seventeen

VISITORS FROM ENGLAND

ALAN sat on a tree stump and watched the men felling a
tree. Another bite into the forest, he thought, as the
tree swayed and crashed to the ground.

He surveyed the land with a contented happiness. In a
year he would have added two more fields of corn to Ashwater ;
in five years . . . he smiled. There would be no end to this
gradual expansion.

Horses came clip-clopping up the track. That must be
Harry ; he had returned to Albany with Alan after the fall of
Quebec, for the fighting in North America was practically ended
now. Quebec was garrisoned, and the French would probably
make an effort to recapture it, but their bases were dwindling
away, and they could not offer much more resistance.

Meanwhile the settlers were streaming up the Mohawk,
cutting into the forest with their modest clearings, felling trees,
sowing crops, mere specks as yet in the great wilderness of
trees, but one day, Alan knew, these tiny plots would spread
and mingle until the forest had vanished, and the whole land
was cultivated and civilized.

Harry was dismounting inside the stockade, and he shouted
cheerfully to Alan. There were two other riders with him,
one of them elderly and well dressed, his clothes altogether
too magnificent for the Mohawk, Alan thought, as he saw the
plum-coloured coat, cut in London by a good tailor, too.
Who could this be ?

The man turned, and Alan gasped, running forward. It
was the Earl of Aubigny.

' Ah, Alan, there you are,' he said calmly, as if he had
parted from Alan a few weeks ago.

' Father ! ' Alan shook hands, and laughed. ' But how . . .
where . . . ? '

The Earl examined Alan with the greatest deliberation, taking in his great height and wide shoulders, his tanned face and air of superb fitness and confidence, and his favourite dress of buckskin and moccasins.

' I can't admire your tailor, Alan,' he said, ' but I suppose those clothes are comfortable.'

' Very, sir.' Alan smiled at his father's servant who was standing by the horses. ' Hullo, Davies, you're a long way from Llanstephan.'

' Yes, indeed, Mr Alan. It's good to see you again.'

Alan shouted for men to take the horses and unload the baggage. His father was not travelling light, he noticed, for there was a spare horse loaded with his bags. Then he ushered them inside.

The Earl surveyed the main living-room in silence, the wood floors and walls, the wide stone fire-place, the heavy furniture and the magnificent furs.

' Quite feudal,' he remarked. ' I imagine my ancestors at Llanstephan Castle must have lived in this style.'

' This is a new country, sir,' Alan said. ' But we're moving fast.' He guided his father to a chair by the fire-place, and the Earl sat down a little stiffly, for he had spent a long day in the saddle. Harry had gone out to find Jake and Bless.

' Do sit down, Alan,' the Earl said. ' I find it a strain looking up at you. You must have grown another six inches at least.'

Alan laughed, and pulled up a chair by his father.

' Yes, you've grown in more ways than one,' the Earl said, his shrewd faded eyes on his son. ' I would trust you with a couple of Troops of Dragoons, now. And a regiment, too, in a few years' time.'

Alan flushed and changed the subject quickly. ' But how did you get here, sir ? ' he asked.

' By ship, boat, and by horse,' the Earl said, taking out his snuff box. ' How else ? '

' But it's a tremendous journey, sir ! '

' I am not in my grave yet, if that is what you mean,' the Earl said a trifle tartly. ' I crossed in a ship of the line, thanks to a friend at the Admiralty. I landed at New York, and came by boat up the Hudson River, and then by horse from Albany to Schenectady, and by boat up the Mohawk. Your friend, young Napier, escorted me from Albany.' He sighed and flicked away some grains of snuff from his breeches. ' I had thought the inns of Italy the worst in the world. They are now second on my list.'

Alan grinned. ' Yes, our inns are dreadful,' he said.

' I met some old friends in the Army at New York,' the Earl said. ' They spoke well of you, Alan. Townshend and Admiral Saunders mentioned you in their dispatches from Quebec. There's a career waiting for you in the Army.'

Alan sat up in his chair. Nothing had been farther from his thoughts. The idea appalled him, but would his father be hurt if he refused the offer? But Jake and Bless came in at that moment.

' Say, Mister Carey,' Jake drawled, ' have you seen the new consignment of furs?' He spat accurately into the fire, and the Earl started and looked up.

' Not yet, Jake. This is my father. Father, this is Jake Winter and Bless Winter.'

Alan's eyes gleamed with amusement as the Earl shook hands with Jake and Bless and inspected them carefully.

Jake was inspecting the Earl, too, with equal curiosity, two men from different worlds eyeing each other with open interest. The Earl was an impressive sight in the big chair, with an air of great distinction and authority, and Jake must have thought so, for he checked his usual spit into the fire, and drew himself up with infinitely more respect than he ever displayed towards Alan. He raised his hand in a rough salute, and Alan choked down his laughter.

' How do, sir,' he said. ' I guess I ain't familiar with the way you talk to a lord from England. They ain't very plentiful round these parts.'

The Earl's face relaxed in a smile, and Alan sighed gently with relief, though he should not have questioned his father's judgement of character; he could recognize a man when he saw one.

' My son has told me a great deal about you, Mr Winter, in his letters,' the Earl said. ' I think he owes much to you. Please sit down. And don't worry about my correct title. " Sir " will do very well.'

Alan sent for Sam, and the Negro brought wine. The Earl and Jake were talking animatedly by this time, and Alan listened to them, still smiling. But how could he break the news to his father that he did not want to enter the Army ?

They spent an hour inspecting the house, the stockade, and the fur warehouse, but the Earl was tired, and Alan took him back to his chair by the fire.

' You were fortunate to find a man like that, Alan,' the Earl said.

' You like him, sir ? '

' Very much. An interesting type, too. We have nothing like that at home.' The Earl smiled. ' That air of independence ; that damn-your-eyes attitude, I'm a free man, and I say what I please. Yes, you're breeding a new race over here, Alan.'

Harry joined them at dinner, the usual Ashwater meal, simple, well cooked food with an ample and varied choice. Afterwards the Earl strolled out with Alan and sat down in the evening sunshine outside the stockade.

' And what are your plans now, Alan ? ' he asked, settling down on a stump of a tree, but not before he had carefully brushed away any dust that might spoil his immaculate breeches.

Alan hesitated, and the Earl glanced at him keenly.

' There is nothing to prevent you returning to England now,' he said. ' I understand from Sir Harry that the card business has been cleared up. And you are regarded by many men whose opinion I respect as an extremely brave and capable soldier.'

' Yes, sir,' Alan said slowly.

' I will put up the money for a commission in any regiment you choose.'

Alan shook his head. ' I would rather not be a professional soldier, sir.'

' Politics, then ? You can have one of my pocket boroughs.'

' Thank you, sir, but I would not make a good politician.'

The Earl shut his snuff box with a snap. He smiled up
at Alan. ' It is perfectly clear to me that you have already
made up your mind,' he said. ' Why not save my breath and
tell me what you propose to do ? '

Alan was looking across the freshly cleared field below
them, over the trees, towards the Mohawk River and the hills
in the distance. He turned to the north, with the sea of green
running away without a break to the blue mountains on the
skyline. All around was the scent of pines, of freshly cut wood,
the clean evening breeze rustling the trees, and the rich earth
under his moccasins.

' I want to make this my home, sir,' he said abruptly.

' I thought that was what you would say,' the Earl said
unexpectedly.

Alan stared at him in astonishment, and the Earl smiled.
' What will you do here ? ' he asked.

' I want to extend all this,' and Alan swung his long arm
around the forest and the clearings. ' There's a lifetime of
work to be done. I want to build, too. Did you see any of
the bigger colonial houses, sir ? '

' I did.'

' That's the sort of house I want here.' Alan stopped.
' But that would need money.'

' Mr Brewster met me in New York,' the Earl said. ' He
was on business there. He showed me the books for Ashwater.'

' Yes, they have been quite satisfactory, I believe,' Alan
said.

' Satisfactory ! ' The Earl took a large pinch of snuff and
sneezed loudly. ' Satisfactory ! In the last three years the
profits from the fur business here have been enormous. I
haven't touched any of it. I will make over to you, Alan, the
whole of the Ashwater estates, the balance in the banks of the
last three years' trading, and you will find yourself a wealthy
man.'

Alan flushed and stammered his thanks.

' Don't thank me, my dear Alan. You have more than

earned it all. Then there is your mother's money. That is yours now that you are of age.'

' But what about George and Rupert, sir ? '

' They are well provided for,' the Earl said. ' George will inherit all Llanstephan and all my estates in England. Rupert will have his share, of course, but he has made a vast fortune in India, so I understand.'

Alan nodded. His head was full of plans, enough to keep him busy for the rest of his life.

' I was hoping that you might sail home with me for a visit to England,' the Earl said. ' Rupert will be home for a few months this year, I think.'

' Yes, I should like to do that, sir.'

' Good ! You can pick what you want in the way of furniture from Llanstephan, too. There is far more than we want.' The Earl put away his snuff box, and took Alan's arm. ' Now, where shall we build this house of yours ? '

They walked back to the house, the Earl leaning on Alan's arm. The sun was setting now behind the forest, and the outlines of the hills were becoming blurred and hazy. As Alan turned, just before he followed his father inside the stockade, he looked up and saw that the stars were beginning to sparkle overhead. He sniffed at the cool night air with deep content, and went into his home.